FILTERED

GREAT SOCIETY TRILOGY: BOOK ONE

G.K. LAMB

MONOLITH

Filtered

Copyright © 2018 by Monolith Books.

Filtered/G.K. Lamb
ISBN-13: 978-1-7339376-1-0

First Edition: November 2015
Second Edition: April 2019

CONTENTS

"Sometime they'll give a war and nobody will come."
— Carl Sandburg

CHAPTER ONE

WEAR YOUR MASK commands the massive neon billboard. I've only just stepped out of my bedroom, but the floor-to-ceiling windows of the penthouse make it impossible to escape the sign's crimson cries for attention. Below the neon, a cartoon depiction of a dead schoolgirl twisted on the sidewalk drives the point home.

Snared by its phantom hooks, I glide across the polished marble floor. Warmth leaches out through my bare feet forcing a shiver.

I press my nose against the wall of glass and observe the soot-and-smog-obscured buildings of the city below. Haphazardly erected with little space between them, skyscrapers strain to break free of the blanket of smoke and reach the fresh air above. Advertisements add splashes of color to the drab gray city. Their slogans, however, do little to add any cheer.

Perched atop a high-rise, just visible through the thick miasma, is a faded poster of a Peace Officer. He looms three stories tall in his ankle-length brown trench coat and gloss-black rebreather sternly pointing a finger at me. Above him is a warning in huge bold letters: *Keep your opinions to yourself! Your business should stay your business.*

The billboard straight across from me depicts a housewife, dressed to the nines, posed next to a tall stack of Mountain Air mask filters. *Remember, a filter a day keeps death at bay!*

Her red dress is peeking out from underneath layers of soot and ash—the first time I saw her swirls in my mind. Most of my young memories are fragmented at best, but this one is just as visceral as the day it happened. I must have been seven when we moved into the penthouse. I remember the boxes stacked in the middle of the living room—I felt so small. I ran to the seamless wall of glass the instant I laid my eyes on it—the same spot where I'm standing now. Visions of sweeping vistas danced in my little head. But instead of an awe-inspiring view, I was greeted by the sight of cheery Miss Housewife and her cavalier demeanor toward looming death—always a filter away. My tears splashed on the black marble beneath me.

Mother was horrified. She pleaded with me, "What's wrong? What's wrong?" Her words fought through strained breaths— her arms wrapped around me like a straitjacket.

I asked her through my sobs, "What if we run out of filters? I don't want to die—don't let me die, Mommy." The expression on Mother's face still haunts me. Her lips quivered—cheeks and ears pulled back, startled and alert. Her pallor waned as though a veil had been draped over her face. But mostly it was her eyes. Her eyes burned with ferocious determination. She held me so tight I can still feel the bruises.

Something awoke inside Mother that day and it hasn't rested since.

It's odd though. I can't picture anything before that with any real clarity. I have a few misty visions. Watching cartoons on the living room carpet. The first time I slid onto the cold metal beds of the imprint cradles at school. Dad holding me in his arms when I was sick reassuring me that everything would be okay. But there's nothing of our first house or much of anything else.

I massage the familiar pain in my temples. Every time I dive that far back into my memories, a loose wire starts sparking in my head. I can never stay down long—the pain doesn't stop building until I get back up to the surface. Thankfully though, the headaches melt away as suddenly as they appear.

I turn my gaze away from the window. The door to the spare bedroom is locked up tight concealing the towering stack of Mountain Air filters—youth-small—heaped inside the otherwise barren room. Every morning Mother grabs a filter from the mound and then watches me while I swap it out for the barely used one she watched me put on the day before. Our morning ritual is a constant reminder of the horror on her face.

She wants to protect me—I get that—but it frustrates the hell out of me. Yes, she ensures that I change my mask's filter, but she can't bother herself to be involved in any other part of my life. She never asks about school, what music I'm listening to, nothing. Not even the serious stuff the parents on television are always talking to their teenagers about. "Are you thinking about your future? University entrance exams are no laughing matter. Have you considered a term of service?"

Every time I confront her on her glaring inconsistencies, she says some crap like "Children should be free to live." She always places an exaggeration on 'live' as if the word itself were magic and merely at its utterance, some fountain of opportunity will come shooting up, out of the ground, and whisk me away.

I am free I suppose, but it feels wrong every time I look out the window, turn on the television, or step outside my bedroom door. Everywhere I look, someone is telling me what to do—what to think. Don't do that, buy this, obey that, walk here, stand there. It's overwhelming, suffocating, like the air you are not allowed to breathe.

Between the monitors at Neptus Memorial—the ritually-disciplined school that Father insists will 'take me places'—and the ever-vigilant eyes of Peace Officers scanning the streets, there is no room for deviation—for choice. And yet, when I lock the penthouse door behind me, I enter a world of paralyzing freedom. I can't mesh them together. There is only a thin pane of glass between them, but they might as well be separate planets.

Trapped behind my mask, my daily routines, and the penthouse glass, I've been studying the city for a way out.

Having just noticed it, I shift my gaze to the reflection of the television in the glass. Swirling forms in every color flash obnoxiously. The speakers are blaring but, thankfully, the cacophony can only be heard when you're sitting on the couch. Mother and I had, in a one-time cosmic coincidence, agreed that the sound system was a waste of money. Father spent twenty-thousand Marks on the thing and technicians were in and out for a week while they 'calibrated.' But, to their credit, it has finally allowed me to observe the city in silence. Now I'm only subjected to the television's assault when I'm sitting in front of it—an occurrence becoming less and less frequent.

Burrowed into the couch, Mother's attention is firmly glued to the screen. Flashes of light explode in her eyes. She looks dazed. How can she sit there every day—for hours on end—and not grow weary of the relentlessness of it?

The silence is broken by the dull, metal *thunk* of the deadbolt sliding out of the wall. Father is home late. Again.

Turning away from the cityscape, I move across the polished floor to welcome him home. He's been going in early and getting home late for months now. The strain of whatever he's doing—that can never be discussed—is clearly visible in the puce bags under his eyes. Looking up at me from the doorway, he gives me a slight smile.

"Hi there, darling. Food in the fridge?"

"Yeah, but it's probably frozen by now."

"That's fine," he says, hanging his overcoat and mask

on the hooks in the foyer.

Father disappears into the kitchen for a moment, then returns with a plate of food straight from the refrigerator. He passes me pausing briefly to kiss my cheek. He smells of coffee and cigarettes.

He plops onto the couch with a sigh. Mindlessly, he starts digging into his food. The vibrant colors of the television now dance in his placid eyes too. Mother hardly looks away from the screen. The gap between them is big enough for two of me in more ways than one.

I step in front of the couch and take my seat in the void between them. As I cross the invisible barrier that keeps the sound contained, my ears are bombarded by the opening fanfare of the Nightly News. This is hardly how I'd like to spend time with my parents, but this is the only time, and the only place, we cross paths anymore.

The intro shows broad aerial sweeps of the city with momentary cutaways to the flag of the Great Society—a man and woman embroidered in silver thread reach for a lump of coal against a field of cobalt blue. With a final flurry of trumpets, the camera focuses on a simple steel desk. Behind it sits middle-aged Desmond Rourke. His gray collarless suit is pressed and perfect, a stark contrast to his thinning hair. His face is smooth and plucked free of imperfections in a poor attempt to mask his age. Shuffling the notes in his hands, he begins in a slow, steady voice.

"Good evening everyone. Before we begin our program tonight, it pains me to inform you of a tragic loss. Twelve school-age children died today when their classroom's air filters failed. We are unable to bring you any footage or photographs at this time, but I'm being told that the school's maintenance staff is in the custody of Peace Officers pending the results of the ongoing investigation. Please do not be alarmed or hold your children back from school tomorrow. The situation is under control. We do advise, however, that while the investigation is underway, everyone should wear their masks—at all times—until the threat of further air filter incidents can be determined. This news grieves us all, but High Caretaker Domhnall has released a statement saying: 'There is nothing to fear. Go about your daily business and demonstrate your grief through hard work and your continued dedication to each other and our Great Society.' I for one intend to follow the High Caretaker's advice." Pausing for a moment, Rourke shuffles the papers in his hands. In a flash, his face snaps from morose to ecstatic, "Now, on to sports."

Rourke's words sit in my stomach like a rock. I tear my eyes away from the television and look to my parents. Mother has bolted up in complete shock, Father sits unfazed still mechanically shoveling cold food into his mouth. Mother's eyes narrow on him with a searing focus. Clearly, she doesn't think everything is all right, with the news or Father. But it can't be that bad if he's just sitting there. Can it?

There is a fleeting moment of absolute stillness before Mother storms off toward the master bedroom.

"Carol," Father's eyes snap away from his fork. "Where are you going? You'll miss the rest of the news."

"I'm getting my mask, Allen." His name oozes over her lips like poison. "How can you sit there? You heard what Rourke said—we all need to be wearing our masks. That goes for you too, Evelyn. Go get your mask on." A shiver runs down my spine when our eyes meet.

"Calm down, you don't need to panic. He advised it, that's all. The filters in this building are top-notch. We even have redundant systems here."

"I don't care if the redundant systems have redundant systems—there are subversives out there killing people."

"They never said that." Highlights of tonight's Brawl Ball game pull his attention back to the screen. "You're reading too much into this."

"I'm not reading anything into it. They said they already had some men in custody and that they needed to do a more thorough investigation. Why would they tell us that unless they thought there was something sinister going on? It's those damn subversives, just like before."

"It was one school, one incident." Father skewers a potato onto his fork. "This is hardly the start of an uprising. Where are the fire-bombings? Murder sprees? Sit down and watch the news with us—it was just an accident."

Her cheeks quiver as she chews back rage. "I'm not letting

them take anything else from me, not this time. I can't." Tears splash on her trembling hands.

"Are you serious right now?" The potatoes have lost their appeal. "You're taking this too far, and you know it."

She takes a step forward, ire burns away her tears. "What if it was Evelyn's school? What if she was lying in the morgue?"

"But she isn't, Carol, she's right here."

Mother's eyes dart over to me.

"Damn it, Evelyn! Put your mask on!"

Father bolts up from the couch sending his dinner flying. The plate shatters showering the floor in jagged shards and lumps of cold potato. "Don't yell at her. She can make up her own mind. I'm not going to wear one and that's final."

Embers smolder on my temples. The television continues to discharge its oversaturated rainbow. Their muscles tense and eyes narrow as they square up on either side of me itching for a fight. The hostility swelling between fills the air with needles. A brushbot appears from its concealed home in the baseboard and begins vacuuming up the mess.

Trapped between them, paralysis grips me.

I know it's coming. Like the stillness before a downpour, a fight is brewing, and it's going to be ugly. Normally I'm a buffer for this kind of thing, but tonight's conflict has roots deeper than what Rourke said. What did she mean by losing something last time?

Fire ignites in my brain.

Searing silver flashes add a new layer of chaos to the already erupting room. Pinching the bridge of my nose, I slam my eyes shut and try to shake away the pain. It's no use—silver lines continue to crisscross the pale red darkness behind my eyelids.

I spring from the couch. "Keep me out of this."

I step over the brushbot and make for my room with long strides. My interruption stokes the tension pressing the remaining air out of the living room. Anxiety skitters down my back. I throw my bedroom door open and slam it shut.

The bubble bursts.

Accusations fly. Old wounds are torn open. Exchanges of familiar insults are peppered with new ones that have no doubt been brewing on their tongues for weeks.

The walls aren't enough to silence them, and the headache is getting worse.

I could drown them out with music, blast something obnoxious, but that would only compound the problem. I need quiet. I need stillness. And nothing in this house will give me that.

The glow of advertisements streams through the window demanding my attention. University applications and internship pamphlets lie scattered across my desk demanding I decide my future right this instant. The open closet reveals rows of uniforms and trench coats demanding my compliance.

The headache swells into a migraine. Light and sound fuel the pressure cooker in my head—my eyes throb with each surging heartbeat.

Desperate, I dive into bed and mound the pillows and blankets over my head. The muffled darkness opens a relief valve on my temples. I pull the bedding in tighter pressing them down on my ears to drown out the fight still on the crescendo.

I linger for what feels like hours before sleep takes me.

Instructor Speer looms at the head of class veiled behind his rebreather. A projected video of the flag bathes him in flickering blue light that shimmers in his glass eye slits. Everyone is sitting with their heads forward, hands flat on their desks. The video's reflection cuts their outlines against the black. I look down at my gloved hands through the glass circles of my mask.

I scan the room. I'm the only student wearing one.

My throat tightens—Speer is staring right at me. A flash of rebellion bursts then flickers away leaving me limp and powerless, quivering in my chair.

Something pricks my ankle.

The sting blisters and spreads over my foot. Now it's chewing, stinging, biting at my legs. My classmates start to squirm trying to stem the blistering's unrelenting march. The urge to scratch pushes out every thought in my brain but Speer's lifeless eyes stay my hands.

It's snaking up my stomach and onto my breasts. Buttons fly as students tear at their overcoats desperate to sink their fingernails into the prickling blisters. Someone thrashes out of their chair.

It's consumed me now—only my face, safe behind the gas mask, remains untouched.

The wailing starts.

Students are clawing at their throats leaving behind streaks of red where their fingernails bit too deep. Hyperventilating through the shorts gasps the mask allows, I rush for the door.

Everyone that isn't twitching on the ground is scrambling for the door too. I push a boy out of the way and get my hand on the handle but it's too late—they are on me before I can think to turn it. Their collective weight spins me around and smashes me up against the wall. I'm ringed by ravenous, bloodshot eyes.

A dozen hands claw for the mask on my face. Hot blood pours down my neck.

I can't hear myself scream over Speer's guttural, crackling laughter.

CHAPTER TWO

WAKING UP HURTS. The position I slept in left a kink in my neck and my right arm is completely numb. I swipe the pillows and covers from my head sending them to the floor with a thud. I sit on the edge of the bed and try to rub the dancing needles out of my shoulder and the nightmare out of my head.

The indistinct glow of the sun crests the skyscrapers and pours through the blinds. I slam my eyes shut and grimace as the light reawakens the dying embers of last night's migraine.

When the fire fades, I glance at the clock on the nightstand: Seven forty-five.

I wish I could go back to the moment before Father opened the door and live there in that stillness.

Any moment now Mother will come through the door with a new filter and pretend like nothing happened. Father will already be off to work, I'll go to school, come home, and for the briefest of moments, I'll live in that stillness again before Father opens the door.

I've had enough. I'm done living yesterday waiting for someone else's idea of my future to begin. I don't know how, but I'm getting off this loop.

Today.

Mother creeps into my room like clockwork holding a filter in her outstretched hand. But already something's off. She's wearing her mask—her eyes obscured behind its two reflective glass circles. Her breathing is rasping and rhythmic.

No 'Good morning sleepy head' or 'do you want eggs for breakfast? I can make you a couple of eggs.' Today all I get is the sound of her unnatural breaths.

I grab my mask from the nightstand and then take the new filter from her. With the speed and enthusiasm I give to all my tedious and repetitive tasks, I open the filter and twist it into place at the front of my mask.

Satisfied, Mother retreats into the living room leaving the door wide open behind her. There is no evidence other than the interaction we just had, but something major snapped in her last night.

The clock catches my attention. I only have fifteen minutes before I have to leave for school. I can worry about Mother later.

Showered and changed, I dip into the kitchen to grab the toast she set out for me. The bread is far past toasted and the thin smear of butter and raspberry jam doesn't quite reach to the ends.

I scarf down the toast before I reach the elevator. With my backpack slung over my shoulder I swing my mask back and forth by its straps and wait for the elevator. *Ding.* I step through while the doors are still opening, tap the lobby button, and then lean against the back wall. It smells of lemon cleaner and coal. The descent is smooth and silent except for the faint whirring of pulleys and gears.

The doors open onto the lobby and the noise of hundreds of shuffling feet floods in. Throngs of people waddle through the long lines stretched out behind the building's six airlocks. I step out onto the dark polished floors and take my place among them in line. No one looks around. Heads straight, eyes fixed on the floor, we all shuffle forward a single step at a time. Shuffle. Shuffle. Shuffle.

My mask hangs heavy in my hands. It's plain—one I picked over Mother's pleas that I get a deluxe model instead—with only a red strip around the edge of the gray filter to break up the solid black of the rubber. A serial number is stamped into it above the forehead *PPS 174517.* I guess that serves to personalize it.

I twist it around and examine its two glass lenses. It's hard to imagine why Mother would willingly lock herself in one of these when she's safe at home.

"Hey, watch it!"

His bark yanks me out of my head. Shuffling automatically, I ran into the man in front of me. He was fumbling with his mask and my minor bump knocked it from his gaunt gloved hands. There's too much pomade in his hair and his features are too small for his face.

His eyes dance over me lingering too long where they shouldn't. "What the hell's wrong with you?"

I stare him down fighting back the urge to snap at him.

"Sorry—it was an accident."

He pulls on his mask and shakes his head.

"*Bitch*." His mask garbles his insult, but it does nothing to dull the sting.

Fuming, I watch him step into the airlock and disappear behind its hissing doors. Rooted in place, I envision a thousand unpleasant ends for that jerk. Some combination of road accident and choking to death would suit him just fine.

There's a jab in my ribs.

"It's your turn," says the woman behind me already shrouded in her mask—her overcoat's large cowl pulled up to protect her coifed hair from soot.

"Right, sorry." I give her a curt smile, but the only thing she's interested in is getting through the airlock.

Flipping the mask back around, I shake that blood-boiling man from my head, look out through the eye holes, then plunge my face into the rubber. It's loose, so I tug on the four straps until it presses firmly against my face. I hold my hand over the filter's vent and blow out hard. The air rushes out under the edges, forming a seal on my face. In the instant before I pull my hand away from the vent, I am empty. My lungs are drained, and I'm trapped in an airtight prison. I move my hand away from the vent and draw in a deep breath. Air, with the faint taste of charcoal and the pungent odor of rubber, fills my nostrils.

The airlock doors open with a hiss of escaping air. I step inside and they close automatically behind me. The cramped cylinder hisses with changing pressures for a moment then becomes eerily still. The airlock surrounds me with an oppressive silence and makes me conscious of being trapped—caged within a cage.

The doors open and the soot-filled air of the streets rushes in. I scan back and forth for the silver transport that will take me to school. The swarm of people weaving here and there makes the search difficult, but shining silver is hard to miss in a city of soot and ash, and its twinkling in the fragments of sunlight show me the way.

Eyes fixed on my target, I head straight toward it cutting across the overlapping streams of equally self-engrossed pedestrians. The transport's door opens as I approach. I don't recognize this driver. She's an emaciated woman wearing a short-sleeved butter-yellow dress under her uniform trench coat—each breath reveals chasms where her ribs connect to her sternum. She can't be much older than me. *I wonder what happened to Mrs. Guerra?* Her golden hair is braided into pigtails flopped over her shoulders to dangle on her chest. She turns to look at me. The ominous mask she's wearing is jarring next to her pigtails and regulation-defiant dress. I avoid her gaze and climb in.

The hierarchy of the bus follows the classic pattern. Little kids at the front and twelfth years in the back. Normally I force myself back there and pretend to fit in, but I have no stomach for that today.

I take a seat halfway down the driver's side blocking the seat beside me with my backpack. Murmurs ripple out from the wedge I cut between the seventh and eighth years. A surge of excitement flutters in my chest.

The ride to school is agonizing in the ceaseless city traffic. The streets were built long before automobiles took the place of horses and in the time between no one thought it would be a good idea to take a break from building and plan things out. The resulting city is one where everything new is precariously built on the crumbling bones of the old.

Advertisements, television, the Caretakers, they always want you to have something new, something more. They're always pressing more and more down the city's throat with no thought of consequence. Last week's filters are pushed off the shelves to make room for *new* ones. No restock would be complete without accompanying masks of every size, shape, and fashion—of course. Custom fit, premium: you name it, they'll make it. But it's always the same thing. It's always the same masks, same filters, and same trench coats with just enough changes to make you want them. Mother always insists on having the newest mask, the newest filters, and I usually indulge her. Twice a year or more she throws away all the filters in the spare bedroom to buy this month's version of *Mountain Air filters, youth-small.* Somewhere there is a mountain of discarded things, still good, still working, but garbage nonetheless.

Traffic eases and the bus lurches forward. Coming out of my head, I look around at the other students. There are kids from nearly every grade on the bus, but the masks and trench coats make it difficult to tell anyone apart. And worse, the masks make it nearly impossible to understand each other with the way they garble your words and dampen your hearing. Isolated in the mask's custody, we sit alone, stare out the window alone, and converse to ourselves. I shift my gaze back out the window to watch blurs of people, cars, and propaganda posters pass me by.

The transport slows, and I see the familiar landmark that lets me know school is only moments away. Beyond the parade grounds on the far side of school is an outsized flickering *diner* sign—its cyan neon cuts through the smog like a lighthouse. And if somehow I missed its distinct blue glow, the diner's accompanying arrow—cascading down from tail to tip in an endless loop—ensures that I don't.

I pull the straps of my mask again to ensure they're tight. Looking around, I watch the other kids perform their own last-minute checks. Some are even going so far as to reform their seals by momentarily depriving themselves of air.

The transport glides to a stop. We wait for a moment while the bus sits idle with the doors closed. I wring the straps of my backpack holding it tight to my chest. The driver gives the signal by raising her arm out toward the door—it opens at her command. Starting with the first row, right to left, we each wait patiently—sitting up straight, eyes forward—for our turn to exit. Ordinary, uniform, disciplined.

Eyes fixed on the girl sitting one row up and opposite me, my earlier rebellion has been replaced by a gnawing anxiety that I might screw up the pattern. When she goes, I count a single breath then follow. Shuffling down the narrow walkway, I keep my eyes fixed to my feet. Off the bus, I join the line for the airlocks.

Monitors stand along the edges of the line in brown uniforms under midnight-blue trench coats permanently stained black from ash. Their rebreathers are jet-black like the ones the Peace Officers wear, only less ominous. My eyes haven't moved from my feet, and my legs have shuffled me forward out of reflex. The school frowns on disobedience and praises strict discipline above all other subjects. I hate the school's stifling rules, but the fear of repercussions and detention force me to bite my tongue and step in line.

Approaching the door, I dare a glance over at one of the monitors standing by the airlocks. The roughness of her soot-covered trench coat and harsh angles of her rebreather make her appear like a hyper-masculine soldier from the posters littering the industrial park. Her head turns, and though it is impossible to tell, I'm certain I feel her eyes piercing through me. Fear snakes through my spine like hot poison. I look away, back at my feet—it's too close to look around now. I hate this feeling of helplessness and isolation but what can I do? They are always there and always watching.

Ahead of the boy's feet in front of me is the silver lip of the airlock. He steps in and disappears as the door revolves around him. I'm next.

I take a gulp of carbonized air and hope the monitor won't pull me aside to chew me out or give me a demerit for looking up at her. I shuffle forward—the airlock's silver maw stands ready to swallow me up.

I lift a cautious foot. Just as it lands, a hand falls on my shoulder. I jump out of my skin and turn to stone all at once. I force myself to look—it's the monitor I made eye contact with. Behind the veil of my mask, I grimace in anticipation of her scolding.

"Do not take off your mask once you've stepped through the airlock. I repeat, do not take off your mask once you've stepped through the airlock. Do you understand? Nod your head to comply."

It's a moment before I realize her words are not a reprimand but a warning. As soon as I piece it together, I nod.

"Step through," she says, removing her hand from my shoulder.

I obey and step in. The system depressurizes like normal and pumps in clean air. The airlocks aren't broken, so they must be taking precautions after yesterday's incident. Before I can think of anything else, the door opens, and I'm face to face with a towering male monitor. He leans down to my level, placing the glass eye slits of his mask in line with the circles of mine.

"Head to the auditorium. Do not remove your mask. Repeat, do not remove your mask. Nod to comply."

I understand the redundancy is for our protection, but every reminder of my powerlessness lands like a hammer blow. I can't stop a sour look from forming on my face. Yet behind my mask, this mini-rebellion is concealed. These masks are good for some things I suppose.

I nod out of deeply ingrained habit and walk past him down the hall. The kid who entered before me must only be in his third or fourth year. I walk fast, following his form down the hallway. At that age, everything towers over you and nothing in your life is yours to control.

Graduation is approaching in a few short months and even though I'll be forced to go out into the world—a leap I'm ill-prepared to make—I don't envy him. Being that young and coming from an earlier life of cartoons and bliss into this kind of regimented asylum for 'the chronically under-disciplined' was a shock I'm still reeling from. It nearly drained the curiosity out of me. Almost.

I watch the boy press open the auditorium's double doors and enter. They swing closed behind him, and for a moment I feel alone in the hallway. The thought of running away into the bathroom flashes in my mind. I could sit out the rest of the day in silence and avoid whatever awaits me in the auditorium.

I entertain the thought for a few rebellious seconds before the burning press of the countless eyes of the students behind me drive it from my mind. I put my hand on the door handle and push—anxiety squeezes my lungs.

I want to break free from the confines of school and its day-to-day monotony, from the masks we all wear, and the ceaseless fear that grips us all—desperately so. But I don't know where I'd even start. My ignorance and doubt feed my timidity, and the rising tide of action fizzles away. I don't know what's holding me back more, the Great Society or myself?

Sensing the presence of the seats to my left, I pull out of my head and back into the auditorium.

The cold, unforgiving concrete bleachers are rapidly filling up. Feeling the throng pushing at my back, I scan the benches for the closest open space and press toward it. Ten rows up, I shuffle down to a gap between two cliques of primary kids. *Great.*

I do my best to sit still and wait here obediently like they want. But if I have to keep looking at my feet I'm going to burst into flames. Surely looking around is less disruptive than spontaneous combustion?

Keeping my head low I lift my eyes and scan the auditorium. The bleachers take up the entire length of one wall. The two walls running perpendicular are plain concrete except for the identical sets of double doors in their centers. At the base of the far wall is a stage made of polished, chestnut brown wood—an odd relic in this city of steel and glass. The wall behind it is decorated with sports banners and pennants radiating out from an enormous, silver-fringed flag of the Great Society. The auditorium's brutalist-gray walls make all the flags and banners, but especially the flag of the Great Society, really *pop*.

The monitors have moved from the hall to take up positions around the circumference of the room. Arms crossed, they stand along the walls forming a cage of muscle. Two of the largest monitors are blocking the two sets of double doors. The auditorium vibrates with an unnerving hum; the sounds of shifting seats and scuffling feet swell the room with unbearable anticipation.

The Authoritarian marches onto the stage. His polished boots echo like thunder in the stillness of the room releasing the tension like rain. He takes his place behind the obsidian podium. Display panels unfurl from the ceiling and the overhead projection system flickers to life. The podium's built-in camera projects him onto the screens. This is the best look at him I've had in years. He is an old, stately man. Even through the glass disks of his mask, his eyes are piercing and as dark as the wood he's standing on. Some of his gray hair is poking out under the straps of his mask. He wears the brown uniform of the instructors, but it's made of premium fabric and stitched and tailored perfectly. His chest is covered in blue and black ribbons, and the golden braids of an aiguillette hang over his right shoulder. The contempt for us glistening in his cruel eyes is unmistakable.

"Rise for the Anthem," he commands—his voice projected and amplified from a microphone in his mask.

A great noise—a thousand students rising in unison to the Authoritarian's voice—shatters the silence. I find myself standing among them, without having given it conscious thought.

The projectors switch from the podium feed to a recording of the Einsam Children's Choir. Hidden speakers in the vaulted room crackle to life. The choir guides us along as we struggle to sing—our voices muffled. Habit brings the words to my lips, but no sound passes through them.

From the ashes of barbarity,
Born our Great Society.

To our freedoms save,
Countless martyrs gave.

Arise patriots arise.
Arise patriots arise.

Lands endless yielding,
Energies boundless building.
Through mother and babe,
Our nation will never fade!

Arise! Patriots arise!
Arm yourself for the fight.

Righteous and glorious,
We march victorious!
United we stand
Against all foreign lands!

Arise!
Arise!
Arise!

The speakers crackle again then fall silent. A few students have lifted their heads as if inspired by the song. No patriotism twinges in my heart, only bewilderment at the absurdity of a recorded anthem played atop a muffled mess. *Who even writes this garbage anyway?*

"Sit!" The Authoritarian's voice booms through the speakers. Startled, I sit obediently. Once again, the silence of the auditorium is disturbed by the settling of a thousand seats.

The Authoritarian waits until the rumbling echoes away and the projectors switch back to him. "As I am sure you are aware, yesterday there was a tragedy at one of the city's other schools. Their air filters failed, and it resulted in the death of twelve students. As a precaution, I have ordered that until our school's air filters are checked, and the redundant systems installed, students and faculty will wear their masks—at all times. I understand the difficulty the instructors and yourselves will have in communicating with your masks on, so I have arranged for us to watch some of the great films our Caretakers have created for us. Do not, under any circumstances, remove your masks. Any student found removing their own, or attempting to remove the mask of another student, will be severely punished and handed over to the authority of Peace Officers under suspicion of sedition. If you do what you are told this will be an easy few weeks for all of you. Do you comply?"

In a thunderous roar, hundreds of filtered voices shout in chorus.

"Yes, sir!"

My lips stay pressed together.

"Starting from the right, exit row by row in an orderly fashion toward your respective classrooms. You are dismissed."

The students sitting at the far-right end of the first row begin the process while the rest of us—the majority—remain perfectly still. No hand, head, nor foot dares to move out of sequence. Sitting dutifully, we wait minute after agonizing minute in the silence of our minds.

After what felt like an eternity, it's finally my turn. I rise and fall lockstep into the line of students swapping one room for the confines of another. Our rhythmic, purified breaths keep the time like a paradiddle.

I linger at the fork that divides the primary and secondary levels and look down the hallway I used to walk. The day I moved up to secondary classes was exciting. I came to the fork, and for the first time instead of going left to the imprint rooms, I veered right toward the classrooms.

I was so excited for the change. Imprint cradles are cold, uncomfortable, and smell like chlorine. You get used to them after a while, and then it's not that bad, really. Lay back, mesh in, and away you go. Four hours later you snap awake dizzy—tongue grating against the roof of your mouth like sand—yet suddenly able to do the multiplication table backwards and forwards or whatever else was loaded on the impress that day. But one discomfort never went away: the teasing. Cradles are for babies.

The joke was entirely lost on our monitors and instructors who seemed impervious to humor—all mischief is swiftly punished. That never stopped the kids the year above us though and they did it any chance they got. If we crossed paths with a higher class on the way to the imprint rooms a few of them would pop out of line, throw their best jab—invariably some iteration of "Baby needs a nap?"—then would rub their eyes dramatically, feigning silent sobs. They'd draw out the bit until a spotter tugged on their coat then they'd bolt back into line before they were caught.

Once we made it through the first year, we took everything the higher classes poured on us, bottled it up, and dumped it straight back down on the new 'babies.' In our sixth year, we finally made it to the headwaters of the childish taunt only to discover that it had always been a self-inflicted wound.

Graduating to secondary classes, I had hoped that in the classroom we would finally have an opportunity to participate in our education. What was I thinking? Like they would ever let that happen. Sure, they don't literally jam thoughts into our heads anymore, but what's the real difference between rote memorization of Caretaker-approved lectures and preprogrammed data stored in a crystalline robin's egg?

A monitor cranes their head in my direction. I drop my eyes to my feet to avoid their gaze and follow the other twelfth-year students down the hallway to the right.

Step, step, step.

I shuffle along envisioning myself as a member of a chain gang like the ones the Nightly News is always showing in the Pits.

Reaching the classroom, I take my seat and relish in the end of our march. I scratch at the itch created by the imaginary manacles on my wrists.

After blissful moments of peace and quiet spent scratching my imaginary itch, the last student enters the room and takes his seat—Instructor Speer enters on his heels. Already, I long for those precious seconds of stillness. He closes the door behind him with a crash. Taking his place behind his desk, he stands observing us through his rebreather's glass eye-slits. Last night's nightmare rushes back and slithers through me.

The sound of his rebreather's whirring recycler fills the room. Why must the silence always be broken by shallow and meaningless noises? I'm positive I could learn more from my own silent and still mind than the gruff and trivial words of Speer.

Normally his young face is visible, and his expertly styled brown hair bounces gently while he pontificates and gesticulates. There's no debating he's handsome—most of the girls, and even some of the boys, have crushes on him. Unlike the rest of them, I haven't been beguiled. Despite his youth, he is cruel and vindictive. The rebreather seems at home on his body and makes him look the way I imagine he should.

"I understand how sad and scared you must feel. But feeling scared—or shedding tears after such a tragedy as befell your contemporaries—is a sign of immaturity and weakness. A wise and strong person, such as myself, feels overjoyed. And I am overjoyed because now measures will be taken to prevent further tragedies. Your fellow students may have died a gagging, screaming death. But their sacrifice means you will live in a world that is safer and more vigilant than the one they departed. Be thankful and rejoice that you have such good Caretakers who respond swiftly in a crisis. Now, how is class doing today?"

In a chaotic roar, each student responds boisterously with their own expression of "joy."

Letting my lips crack open, I mutter the truth, "Suffocated."

Speer's reaction to the outcry is impossible to gauge with his face hidden behind his mask, but by his smug, shoulders-back bravado he is relishing in their sycophantic praise. Now that his ego has been preened, Speer turns to the wall behind him and presses his hand into the projector's command module. His fingers dance in the projected light interface awakening the aging projector in a flicker of prismatic color. The equally antiquated speakers crackle like the ones in the auditorium. As the projector warms up, the start screen for a Great Society film comes into focus.

"Because we will be watching films for the next week or so, I decided to start at the beginning. Today we're going to watch one of my favorite films. *Year One, the Origins of Our Great Society.* This film tells the tale of how the Great Society formed itself from the ashes of oppression and foreign invasion. You should take the whole film in and appreciate it. But pay special attention to the story of our first High Caretaker Antonius Neptus. He is truly our greatest hero, having single-handedly formed the nation and created a great and lasting peace."

This again? How many times do we have to hear this story? I know I'm not alone in my frustration, but after twelve years we've all become experts at pressing everything down and nailing a lid on it. No one makes a peep, not even me.

"Remain awake, remain attentive. When this week of movies and vacation is over, there will be a test, a detailed one."

This could be my chance to live out one of my long-held fantasies. In it, every student springs from their desk, charges Speer, straps him to his chair then runs out of the school. We run and run until the thick smog clouds of the city disappear, and the towering outlines of skyscrapers fade into the horizon. We don't stop until we reach that mythic *Mountain Air*. But deep down I know it will always be a fantasy. I have never even stood up out of turn, let alone assault the instructor and flee. Even if I worked up the courage and did it right this second, none of my classmates would join me. They'd be the first to hold me back.

The projected image dances to life as the narrator's velvety voice fills the room.

"In the fourth century of the Great Society, many take for granted the wonders and bounty we have been born into. From time to time, however, we should all pause and remember the great patriots and martyrs upon whose blood and bone our civilization is built. Be thankful and appreciative of what they have given you…"

The film continues for almost two hours, but little to none of it sticks. Drifting off into my own world, I watch the re-enacted scenes of the great evils of barbarity and hedonism in the old world and the heroic battles that were fought to eradicate them. I witness walls and blockades, made from the bodies of an untold number of patriotic martyrs, holding the rest of the uncivilized world at bay. The narrator names a dozen heroes and heroines, a hundred battles, and a thousand enemies, but their names all fail to imprint themselves in my mind. Only his final words work themselves out of the regular muck and propaganda that saturates everything that passes through his lips.

"The greatest sacrifices of our Great Society have yet to be made. Are you willing to give everything to ensure the survival of humanities shining achievement?"

After his words finally echo away, an image of a Peace Officer's recruitment facility and Guardian's barracks fill up the front wall of the classroom. The image lingers there, blaring, "Join Today," even after Speer switches on the lights.

Confidently standing in the diminishing light of the projector, Speer addresses us, his voice filled with energetic patriotism no doubt put there by the film.

"I want all of you to take a moment and contemplate the heritage of sacrifice and turmoil our Great Society has endured. No matter which path you choose when you graduate and join the ranks of ours, the greatest of societies, always remember that giving your life in service to the nation is the least you can do."

The room falls silent. A few of the boys fidget with their sweaty palms under their desks. They've probably eaten the whole story up, taking each word as truth. I bet they've already planned what they'll do the day after our rapidly approaching graduation. They'll wake up early, eat one last home-cooked meal from mommy then race off into the muck-filled streets for the recruiting offices. Inevitably there will already be a line, and they'll stand there for hours shuffling and soot-covered in their haste to become thralls of the state. No doubt everyone who doesn't get into university will be standing in them before the ink on their diplomas is dry. It seems like every year those lines get longer.

I could still join them. Stand there in line dreaming of being a heroine of the state—my likeness cast in bronze to stand vigil over my martyr's grave.

I don't know what my path is, but I know for damn sure it's not that.

Class buzzes as Speer readies the next documentary— dread bubbles in my guts. Instead of patriotism, the film has filled me with new doubts.

Were the walls built to keep them out or us in?

CHAPTER THREE

"WE WILL PROCEED TO THE DINING HALL. The Caretakers have graciously supplied us with emergency rations. I trust you all know how to use the liquid ports on your masks?"

Speer's words force me to put aside the questions still gnawing at my sides.

"Rise and proceed single file."

The room fills with the squeaks of chairs being pushed against the concrete floors. In silent choreography, the class lines up with mechanical precision. I do my part and fit effortlessly into the flow.

The march down the hall is devoid of incident. Lockstep and staring at the person's feet in front of us, the only conversations that take place are safely contained within our individual minds.

The dining hall is large enough to feed the entire student body at once. I take my place in line and switch on autopilot.

Carved stone arches draw my eyes to the vaulted ceiling.

It's the only beautiful part of the school. The basalt walls are carved with long, flowing lines and inlaid with white marble. This room's beauty stands in stark contrast to the rest of the school's rectilinear concrete monotony. Speer told us that the whole school used to look like this but most of it was destroyed in a fire and when they rebuilt it, they did so in a more modern style. He says that the uniform concrete architecture is supposed to make us feel safe in its regularity and simplicity, but it feels just as suffocating as our masks.

"Student, take your ration. You're holding up the line."

The server is holding out a box of rations gesturing sharply with his head for me to grab one. He looks so out of place in his mask. I blink myself back into the moment. He shakes the box again. The line behind me breaks rank to lean out and see what the commotion is all about. Snickers and muffled laughter ripple down the line.

"Sorry." Tendrils of white-hot embarrassment dart across my face.

I grab the small silver pouch and dash for a table, but the way is blocked by a gaggle of students. Wishing I could melt into the floor, I stand awkwardly looking for a way through.

"If she were any more air-brained she'd blow away," says a muffled voice from behind me. The twelfth years behind me laugh as loud as they dare with the monitors watching from the corners.

Embarrassment explodes into columns of stinging insects shooting down my neck. I don't mean to zone out, but there is no little life outside my head. What am I supposed to do, just stare at the back of people's heads?

I push through a roadblock of ninth years trying to elbow their way into the joke and make for the nearest table keeping my head low and my eyes fixed forward.

I find a seat at an empty table and throw the silver pouch down in front of me. It lands with a wet thud and jiggles for a minute before lying still. I try not to look at the students passing me so as not to draw the attention of whoever made fun of me, but it's too late. She steps right up next to me, bends over and forces our eyes to meet. Slim, tall, and flanked by other girls, Victoriana Zarrov is hard not to recognize with her buttermilk-blonde hair flowing out from under her mask down to the middle of her back. She stares intently at me—moments grind into seconds. It's impossible to tell if she's going to say something.

"Oh, sorry," she says rolling her eyes theatrically. "Just zoned out there for a second. Silly me."

Her voice, normally too sweet to be genuine, sounds glassy and dark as it resonates through her mask. Her gaggle of friends erupts into a chorus of scratching, smoky laughter. The troop follows on Victoriana's heels as she walks away, her shoulders back and proud. I close my eyes finding calm in the stillness of my mind. She's a terrible person, and I just need to let her words go. At least she couldn't see me blush today.

I look down at the pouch. Its liquid contents jiggle when I pick it up. It's thick, and after my encounter with Victoriana, I have little desire to eat.

My thoughts return to the documentary and the images of violence, war, and death. So much pain and suffering went into the construction of this world that I feel it seeps through the very walls.

Lunch hour drags on too long but ends before I'm ready. We return to class with the same automated enthusiasm and retake our seats. Speer sits waiting, reading the newest copy of *Drumbeat* magazine. The projector is already warmed up, casting him in the dark blue shade of the flag. A wave of vertigo hits me. Am I back in my nightmare or am I still at school? What's the difference?

When the last student enters, Speer sits up and folds his magazine. He waits until Hector takes his seat across from mine before he gets up and presses 'play' on the command terminal.

"Two more documentaries today. The first will explore the boundless wonders of coal. And the second will explore the history of our gas masks and the airlock systems. Remember to pay close attention. I highly advise you take notes."

The documentary starts with typical bombast. Speer retakes his seat at the head of class, contorting himself around to watch the video projected behind him.

Neither of these documentaries are as captivating as the first, and I struggle to recall a single scene from either. The information is so perfunctory and obvious that it's hardly worth taking up space in my brain.

The end of day bell rings. Speer waits until all the excitement has bled out of us before we're excused. Orderly, we rise and march toward the exit and the silver transports that await us. The line at the airlock moves quickly, and I soon find myself outside. The contrast is stark. The wind is strong today. Ash and soot swirl wildly, obscuring anything more than an arm's length away. I double check the buttons on my overcoat, pull my backpack straps tighter, and press through the wind toward the transports.

The outline of the transport emerges through the blowing soot. A few more steps and I'll be right back where I started. Back at the window holding tight onto each second trying to make them last forever. Back wishing there was a way out. *How many times have I been here before?*

The dread, still simmering from earlier, boils over and floods into my veins. I'm at the threshold, I could reach out and touch it. Everyone, and everything, around me demands I press forward.

Step on! Step on! Step on!

"Enough!"

I'm walking away. *Did I just shout that?* Who cares! I'm tingling, electric, and alive.

Tucking my chin to my chest to guard my neck against the rough and stinging soot, I dash across the street and into the unknown. In all twelve years of going to school here, I've never even stepped foot on this side of the street. Near my apartment tower, sure—I've walked those roads a thousand times. But I've never ventured this far from home and familiarity. This is exactly what I needed to do.

The wind eases as I walk, and the ash leisurely settles back onto the ground. Sweepers emerge almost as soon as it does and begin removing the heaping mounds. But no matter how frantically they sweep, the streets seem to forever remain black and slick with slag.

The buildings here are just as choked and cramped as every other part of the city. Making matters worse is the black-gray grime obscuring every sign and banner that could clue me into my location. I'm lost, but I guess it doesn't really matter because I don't know where I'm going. Just as long as it's not familiar and not home.

As my exhilaration winds down, thoughts of the dead school kids creep in. I imagine being in my classroom, surrounded by the other students I hardly know, and choking to death on poison air as Speer looks on from behind his rebreather. In my last gasping moments, I would be alone in a room of strangers. I have no friends or anyone that I could hang onto for comfort in those final agonizing moments. Victoriana would at least have her toadies so she wouldn't have to die alone.

Death, choking, sacrifice. The foundations of our Great Society. My imaginary demise mingles with depictions of lifeless, mounded martyrs from the documentary—their bright red blood covering the ground as the ash does now. I try to push these morbid thoughts away, but everywhere I look, and with every breath I take, I'm reminded by death's looming presence. Just a filter away.

Beginning to think I would aimlessly wander the streets with these horrific thoughts forever, the muted thumping of heavy music stirs me out of my mind. I follow the sound around the corner and look down.

A steep staircase delves below street level. At the landing is a door that was probably painted blue when it was new. A sign hangs above it, but its words are incomprehensible under a thick covering of soot. The music is coming from behind the door and entices me toward it like a siren. Normally music—or really any unpleasantly loud and demanding sound—doesn't interest me. But this feels different. It's deliberate and foreign. I've never heard anything like it, and I have to know where it's coming from.

I slip and nearly fall on my way down the staircase, but the handrail is there to catch me. My hand hovers over the doorknob—anticipation rises so fast I'm ready to explode. Fingers tingling, I grasp the handle and press inside.

CHAPTER FOUR

THE MUSIC—muted from behind the door—hits me with its full voice and vigor as I cross the threshold. There is no airlock. That should be sinking in an sending me into a panic, but a torrent of indigestible stimuli has me awestruck.

A throng of mask-less people jump and thrash about wildly. Sweat beads on their skin as they press together in an organic, undulating mass. Nevertheless, they don't appear to be rhythmic or orderly, but syncopated and chaotically individual. Their clothes, too, are not trench coats, stained black from daily use, but bright, revealing fashions of all cuts. It's cramped, hot, uncomfortably alien, and everything I didn't know I needed.

Enraptured and overstimulated both, I push my way through the dancing bodies. Every footfall is labored with the suction of the sticky floor. Each step draws me deeper like an undertow pulling me into a sea of music, light, heat, and humanity.

I spot a bar to my right serving drinks of every color in tall, thick glasses, undoubtedly the culprit for the sticky floors.

I contemplate getting one, but the current is too strong, and I don't want to fight it. Pressing through a cluster of dancers sloshing their drinks, I emerge from the pack and find, against the back wall, a row of empty tables. It seems I'm the only one who feels like sitting.

I sit in the corner behind the stage and pause a moment to take in my strange surroundings. On opposite sides of the room stand an antique-wood bar and a metal and plexiglass stage bathed in saturated orange light. I'd like to run my fingers across the bar's smooth scars in the hope of coaxing out the knowledge trapped under its patina—I can only imagine the things it must have witnessed as the city swelled and the ash thickened.

But the pull of dancing, light, and sound is too intoxicating to ignore. Up on stage, a man is operating a musical input device—it's like nothing I've ever seen. His fingers sweep, dodge, and weave through the projected light. Immediately, I recognize its connection with the ebb and flow of the rhythms within the music. I close my eyes and let it wash over me. I sway, letting the beat drift me away.

Rip.

My tranquility ends in an instant with the forceful sting of my mask being ripped from my face. Panic pulls me back into reality, and I clutch at my mouth and nose in a pathetic attempt to keep the poisons out. A pungent aroma of alcohol, sugar, and sweat overwhelms me. I know I should have nothing to fear, all these people are dancing wildly, gulping deep breaths of unfiltered air, but I'm so conditioned against the idea of breathing in buildings without airlocks that my hands remain glued over my lips.

Turning to see who pulled off my mask, I come face to face with a woman not much older than myself. She's striking. Plump cheeks soften her chiseled teardrop face. Orange light reflecting from the stage burns in her downturned eyes.

"If you're going to try and fit in here you might want to at least look the part." She practically shouts to make herself heard over the thundering noise of the music.

"But there's no airlock." They are the only words I can think to reply, and I immediately regret them.

The woman tilts her head back and roars with laughter.

"You are definitely not from around here. How old are you? I bet you're still in school."

"Neptus Memorial. But I'm graduating soon."

Her face turns up in amused understanding.

"Rich kid. I don't think mommy and daddy would like to find out you've been hanging around a place like this."

"My parents don't care what I do."

"Tell them you've been here and I'm sure you won't have that smug look on your face."

I notice my smirk and drop it. Shouting to hear each other escalated the conversation faster than I think either of us intended.

The woman takes a deep breath and relaxes her furrowed brow.

"I'm sorry kid, what's your name?"

"Evelyn. Evelyn Brennan. And you are?"

Her face lights up with a smile.

"Delia. Pleasure to meet you, Evelyn."

She offers me her hand. I pull off my glove and take it trying to squeeze firm enough that she takes me seriously without going overboard, or worse giving her the dead fish. She looks me over, shaking her head with an inscrutable grin. She drops my hand—the music overtakes the silence growing between us.

"If you want to talk, there is a quieter place," she says motioning behind her with a jerk of her head.

"Sure," I say, standing.

Anticipation twirls in my stomach. She moves through the dancers like smoke. I follow her bumping into nearly everyone I pass exchanging soot for sweat with each collision. She pulls open the door to the back. The light pouring through it is so bright it's like a portal to another world. She's moving quick and doesn't stop to see if I'm still behind her. Heavy springs over the door start to pull it closed. I rush forward nearly spilling a guy's beer.

"Watch it!"

I manage to grab the door before it closes. Holding it open with both hands, I cross the threshold. The thick door springs shut behind me cutting the volume of the driving music to a muffled rumble. I let out a sigh of relief happy that I can hear myself think again. She's already halfway down the hallway so I jog to keep up.

I rush past open doors along the hallway framing vignettes of things I'm struggling to comprehend: life. Each room is decorated with a dizzying array of fabrics, colors, textures, furniture, and paintings but no two rooms are the least bit alike. In one room, men and women not much older than I am sit around an old-school turntable sipping on dark spirits. In another, they sit in a circle on the floor talking, laughing, playing music on well-worn guitars. Each room is an intimate huddle as unique as the styled-up people inside.

My pace begins to lag as I try to drink it all in.

"Come on kid."

Embarrassment tempers my stupor. I pick up the pace following her to the large, dimly lit room at the end. I pass through the beaded curtain and pause a moment to take it all in. The wall and ceiling are draped in bright patterned fabrics making the whole room feel like the inside of the world's biggest blanket fort. Paper lanterns hanging all over at various heights wash the room in a warm amber light. Tiny slivers of the concrete floor peek out from under an array of plush carpets. They appear to have been vividly colored at some point, but soot-covered feet have painted them a uniform reddish gray. Pillows of assorted sizes and wild patterns dot the room. A half-dozen people are curled out around the perimeter fast asleep.

Delia plops down on a particularly large and comfortable looking pillow with her back up against the far wall. She beckons me to do the same on a clean pillow next to her. My movement disturbs the haze of incense and tobacco. The smell rushes to my head and the room wobbles a little. The unfamiliar incense and all too familiar tobacco stir up an uncomfortable mixture of curiosity and disgust. I stop in front of her. She turns my mask over and over in her hands.

I gesture around the room, "Are you sure we can talk in here?"

She looks up from the mask and smirks. "Absolutely. Believe me, they're passed out—you couldn't wake them up if you wanted to."

Trusting her, and growing more embarrassed by the second, I drop my backpack then fall onto the pillow. It wraps me in its velvety embrace. The weight on my chest lifts away in an instant. Now I understand why everyone else in the room is fast asleep. Eyes drifting shut, the tension in my muscles starts to liquify then hardens in a snap—I still have my filthy overcoat on! I jump back up, scrambling to unbutton it and pull it off. Two buttons free, I stop and look down at the now soiled pillow.

"Don't worry about it, we aren't exactly at the Savoy."

I sigh and plop back down. "Thanks, but I still feel bad—everything in here is just so beautiful. I've never been any place like this or seen…" My words trail off as I struggle to take in the radical vibrancy of the room.

"Take a deep breath kid, relax. There are a lot of things to get worked up about in this world, but dirty pillows aren't one of them."

The muffled bass rumbles through the floor marking time in rhythmic pulses. I'm overwhelmed with the urge to shout, cry, laugh, and scream. I feel like I fell through the mirror into another world and I can't seem to catch my breath. Even so, I never want to go back.

Delia shifts around, itching to get the conversation moving again.

"So, Neptus Memorial, huh? I haven't been there myself, but I hear it's not much cozier than a mortuary."

"Basically. Everything is so uniformly gray in there it's impossible to even tell where you're going. You might as well be walking in place—the scenery doesn't change."

She chuckles. "And I bet you live in one of those sleek modern apartments so clean and sterile you could do an operation on somebody right there on the bathroom floor."

I nod in full agreement. Where I live and where I am couldn't be further apart from each other. I've seen pictures of ballrooms and palaces and lavish sets in the fantasy serials. But the idea of the thing and the reality of it are wholly different. Velvet crumples under my fingers, a jumbled mix of aromas swirls in my nose, and the glorious bass track hammers through my bones. None of that comes through in the pictures.

Delia fishes through her pockets and pulls out a tarnished silver cigarette case. She pops it open and holds it out offering me one.

I contemplate it for a moment, even stretching my fingers out eager to indulge in one more act of disobedience. But I stop myself short. The sight of her hand-rolled cigarettes conjures an amalgamation of sense memories and dumps them on my tongue. Father's stained fingers. Their fights about quitting. Mother's desperate pleas to keep me from smoking and his absentminded offerings of a puff.

"No, thanks."

She shrugs and pulls one free. She strikes a flimsy paper match bringing it crackling to life—her eyes dance with fire. She takes a few drags then rummages around under the pillows next to her, retrieves an ashtray made from the lid of an old can, and snuffs it out.

"I'm always one away from quitting…" She chuckles to herself picking up my mask again. "But then I think, what better way to give a big middle finger to the Caretakers?"

"I hadn't thought of it like that, but in the end aren't you just hurting yourself?"

She points at me, bouncing her head to concede the point.

"So what brought you down here, just curiosity? Or were you hoping to jab the Caretakers in the side a little too?"

The compulsion to break myself free is the strongest, surest thing I've ever felt. But to put it in words? I don't even know where I'd start.

"Both, sure. But it's more than that. I don't know, I've just always felt it. That something's not right. The way things are…" I shake my head. I haven't spoken this out loud to anyone, not even myself, and it's showing.

"Hey, it's all right." She leans forward putting a comforting hand on my knee. "Growing up you just accept things, it all starts to feel normal. But it isn't normal. You don't need to explain yourself to anyone. You're new to all this, but you've already done a hell of a lot more than most people ever do. They live their whole lives turning a blind eye."

I linger on her words. The way things are. The Caretakers, our Great Society. Regimented, isolated, dark, terrifying.

"I just can't fit these worlds together," I say looking away from her piercing gaze. "Everything up there, and this here," I pat my pillow. "They're as different as night and day. I have a life up there, but down here… I feel alive."

"Unbearable, isn't it?"

"It's overwhelming."

"I pulled myself out of their crap years ago. I don't regret it for a second. But I'd be lying if I told you that life down here is always like this. I don't know what kind of fantasy Isadore promised you." *Isadore? Who is she talking about?* "But this isn't a path to be taken lightly. No matter how much space you carve out for yourself down here, they'll always be just up there pressing you down with their boots."

She opens her mouth to continue, then stops—the confusion on my face creeps onto hers.

"Wait a second. Isadore sent you, right?"

A prickling itch spreads down my back. *Oh no, what have I stumbled into?* Everything kicked up inside me implodes into a boulder that comes crashing down on my chest.

I can't drop the mortified look from my face. All I can manage to do is shake my head no.

"Hold on—Hold on," she puts her hand up imploring the universe to make her a one-time exemption and turn the clocks off. "You're that minister's kid, right? He said you'd be about seventeen…" She jumps up and starts running her fingers through her hair—her other hand constricts around the straps of my mask. "How did you find us then?"

I gulp hard. There was never any doubt in my mind that this place is totally prohibited, if not downright illegal. But I've been so caught up in it that I haven't thought to put two and two together—any place like this can't have uninvited guests.

"I was wandering around and heard the music—"

"What?"

"—I was curious, so I followed it down here."

My words land like a sucker punch. She starts mumbling to herself trying to talk her way through it. It comes to her in a flash and her face morphs into horror—the blood drains from her olive skin.

She bursts into action sprinting flat-out back to the dance floor. My heart is throwing itself against my ribs. Dread pours over me as I look around and realize that I'm trapped. I pull myself out of the pillow, throw my backpack on, and get everything rebuttoned ready to run.

Heads pop out of the rooms as Delia runs past them. She throws open the door without breaking stride. The music rises then recedes as the door pulls itself shut.

Panicked murmuring streams out of the rooms. A man steps into the hallway. He looks intently at the door then turns to stare at me. He looks back to the door, then whips back around.

The baseline stops. Without it, I notice my trembling.

His eyes balloon. He stumbles over himself, falls, then he's on his feet again flying to the door.

"Bug out!" He throws the door open and disappears.

The rest of them come rushing out, getting jammed in the

doorways as they push past each other desperate to flee.

Numb I take a step back, then forward, unsure which is the safest way to go.

All of them rush for the door at once, some pushing, some pulling. The door stands fast. Something cuts through the screams, a shrill razor at the top of my hearing.

The door bursts open and the gaggle tumbles over. Delia emerges climbing over the writhing mass of flailing arms and kicking legs. She blows through the beaded curtain and hurls my mask at me. I catch it, stinging my hands.

"Help me get them up."

Her words give my adrenaline an outlet. I throw myself into the task, rushing from person to person shaking them by the shoulders to get them up.

"Wake up! Get up! Quick, Quick!"

A few of them blink awake, sitting up slow and rubbing their eyes until they grasp what's happening then they burst to their feet.

"Get up!"

I'm shaking her as hard as I can, but she won't wake up.

"Wake up!"

Delia grabs me by the arm.

"We did our best, come on. We have to get out of here."

She pulls me down the hallway our speed building as we go. I catch only the briefest of flashes of one of the rooms. The chairs are all upended and awkward. Spilled alcohol drips off the couch.

There it is again, that stabbing I can only just hear.

The doorway has cleared up some but it's still a logjam. We fight our way through the frantic swarm and make it through the door. I keep my eyes on her green shirt, so we don't get pulled apart in the tide.

The atmosphere, so inviting before, has vanished replaced by terror and stinking panic. Daylight streams through the front door now swung wide open—everyone is making a mad dash for it crushing themselves into an impassible blob.

My heart sinks at the sight of the open door and the falling ash outside.

I pull on my mask—my fingers fumbling like sausages. Hair snags painfully in the straps. Fear grips me. Everything is over-saturated, loud, and confusing. What do I do?

A wild elbow catches me in the gut. Wind knocked out, I double over. A knee catches the side of my face showering the world in silver stars. Below the sight line, someone crashes into me sending us both sprawling to the floor.

The world narrows. *Is this where it ends, trampled to death on a sticky concrete dance floor?*

A hand takes me firmly by the collar and yanks me up enough for me to get my feet under me.

"Get up, Evelyn!" Delia guides me out of the chaos to a pocket of calm next to the bar.

Bleeet!

The Peace Officer's whistle slices clean through the din. I throw my hands over my ears as panic explodes into pandemonium. The shadows of Peace Officers reach down the stairs in staccato flashes of red siren light. Those closest to the door see what's coming and turn to run. Unable to see over each other, the people at the back are still pushing to get through.

Delia pulls my arm so hard it nearly pops out of the socket.

"Out the back way!" I can see that she's screaming but her voice sounds like its coming from under the ocean.

"Stop where you are. You are under arrest. The law compels you to comply." The modulated roar of the loudspeaker makes it to our ears just as the first baton finds its mark.

Batons crack. Bones crunch. Blood sprays.

The throng collapses in the middle. A crest of bodies forms as both ends desperately scramble to reach the assumed safety of the other side. The screams of the trampled push me over the edge and everything falls to static—the world shifts and slides over itself.

We get to the door a few strides ahead of everyone else.

She lets go of me once we're through. Arms free to pump, I fly down the hallway. I stop just short of the back wall.

"Help me take it down!"

Delia tugs on the curtain covering the back wall. I join her and our combined force tears the fabric from the wall taking its haphazard anchors with it. It falls away revealing a steel door with a heavy bolt securing it to the door jamb.

I take the bolt in both hands and heave.

"It won't budge!"

"Out of the way!" She shoulders me aside and pulls on the bolt. Veins bulge in her forehead. Nothing.

"Fuck! We need a lever. Look around for something!"

I turn, ready to sprint to one of the rooms but there's no way that's going to happen. People are starting to spill into the hallway—their faces twisted and pained.

"No time!"

I rush back and add my strength to hers.

Clunk.

A wave of euphoria washes over me. Our combined force was just enough to unbind the bolt.

A Peace Officer, baton raised and spattered in blood, enters the hallway.

Out of options, people are falling to their knees and offering their hands up in submission. Unwilling to surrender, a big man surges down the hallway, blows past the beaded curtain, and slams into the door knocking us aside. In his panic, he tries to *push* the door open.

"Out of the way!" Delia drives her knee into his leg just behind the knee. Staggered, she grabs his shoulders and throws him back.

"Take my hand!" Delia tugs me to her side then throws open the door. She pulls me through, and we bolt like rabbits.

It's near total darkness—a handful of faint utility bulbs paint the edges of the boxes in the basement storeroom. The sound of the chase nips at our heels.

Rounding a corner, a shaft of light streams down a staircase guiding us in like a beacon. We race up the stairs with reckless haste. We emerge into a shop that's clearly been out of business for some time. The displays and counters are draped in heavy cotton covered in a quarter inch layer of dust.

Our pace doesn't slow, we surge toward the light coming from the front window display. The lock twists and she throws the door open. Two boards have been nailed in a zigzag on the outside.

"You've got to be kidding me."

Bracing herself on both sides of the door, Delia smashes her foot through the bottom board. We crawl through the gap onto the sidewalk.

One street over from the club, the commotion has brought traffic to a complete standstill. Chrome hulks rumble and belch their displeasure in putrid clouds of black smoke. There is a moment's hesitation as we scan for our next move.

"There!" Delia points across the street to a narrow alleyway. She takes off weaving and jumping her way through the cars. Motorists lay on their horns. I follow her as fast as I can, keeping my eyes fixed on her green shirt to guide me through the sea of gray and black.

We pass through the traffic jam and dip into the alley unseen by the gaggle of pedestrians clustering up at the barricades. Approaching sirens echo in the claustrophobic city canyons. Darting left and right into connecting branches, we quickly lose sight of the street and rapidly increase the distance between us and anyone still giving chase.

"Keep moving—we need to keep moving," Delia says.

I'm trying to keep up, but each breath is a ragged gasp—my throat coppery and raw. My lungs feel ready to catch fire and my legs are quickly turning into cooked noodles. She doesn't give up the pace and I don't want to let her down.

She leads us through the confusing maze of alleys with almost too much confidence. I dare a glance over my shoulder—no one else seems to have picked this way. But it's too late to change course now.

Delia takes us into a small, blind alley partly obscured by a dumpster. Delia presses her back to the wall and slides to the ground. She pulls a disposable gas mask out from a small pouch on her waist and fastens it over her nose and mouth.

Everything hurts and I'm gasping for air, but I'm bursting with life and I can't stop smiling.

"Are you okay? Do we need to get you to a hospital?" I say panicked. I've never seen anyone outside without their mask. You'll die. It's that simple. Or at least it was until a few moments ago.

"No, I'm okay," she fights to catch her breath. "We need to lay low as long as possible. They're on high alert now."

Delia looks down at her vibrant shirt steadily turning black in the falling ash.

"What now?" I ask.

"I can't be seen right now—I'm a dead giveaway in this green shirt. I'll need to wait until dark before I can get out of here. You, on the other hand, can still slip onto the sidewalk and blend in. You need to get home. You need to get back to your parents."

"Like they care," I say still catching my breath and feeling too many things to filter myself.

She sighs shaking her head. "You just need to cool down for a little while, get your head back on your shoulders."

"But, can't I come with you?"

Her laugh turns into a cough. "No. I know you're still fired up right now, that adrenaline feels good—there's nothing quite like getting away. But you're not thinking straight. Sleep it off, reflect on it, then table it for a year. This life," she gestures to the formless gray sky and the gently falling ash. "My life isn't something you just jump into."

I shake her words out of my ears. "You know things. Things I want to know. I mean look at you, your mask—you didn't need a mask! I know I'm amped up, but why the hell not? We're alive! Nothing makes sense, but that doesn't matter. I can finally get to the truth."

Delia lifts her head locking her eyes with mine.

"You don't know what you're talking about kid. We were so lucky today. Things could've turned out a hell of a lot different. You want the truth? I'll lay it out for you. This still isn't real for you. You can go home and take a hot shower, eat a nice meal with Mom and Dad, and lose yourself in a primetime hit. But I'll be ducking and hiding in alleyways, digging through dumpsters for dinner, and squatting on rooftops tonight. You think you're ready for all this, but trust me, you're as green as they come. Until you can wrap your head all the way around today, the smartest thing you can do is stop looking for things you aren't ready to understand."

"I'm not going to stop looking."

Delia drops her head. Only the movement of falling ash breaks the stillness while she thinks.

"I'll give you one thing Evelyn, you've got grit."

She looks up at me and I hardly recognize her. The woman who approached me in the club is gone. Her vibrance has turned to stone. She's laid herself bare unveiling her cracking core of grim resolve.

"So tell me then, what's the question that's driving you?"

My answer is automatic. "Why do we wear masks?"

She studies my face.

"I'm not talking about the soot. I mean, how did we get to where we are? How did this," I turn my palms up to catch a sticky ink-black snowflake, "become what life is?"

"That's a big pill to swallow. If you're serious about this," I take a step toward her and nod. "Then you've got to break it down. You're not going to like the answers you find—once you ask this question there's no coming back."

I take another step forward—I'm six feet tall with anticipation.

She lets out a long, deliberate breath. "What's hidden in the silver trucks?"

I gulp hard. Fire courses through my blood. Silver trucks? What is she talking about? Nearly every word I've heard today has revealed something new about the world, yet I can't help but think that I'm understanding it less and less.

She reels forward. A short spasm of hacking coughs leaves her gasping for air. Helplessness tugs at me.

She takes a minute to compose herself. "You've got to be smart about this," soot falls from her shaking head. "Treat this like a loaded gun. Blend in, cover your tracks, and don't make waves."

Her warning sinks home. Peace Officers don't take kindly to abnormal behavior. It's beat out of you your whole life to the point where it becomes unimaginable. And I saw firsthand today what happens to people who cut their own path.

Delia pushes herself out of the filth that's piled up around her. Her pace is weary. Not from the sprint, but from being on the run. I can't shake the feeling that I'm looking at my future self. The thought sinks into the pit of my stomach and does a flip.

She turns away from me taking long strides down the alley. I panic. This has been too much too quick, and I still have so many questions.

"Wait, you can't go." More anxiety seeps into my words than I'd like.

Delia locks eyes with me. I see something there, familiar, yet I cannot express it. Like the look Mother gave me all those years ago, this too will haunt me.

"Tread carefully, Evelyn."

I stand frozen as I watch her turn the corner and disappear. I've hardly stepped foot in her world and it's already slipping away from me. I think of crying out to her but decide better of it—patrols could still be looking for us. Paralysis gnaws at me. If I let her get away now, I may never find my way to the answers. Willing my begrudging body to move, I run after her as fast as the slippery cobblestones allow.

The alley forks and diverges. I pick paths on impulse, then double back when they too turn up empty. Lungs rasping, throat burning, I slow to a walk. Tears pull the world out of focus. I found what I was looking for and I let it slip away.

The weight of the day builds on my shoulders. My heart slows and the last of my adrenaline fades away. I slump against the wall and let myself slide, limp, to the bottom. Swollen tears stream down my face, pooling in the inner seal around my eyes. One piece at a time, I pull all the emotions this encounter unleashed back into place and rise from the cold, stone alley.

I take my time, checking around every corner before I press forward. I wind my way through alleyways and side streets for well over an hour before I stumble across a road I recognize.

Foot traffic is picking up as people hurry home before the last of the daylight fades away. I slip out of the shadows and disappear into the crowd.

The only thing I know for certain is that my life will never be the same. Everything hurts and I still don't have all my wind back, but there's a fire burning inside me, and I can't stop smiling.

CHAPTER FIVE

WITH THE SUN NOW SET, the roads are tricky to navigate in the sickly-yellow glow of the streetlights. In the large gaps between light posts, the darkness is as thick and suffocating as the falling ash.

I keep moving with the thinning crowd until I make it back to familiar surroundings. Across the street from me stands the imposing visage of my apartment complex. Pausing to look at it, I realize its enormity for the first time. Shooting higher into the sky than the buildings around it, it looms over everything in sight.

Everything feels different. The world seems darker, the ash thicker. My mask is heavy and uncomfortable on my face. The sounds of wet soot sloshing under the wheels of passing cars and the dull hum of neon lamps fill me with dread.

It's as if my eyes have been opened for the first time, only instead of seeing the world illuminated, it's now engulfed in total darkness. I am blind.

I pass through the airlock and enter the lobby. A small fleet of mopbots dart across the floor, leaving it polished and clean in their wake. They disappear into hidden panels along the wall.

Mr. Standish glances up at me from behind the concierge desk and cracks a smile before returning to the pages of his *Caretaker's Quarterly*. He's friendly, but I don't feel welcome here.

The elevator whirs its comforting sounds. I exhale completely for the first time in hours. Emptying my lungs of the day, I refill them with filtered, lemon-tinged air. I'm feeling better already. Today has been a whirlwind, and I am floating in the unknown, but at least I have something to orient from. How can the air be poisonous if Delia didn't die? This mystery is certainly bigger than just air you can't breathe, but it's a place to start. If I can answer that I can move on to the bigger questions and maybe one day, I'll no longer be in the dark.

Ding. The elevator doors glide open. Pacing down the hall, I suddenly remember how late it is. Is Mother worried? Has she even noticed? She always tells me to be free, so she shouldn't have a problem with how late I stay out. Unconcerned, I open the door.

Immediately I know I'm wrong. Mother sits on the edge of the couch rocking back and forth. Her hands, clasped tight, are red from wringing them. Seeing me, she jumps up and runs down the hall toward me.

"Evelyn? Darling, I was so worried."

She wraps her arms around me. Her embrace is uncommon but not unwelcome. I hug her back. She pushes herself away to look me in the face, our masks eye port to eye port.

"Never do that again! Do you know how much anguish you caused me? I phoned the school, Peace Officers. I've been here worried sick."

"You called Peace Officers?"

A knot closes up my throat. If I hadn't followed Delia out of there, we'd be having this conversation at a detention center, and the tone would be drastically different. I swallow hard.

"I'm sorry, Mother. I didn't mean to worry you. I walked home from school. That's all."

She embraces me again.

"You could have gotten yourself killed, Evelyn. I don't want you doing that again."

Her grip tightens—all the warmth of the hug is gone.

"You can't let them get you, Evelyn… you can't."

Her fingers dig into my back. I wince, rocking my shoulders to escape.

The fire flashes out of her eyes. She lets go and wanders away.

"I'm going to bed." Her voice, drained of all emotion, is barely audible.

Dazed, I watch her slink off and disappear into her room. I can't make sense of her vacillating tone. She wants me to live and be free, but she also deeply fears the air, the subversives— everything. I know there is a battle raging inside her but how am I supposed to interact with her when I never know which way is up?

She's just as blind as I am. She doesn't know, so she can only fear. I want to empathize with her, but the pain in my back where her fingers dug into me makes it difficult.

I hang my coat up on the rack next to Mother's—my eyes linger on the empty hooks. Father still isn't home. Not wishing to wait for him and risk another indecipherable parental inter- action, I get ready for bed.

All night I dream of the club. The bright colors, the heat, the smell—life. Mother's fingers in my back. The look in Delia's eyes.

Morning slams into me like a truck. Ready or not, Mother enters my room. Still in her mask, still silent. Obediently, I re- place my filter. As soon as I do, she slinks back off to her room.

Getting up and dressed, I push her from my mind while I rub the sleep from my eyes.

Why we wear our masks is all I can think about on the way to school.

<hr>

Three more documentaries today. *C for Citizen* was by far the standout picture. The junky old speakers choked and crackled every time the bombastic soundtrack played. Speer fumbled with the controls trying to anticipate the music and turn it down before it would overload and fill the room with shrieking noise. But for every one success, he had two mishaps. He would inadvertently turn down the narration and then, in an attempt to make it audible, crank the volume just as the music would start.

I literally bit my tongue a few times to keep from bursting into laughter.

The end of day bell rings, and I nearly burst up from my seat. My cheeks ache from muffled laughter and thoughts of the club swim so vividly in front of my eyes I have to restrain myself from reaching out for them.

I take slow, controlled breaths to keep myself from bouncing down the hall.

Wait in line, through the airlock, outside.

A gale of slag veils the city cloaking my movements. I look around to make sure no one notices me stepping out of line. Feeling confident no one can spot me through the impenetrable haze, I avoid the buses and sprint off toward the club.

I tuck my head down and hold my coat collar up to shield my neck from the stinging grit.

Turning the corner out of view of the school, a hot rush of excitement surges through me. Logically I know Delia won't be there. Peace Officers have no doubt scoured the place and sealed it up. But a flicker of hope aches in my chest. Maybe, just maybe, she's there waiting for me, eager to lead me into worlds I can't imagine. Compelled back to the club with reckless haste, I'm untouchable, invisible, and fully alive.

Rush hour traffic is starting to clog the roads. People emerge onto the sidewalk like water seeping from stone. Not a single eye lifts to notice me as I pass.

Anticipation reaching a fever pitch, I nearly break into a run as I round the final corner. Coming around the bend, my journey meets a jarring end. A tall man clasps me on the shoulder and shoves me back. Totally unprepared, I tumble to the sidewalk.

"Not that way," he says.

"What the hell!" I say brushing myself off—his words eluding me.

Collar up, hands shoved into his overcoat's pockets, he keeps moving without so much as turning his head.

I scoff loudly. Agitated, I try to shake it off, but my fantasy is shattered.

Wind howls in the canyon of tower blocks that disappear in the gray-black cloud looming above. Yellow caution tape wrapped around the stairwell flaps violently. Red and blue lights sweep over everything. Realization snaps in. I feel faint.

Crouching low, I dare a glance around the corner. Peace Officers are still swarming the club. Inspectors are furiously punching findings into their data slates while others sift through the soot looking for clues.

My heart is pounding so hard I can scarcely hear the traffic. Shaky, I bounce up and beeline back the way I came. The bustle of the street rages in my head—every flash of light in my periphery sends fresh waves of tingling shivers radiating out from behind my ears.

"Evelyn? What are you doing here?"

I freeze. That tone—smoked honey. Victoriana is standing two paces in front of me disappearing and reappearing as pedestrians flow around us. Shit, she must have followed me. Anxiety constricts my throat. She inches forward—her progress impeded by the current. The instant she crosses out of view, I bolt.

Victoriana calls out. I ignore her and press on. Soon the rumbling of traffic and thundering of shoes on the sidewalk drown her out. I run as fast as I can. I run like devils are chasing me.

I linger with my hand on the door until my heart rate slows to normal. Soft muzak plays in the hallway. Flustered, I can't bring myself to open the door and enter the apartment. What version of Mother awaits me on the other side?

Knowing I have little choice in the matter, and every moment gives her anger more time to boil, I exhale sharply and press inside.

The apartment is cold. The lights flicker on to greet me. Blue light dances under her door. I tiptoe to the bathroom, crank the shower, and lose myself to the steam.

***

Bound like a wire, I get little sleep. Mother shuffles into my room right on cue. Twist, plunk, twist.

By the time I'm ready for school, she's back in her room—blue light already dancing under the door. I check the kitchen—no breakfast set out this morning. Lingering by the door, I run my finger over Father's empty hook.

Retreating into myself, I sigh and give in to the routine.

***

From the moment I stepped into class, Victoriana's eyes have been drilling into the back of my head. After the morning's first film—*Make Mine Freedom*—finished up, I dared a glance back at her. There she was, sitting in the middle of her gaggle like the eye of a hurricane—her sycophants passing notes under their desks around her. Our eyes met, and my throat seized. Her eyes burned like blue neon. I turned around as quick as I could—sweat beading under my collar. I blinked away the afterimage of her piercing eyes as Speer fought with the projector to get *Just Punishment* playing. The image stuttered, and the speakers grumbled, but it smoothed out by the end of the opening credits.

Has she told anyone what she saw yesterday? I mean there wasn't anything to see. Right? She's probably telling her friends that I was at the crime scene to destroy evidence or something. She's probably telling them I'm a subversive.

She has it out for me, and if I'm not careful things could get out hand fast. What if she went to Inspector Aldridge during lunch and told her I was plotting to sabotage the school's air filters? She could have me sent to the pits or worse. Just with a word. I bet she's loving this. Having something to hold over my head, make me squirm. I bet it's just like squashing an ant to her. She probably doesn't even see me as a person. And what have I ever done to her?

I dig back through every memory I have of her. Every passive aggressive comment. Every party invitation snub. I dig all the way back to first year. There is nothing there. Not even a glimmer of friendship or kindness—a gaping cavernous maw. Staring into it, my head begins to throb—a pain like hot needles being shoved between my eyes keeps me from looking any deeper.

Eyes slammed tight, pulsing waves of light flash before them. Nausea pushes me to the brink. I'm desperate to pinch the bridge of my nose or rub my temples. Anything to relieve this headache. But encased in my mask, I hold my head in vain.

The prattle of the projector stops and the classroom's fluorescents flash on. I stifle a whimper.

"How about that class? Good, right? That's one of my favorites. Really shows you the cost of stepping out of line. Now up!"

Still reeling from this fiendish headache, I'm up and marching in line without a thought.

Head in my hands, I shuffle along guiding myself with peeks at the heels in front of me. I've walked this path so many hundreds of times I don't have to look up to know that we're almost there.

Wham! A slam to my shoulders pushes me out of line and through the door of the girl's bathroom. Alert, I pivot around. Victoriana is holding me by the shirt, pushing me back. I reach out and grab the sink before she rams me into it. She lets go of me then rushes over to the stalls. She pushes them open one by one. Empty. She moves to the lock on the door and throws it with a *thunk*.

"What was that all about yesterday? Huh? Have you gotten yourself mixed up in something? You need to be more careful." She pulls off her mask, tousles her hair out of her face, then locks eyes with me. It's like staring into an open flame. Unable to match her gaze, I look down at her boots and step forward. Everything's hot and spinning so I just open my mouth and let fly.

"Oh, so now all of a sudden you give a shit about me? Or are you only a bitch when you've got your little posse around? And how is where I go any business of yours? Where do you get off attacking me? You're the one following me around!"

"What has gotten into you? You've been so," she shakes her head then throws her hands up in exacerbation. "So hostile lately. You keep looking at everyone like they've got the plague or something."

"Well, that's how you treat me."

"I'll admit I haven't been very kind. But I didn't start this. You're the one ghosting all of us. Staring right through us like we don't exist. That hurts, Evelyn."

"Oh please. We aren't friends."

Tears well in her eyes clinging to her long eyelashes like dew.

"What is going on with you? You aren't yourself. You haven't been yourself in a long time. You aren't talking to anyone. Going out after school. And now you're stepping out of bounds, breaking the rules. I don't know who you are anymore."

She might as well be speaking in a long-dead language—I can't make heads or tails of anything she's saying. Rifling through memories, I can't piece together anything like what she's talking about. But there is something there amorphous and hazy. I dive in after them. My brain is screaming. I can almost grasp them—their tendrils are slipping through my fingers but only just. I try harder, but the closer to the memories I come, the more my head pounds. I grab hold of one. Electric fire explodes in my brain ricocheting back and forth between my temples.

The pain throws me into a rage—I latch onto the last words I can remember her saying and explode.

"I'm breaking the rules, look at you!" I cast an accusatory finger. "Taking your mask off—if Speer or Aldridge find out… tsk tsk tsk."

Tears drop from Victoriana eyes. "Evelyn, what are you doing? Why are you being like this? I'm just trying to look out for you."

"What was that?" I cock my head to the side and look her right in the eyes. "I'm sorry I'm so air-brained I didn't catch that."

Aghast, Victoriana shakes her head as she backs up to the door. "What did I ever do to deserve this from you?"

A thousand things come to mind. *You could be nicer to me. You could have invited me in instead of constantly pushing me away.* But I say nothing—I let the silence speak for itself.

"Don't say I never warned you."

"Whatever. Bye Vicky." I twiddle my fingers as mockingly as I can. Shaking her head, she puts her mask on, checks the seals then exits without a backward glance.

As soon as the door closes, I rush to the nearest stall and slam the door. What is going on? Is she going to turn me in? Was she actually trying to help me? What am I going to do? There is no way this is going to end well.

Just breathe, Evelyn.

Pulling myself together, I flush the toilet for anyone who's listening, wash my hands, then head to the dining hall. Nothing out of the ordinary here. Everything is fine.

I grab my emergency ration and sit as far from Victoriana as possible. I close my eyes and try my best to rub the lingering pings of fire racing around on my temples.

The loud crackle of the classroom's speakers coming to life pulls me out of my head. Watching Speer fiddle with the command module, it's clear that something isn't working. The speakers start playing the audio of our next documentary, *Great Occupations in the Great Society,* but the projector isn't firing up.

"Damnable thing!"

Speer slams a fist into the command module and the narration stops. We hold our tongues, but I'm sure I'm not the only one with a smirk on my face.

"Stand by, students."

Speer turns and leaves the room without waiting for our response. He doesn't have to. He knows that we are incapable of anything but obedience, and sadly enough he's right. My mind drifts back to the club.

It was cramped, loud, chaotic, and intimidating, but it was also alluring, sensational, and alive. The contrast between then and now is so strong that I'm starting to doubt if it was real or just a vivid fantasy. Reveries of batons, screaming, and running push those doubts aside. It was all too real. And so easily shattered.

If I can't figure out what to do about Victoriana, I might never have a chance at that kind of freedom again.

Speer returns followed by two gangly men in brown coveralls wearing simple half masks with hoses connecting them to boxy filters clipped to their sides.

"The projector finally crapped out huh? We'll get it up and running again, but it'll take us a while," says one of the disconcertingly similar technicians. The other shakes his head up and down in agreement.

"I thought that might be the case. All right students listen up. The projector needs to be repaired. We will work around this by going to the computer room for some unstructured lab time."

The other students fidget with excitement, but I don't. Oh, I'm excited, but for completely different reasons. I have a plan.

"Settle down. Don't make me regret this. Stand up! Proceed to the computer lab single file."

CHAPTER SIX

AT SPEER'S COMMAND, we rise from our desks and file out into the corridor. We shuffle our way there under the withering stares of monitors patrolling the halls like aimless sharks.

The computer lab is a dreary little box crammed with long tables and more than enough computers for the whole class. I move quickly to get a computer as far from the instructor's desk as possible. Speer always looks, and I can't have him looking today.

He enters last, taking his seat at the front of the room.

"You have an hour of unstructured computer time. I suggest you use it wisely."

Picking up his newest copy of *Drumbeat*, he kicks his feet up and leans back. Most everyone wastes no time logging into their terminals. Unrestricted, they pull up videos and begin instant messaging each other over the intranet.

Normally the computers are highly restricted. When we have access to them, we use them for specific lesson plans. Even then Speer is always leaning over your shoulder checking on you. But today is different.

This unexpected turn of events has me exhilarated. I can search for answers and get Victoriana off my back. Two for one.

Victoriana leads her gaggle to the row of computers in front of me. They don't seem to have any interest in using them though. Victoriana takes her spot in the middle—her unmistakable golden locks bounce as she talks. The girl to her right pulls some markers from her pocket and offers them up. With great zeal, they launch into drawing geometric shapes on each other's masks. I suppress the desire to roll my eyes. What's the point of any of that? That's not real rebellion, that's complacency.

Decorating your mask doesn't change what it is—you can't personalize something that erases your identity. Okay fine, if it brings them some measure of happiness, who am I to stop them? But no one is going to look at a dozen kaleidoscopic patterns and think, "Oh, that's so and so." They'll just see another young woman content in her prison. They might be, but I'm not.

Despite how I feel about it, their distraction has given me the opening I need. Every student must log in with their own individualized user ID and password. Once they've done so, every action they take is copied from their terminal and sent to the school's central database where Inspector Aldridge picks through every line to ensure we aren't looking at restricted materials.

In eighth year, I searched "What makes the Great Society so great?" That little act would have landed me two weeks detention if I hadn't been able to convince the Authoritarian and Inspector Aldridge that I had not meant for my search to be sarcastic and that I actually wanted to compare my own list of what makes the Great Society great with what the computer said. When the Authoritarian commanded me to recite what makes the Great Society 'humanity's crown jewel,' I froze. Aldridge threatened to put me in her imprint device, peel my thoughts open like a can of tuna, and find out for herself. After her threat, I burst open spewing patriotic praise from trembling lips.

I haven't used computers for anything out of bounds since. If I'm caught today, I don't think I'll be able to praise my way out of punishment. It worked when I was twelve, but at seventeen, the authorities start thinking about prison, not detention. Or maybe Aldridge will finally make good on her threat, open my mind up, turn me into a potato, and send me on a one-way trip to the pits. But I have a plan to dodge suspicion, and I think it'll work.

Normally the thought of getting someone else in trouble by using their login wouldn't cross my mind, but with Victoriana?

She treats me like garbage. She manipulates everyone in class. She spreads lies and starts rumors. She is a living embodiment of what's wrong with our society. She's probably never had as much as her pinky toe in hot water. A little dip will get her off my back *and* teach her a lesson. Besides, her parents are powerful people. They're high-level bureaucrats or something—she brags about whatever it is that they do all the time—I'm sure they could convince people to look the other way in the case of one, innocent, transgression.

Plus, she's an easy target. She is the only girl to have ever gone to Neptus Memorial with the initials VZ giving her the username VZ1. Knowing her username wouldn't be enough, but a few weeks back I watched her type in her password: vicky123. She's made this almost too easy. I know it's risky, and Victoriana might get in serious trouble, but this is my best shot at figuring out what Delia was talking about. I have to take it.

I watch her draw detailed patterns onto the mask of whoever is sitting next to her, Barbara or Britney. I don't remember, it's something vapid with a 'b.' Steeling myself, I begin.

My fingers dance through the terminal's projected light interface. I'm in. There is no telling how long they can keep themselves preoccupied with decorating their masks before they decide to use their computers, so I work as fast as I can. My fingers darting like lightning, I type in the question Delia left me with, "What's hidden in the silver trucks?" The search is instantaneous.

The Public Works and Infrastructure informational site opens, zooms down the page, then focuses in on a headline. "GSPWI workers toil around the clock to keep your streets clear of refuse, debris, and obstacles. We keep the city beautiful, so you don't have to."

Fantastic, more lies. More propaganda. What did I expect? The truth that easy? Just type in my burning question and have it instantly gratified with a clear and rational answer? Having wasted my one and only opportunity, I log out.

Heart racing, I lean back in my chair. Staring at the roof, the pockets, cracks, and discolored spots of the concrete scowl back at me with unflinching coolness. Nothing is that easy. I had one shot with that, one shot to find something out, and I threw it away. At least now I know for sure the computers are not to be trusted, and whatever the truth is, they really don't want people to stumble across it. I should have known that nothing is that easy to find, especially when the entire state apparatus is invested in keeping it hidden.

Victoriana finishes drawing a thick golden line completing the zigzag pattern on b-something's mask. As soon as the pen lifts from the rubber, the excitement of decorating the mask fades, and she abruptly turns to her computer terminal and logs in with fast, practiced fingers. Pages of fashion sites, media, and instant messaging clutter up every pixel of her screen.

I let out a sigh. That was close. Unable to look at her, and with apprehension knotting my stomach, I shift over to the empty terminal next to me and log into my own account. Pulling up pictures of the billboards that stare at me through the penthouse glass, I scour them hoping to find the secrets they're hiding.

Without warning, the door to the computer room bursts open. I look at the clock floating in the three dimensions of the illuminated light to see if it's time to go back and watch the documentary. It's only been ten minutes. My ears pull back with fear. Cautiously, I look up to see the towering form of Inspector Aldridge storming in.

All clacking and clicking stops dead. My skin tightens and the hairs on my neck prick up. Speer jerks up but makes sure to set his *Drumbeat* down carefully so as not to lose his place.

A half-dozen monitors spill through the doorway and fan out behind her. Aldridge's thick, muscular build bulges under her white OSS uniform.

"Victoriana Zarrov, come with me immediately."

Victoriana looks up from her screen. She hesitates to move. Hovering over her seat her eyes dart from Speer to Aldridge to me.

"Now!"

The rebreather amplifies the authority in Aldridge's voice sending a bolt of electricity through every spine in the room. Victoriana snaps up and with her head hung low, steps into the aisle. Aldridge grabs her by the scruff of her neck forcing her head down to waist level with a jerk. A monitor takes her by the arm, straightens her up, then leads her out. Her pleas echo down the hallway.

I'm trembling. The room is about to shatter.

Aldridge pivots, turning her inquisitorial gaze on Speer.

"Instructor Speer. You will come with me."

Three monitors step forward cutting off all his avenues of escape.

"Myriam, whatever she—"

"Comply, or I'll drag you out of here."

Speer gulps and scans the room. He's already lost face in front of the class—will he risk losing any more? He considers his options and finds only the one.

"At your command inspector."

Aldridge lifts her hand and the monitors move in. Surrounding him, they shepherd him out. Speer looks pained but offers no protest.

Aldridge and the remaining two monitors study us—her void gaze withers every student it crosses.

"Up! Everything stays exactly where it's at. Touch nothing. Now, back to class. There will be absolute silence. Comply?"

Coiled, everyone springs to their feet but me.

"Yes, ma'am!"

Aldridge turns to the monitors.

"Take them to their classroom and await my commands."

"Affirmative ma'am." Both click their heels in salute. Aldridge passes her eyes over us once more then exits the room.

The slender female monitor steps forward. "Leave everything exactly where it is. Touch nothing as you leave. File in behind me."

Mortified, class obeys without question. I rise from my seat at the last possible moment and slink in at the end of the line. The weight of an ocean presses down on my chest.

The stocky monitor follows us a few paces back. I can feel his eyes burning into the back of my head. He can see my guilt. He can see it written on every raised hair and bead of sweat.

The room is dark, empty, and cold. The automated systems kick on the fluorescent lights. They flicker until they warm up. The technicians have already finished—we probably could have just stayed in the room. They removed the old projector and replaced it with a new one. It's slightly blacker, but otherwise indistinguishable from the old one. New.

We pile into the room clumping up at the front. No one wants to do anything without being told.

The slender monitor barks at us.

"Get to your seats."

There is a collective reluctance to be the first person to move.

"Now!"

Panic surges us into action. There's some bumping but we all find our place. The stocky monitor stands akimbo blocking the door.

"Find a speck on the wall and study it. I don't want to hear so much as a cough."

Even if the monitors weren't here trying to intimidate us,

the lingering shock would be enough to keep us silent.

The clock ticks. Desks moan. Hector coughs then immediately cowers. The slender monitor remains sphinx-like at the front of the room.

I want to explode, grovel at Aldridge's feet and beg her to stop. "I didn't mean it. I just wanted to scare her—get her off my back. Please, please don't hurt her." But what good would that do? They'd drag me down the hallway and Victoriana would still be punished.

Nausea grows with each agonizing minute.

"Affirmative." I dare a glance out of the corner of my eye. The squat monitor has his head cocked to one side straining to understand the instructions sizzling through his earpiece.

"Copy that ma'am. They'll be down shortly." The slender monitor paces down the rows—striking her heel down hard with every step.

"One, two, three, four." She jabs each student as she goes along numbering them.

"One, two—" her bony finger misses my shoulder and hits me in the armpit. Outsized pain radiates into my back.

Finished numbering us she returns to the front.

"Number one's, line up at the door."

This time there's no hesitation—relief washes over the spared.

The slender monitor approaches Hector.

"Coughing boy. While we're gone, you're in charge. If there's as much as a whisper, you'll answer for it. Comply?"

His skin drains of life. He stands and nods in affirmation.

"All right, step to it."

She leads the column out the door.

Chairs and feet scuffle. Muted whimpers ripple around the room.

The door slams closed with a clang.

I focus on the X someone carved into the concrete and retreat into the depths of my mind.

It doesn't take long for Hector's terror to morph into pride. Standing shoulders back, arms crossed, the powerful pose he intends to strike comes off as delusional. He doesn't scare me, and I don't think anyone would keep themselves from talking on his account. Each of us is silent for ourselves.

Shucking off his sheep's skin has revealed a jackal. I bet one day he'll look back on this as the day he knew he would become a Peace Officer. I don't even have to imagine what kind of person he'll be once he's given his uniform and baton.

Lunch comes and goes. Growling stomachs mingle with

the tapping feet of students desperate to pee. The uncertainty of what's happening to Victoriana, the ones, and Speer is eating its way out of my empty stomach.

The door swings open without warning. There is a moment before they step through when anyone, or anything, could come rushing in.

Speer enters at the head of the ones. Is this a good sign or a bad one?

The one's file into their seats. Speer looms over Hector his chest seething.

"Take your seat."

"Yes, sir!" Hector says without hesitation. He nearly knocks his desk over in his haste to sit down. Speer pivots to address us. He's bent and disheveled. His left lapel is ripped and the blood on his collar is still glistening. His mechanical breaths are rapid and heaving.

"Before you all start raising your hands with questions, let me remind you that when a student is removed from class, their crime or punishment is none of your concern. If you prod me, or any other member of staff for answers, we will have to assume that you were an accomplice and take you in for punishment as well. Now, I know that you all understand these rules, I'm simply reiterating them for your own good."

Speer straightens up fussing with his lapel trying to get it back in order. He moves around the desk and retakes his seat.

The room buckles under the grating mechanical sounds of his assisted breaths.

When he finally catches his breath, so do we.

"Victoriana is being questioned by Inspector Aldridge." With his regular bravado missing his voice is tinny. "She will not be returning to class today. Because of her actions, twelfth-year computer lab privileges are being revoked until further notice."

He pulls a handkerchief from the desk drawer and dabs at his neck. He recoils and it comes away red. He stares at it twisting the bloodied cloth into a ball.

"But it's not all bad news." The bravado's back. "We now have more time to watch the Caretaker's videos. In fact, I think with our remaining hour we should be able to squeeze one more in today. We just might get through all of them before the redundant air scrubbers are installed and classes return to normal."

Speer stands and punches in the video at the command module. The new projector stutters on, and once again we are bombarded by the speaker's crackle.

"Listen to the thoughtful words of the narrator. I hope you take them to heart. Remember, you will be tested on all the different ways a citizen can make their life useful to society."

The film begins, and the narrator's voice attempts to grab my attention, but I'm deep below the waves and his sultry tones cannot find me.

What have I done? Is Victoriana being tortured because of me? What did Aldridge do to Speer? And what about the students they pulled out of class? Were they trying to get us to snitch?

It should be me in there.

Glancing up at the film, I can tell they aren't going to show us any of the more nefarious professions of the Great Society like those of the people interrogating Victoriana. Within these walls, at this very moment, she is terrified and in pain while we just sit here, vegetative. I feel like I'm going to flip inside out.

I can't be that carless again—using the computer was a terrible idea. No matter how bad Victoriana can be, she doesn't deserve what I did to her.

CHAPTER SEVEN

I WALLOW IN SHAME for the rest of the day. My mind boils with images of Victoriana in a thousand forms of anguish. I don't remember the end of day bell or following my classmates out of school and onto the bus, but here I am staring glassy-eyed out the window.

Traffic is surprisingly light today. Watching the city pass by in a blur takes my mind away from everything. It's amazing how the normally sad and bleak soot-covered buildings can be turned into swirling art by the movement of the bus. I wish more art looked like this instead of the overly bright and optimistic pictures of men and women working—their faces, like the woman on the Mountain Air billboard, overly enthusiastic. It has been my experience that no one looks like that, without medication anyway. I lose myself in the blurry world beyond the windows.

Slowly it begins to unswirl and reform into the solid shapes of black and gray buildings and the bobbing masked forms of people walking the streets. The bus stops with a jerk. I wait my turn, watching the girl off to my left. When she rises, I do too. Keeping my eyes down, the shuffling of my feet brings my thoughts back to Victoriana. They never really left—they were only momentarily muffled. The disgrace I felt earlier retakes me. I step off the bus and push my way half-heartedly toward the lobby.

The line is short—I'm inside the cylinder in no time greeted by the sounds of hissing air and grinding steel that let me know I'm home.

I stagger out onto the polished floor of the lofty entry hall. Music is playing like normal, but it's muffled and distant—a welcome change with the pounding in my head. There is no line at the elevators. I press the silver call button and the doors open right away. Stepping inside, I press the button for my floor, without looking, and lean back against the wall.

Like normal, like clockwork.

I wonder if Victoriana is home now or if they're still holding her at school? Does she know it was me who logged into her account? And if she does, would she tell them or would she protect me? She has no reason to, but she must have if they haven't come for me already.

The elevator lurches to a stop and the doors slide open. I step out automatically and start the long walk down the hallway to the door at the end. The sound of distant, indistinct voices grows with each step. I don't look up from my feet to investigate, trying instead to focus on the swirling pattern of the floor as I walk. Anything to keep my mind off Victoriana.

From years of walking this hall, I know I'm by my door without having to look. The once-distant voices are right on top of me now.

I look up and search for the handle but my hand swipes through thin air—the door is wide open. Startled, I try to get my bearings. Mother—wearing her mask—is standing with Mr. Standish in the living room. Framed by the doorway, they appear to be arguing—they are gesticulating passionately—but I can't make out what they're saying. Then it dawns on me, I forgot to remove my mask. How could I forget to do something that simple? I'm more shaken up by what happened to Victoriana than I realized.

Lifting my hands up, I run my fingers along the skin of my neck until they poke under the rubber. With a single motion, I pull the mask free, and the intensity of their voices hits me. I duck into the kitchen to eavesdrop.

"I've told you a dozen times already, we've already taken precautions and installed a redundant air safety system."

"I don't care if you've done it already. I want you to do it again! And double check all the seals and doors to this place while you're at it. You may be too thick to remember, but the people who murdered those school children are the same ones who nearly burnt Einsam to the ground a decade ago!"

"What? How does this have anything to do with that? It was an isolated incident—that's what the news said."

"That's what they told us last time too, even when you could look out your own window and see the city burning!"

"Look, lady…"

"That's Mrs. Brennan to you."

"Look, Mrs. Brennan, I do remember those days. This is nothing like that. All the subversives are in prison. This was an isolated incident. You are safe here. You don't need to wear your mask inside."

"Are you that naïve? You think you can simply imprison all of those deranged people and have the problem go away? They're like cancer! Once they enter society, the only way to remove them is to purge the whole body. Every cell, every molecule, must be scoured clean. I know they're back, and I'm not going to have my family choke and die because some penny-pinching custodian won't inspect the building again!" The passion drops from her tone, and it takes up a steely resonance. "If you don't go and ensure the safety of this building, then I'll be forced to call the authorities. For all I know, you could be a subversive attempting to murder every man, woman, and child in this building."

"Wait, what? Hold on a minute, there is no need for any of that. I've already inspected everything. All the building's safety certificates are up to date. Besides, who's going to pay for all of that? You? Do you even know how much a backup air purifying system for a building this size costs?"

"For a moment I thought you would see reason, but I'm

convinced now that you are a subversive. I'm calling you in."

Mother makes a move toward the phone—the phone in the kitchen. She won't be happy if she finds me in here without my mask. Even if I wanted to put it on—which I don't—there's no time. Bracing for her arrival, I'm saved.

Mr. Standish jumps in front of her. Placing a trembling hand on her shoulder, he speaks through quivering lips.

"I'll do it, I'll do it all. Every crack every crevice. The second redundant system is going to take a week or more to install, but I'll have my people get started on it right away. Just please, don't call them."

"Excellent," her voice sends a shiver shooting down my neck. "I knew you'd come to your senses. I expect to be informed of your progress."

Defeated, Mr. Standish, nods, then makes for the open door. His face is weary with a hint of fear in his eyes. Mother's, on the other hand, remain emotionless, veiled behind her mask. He passes the kitchen without noticing me then closes the door gently behind him.

Holding my mask in my hands, I look into the two small glass circles and see my eyes reflected back—the fear I saw in his eyes is there in mine. I stand up from my crouch, unwilling, but ready to face Mother without my mask.

"What are you doing? Get your mask on! Quick before something happens."

"You heard Mr. Standish, Mother, nothing's going to happen. He already checked it."

"How much of that did you hear? Can't you tell how worried I am? You would side with a stranger over your own mother? I love you, Evelyn. That's why I want you to wear your mask. I don't want you to die."

Mother begins to sob. Grief clouds her eye ports.

"I'm not trying to hurt you. I just don't think there's anything to worry about."

"Nothing to worry about? Children are dying in their classrooms. Do you think that's nothing? You were too young to remember, thank the Caretakers, so you don't know how much there really is to worry about out there. I know I let you do what you want, but not today, not this time. You will wear your mask from now on. Period! End of discussion. I'm not going to lose…" her words fade into heaving breaths. She's vibrating like she's about to shatter into a million tiny pieces. I step forward reaching out for her.

"… put your mask on—"

"But…"

She snaps up. "Now!"

I've never heard Mother scream with such fury in all my life. Muffled as it was by her mask, it loses none of its power. My fingers dance on my mask's straps, electrified with the intensity of her voice. Fumbling, I get the straps loose then slip it back over my face. In my haste to get it on, I get some of my hair caught in the straps. It tears out in a clump as I yank down. I keep my pain inside.

I take my backpack off and hold it in one hand while opening my bedroom door with the other. Closing the door in one instant and tossing my backpack across the room in the next, the tension and weight of today crashes down on me full force. I flop ungracefully onto the bed, listening to heavy rasps of stress venting through my mask.

The day boils inside me. Did those students really die? They couldn't have, Delia didn't. But how is Delia now? How is Victoriana? Do they know it was me? Why was Mr. Standish so afraid of having the Peace Officers called? Why is Mother so afraid of subversives? Why is she demanding things of me now when she never has before? Will she fight with Father again tonight? Too many questions, too many emotions.

Overwhelmed, I'm unaware of how long until the world fades and I fall off into a restless sleep.

CHAPTER EIGHT

THE RUMBLING in my stomach forces me awake. Groggy, and still overwhelmed by the events of the day, I sit up on the edge of the bed and wait for the world to stop spinning. My face is sweaty and gross from sleeping in my mask. Still pulling myself back from the edge of sleep—but not wanting to stay in my room any longer—I get up and head to the closet. I pull the doors open and stare at my clothes. Moving my finger along the hooks of the hangers, I search for something comfortable to change into. My finger stops on a purple nightgown. I haven't worn this in forever but it's comfortable and flowing. If my head has to be trapped in this mask why should the rest of me be trapped too?

Pulling it off the hanger, I drape it over my arm. Picking up the rest of the clothing I need, I move to the door. Hand on the doorknob, I take a breath and hold it. I listen for stillness on the other side. Satisfied, I exhale and push through.

The living room is foreboding. Harsh neon light shining through the windows casts everything in sinister red silhouette.

The living room is cold, and every minute sound gets amplified in the lofty, sterile emptiness. An unnerving, yet oddly pleasant change from its normal noise and chaos.

My eyes acclimate a little to the near dark as I walk to the bathroom. I notice the telltale pale flickering of television under my parents' bedroom door. Retreating into her mask, and now into her room, Mother is becoming a prisoner of her fears.

Closing the bathroom door behind me, I linger in the darkness until my eyes adjust well enough that I don't run into anything. As I strip down to shower, my bare feet touch the frigid floor—a cascade of gooseflesh spreads over me. I start to pull off my mask but stop just as my fingers break under the seal. I don't ever want to be a prisoner in my own home. I don't ever want to be terrified of life like she is. My fingers pull against the stretchy rubber. A hair the straps failed to pull out the first time yanks out as I remove the mask. It hurts, but it's minuscule compared to the unknown horrors Victoriana is going through. Having a staring contest with myself in the mirror, I force my emotions back into their bottle.

I step into the shower and turn it on. The icy water tightens my skin and causes involuntary shivers, but I let it wash over me without complaint.

The water turns warm, and the shivers abate.

I slump to the floor of the shower and let the hot water soothe me. I need to keep looking for answers, but I need to do it myself. I can't drag anyone else into my search. If anyone is going to be punished for my curiosity, it needs to be me.

I sit there until steam builds so thick the world disappears. I lie dormant in the swirling, hot haze until the water begins to cool again. I rise feeling more like myself again. My mind is no longer burning, and the tension in my muscles has melted away. I turn the handle to the right cutting off the stream of water. Waiting, I listen until I hear the last drops of water fall from the faucet.

Stepping out onto the still icy floor, I pull a towel off the rack. It's warm and soft against my clean skin. Dried off, I put on deodorant, then dress. Putting my hand on the handle, I prepare to leave. The knob is halfway twisted when I freeze. Turning around, I see my mask's eye ports reflect in the steam-covered mirror. I turn back with a sigh and snatch it up. Taking time with each strap, I loosen them then fix it back over my head. Looking through the mask's filtered perspective, a small amount of the day's tension rebuilds within me.

Taking a deep breath alleviates most of it, but not all. For now, the mask is a necessary evil I must endure. I need to get more comfortable in it, but the very thought of that repulses me.

I open the door and return to the living room. Still dark. Still quiet. I walk on silent feet to the window and survey the city. The billboards project their bloody tinge defining Einsam's countless skyscrapers in vibrant neon against the swallowing darkness of night. Through the combination of glass from my mask's eye ports and the penthouse's windows, the lights of the city are doubly reflected, making the city seem brighter. Through all the distortion, Einsam is almost beautiful. The surreal tableau disappears in a flash as Father opens the front door, flooding the room with light from the hallway. He flips the light switch on, drowning the house with bright white light. The cool stillness of the dark is gone, and the city outside has been obliterated. With nothing to look at but my reflection, I turn around to greet him.

"Sweetie, is everything all right? Why are you wearing your mask?"

I cross the room before I respond. "Everything is fine. Mother is just worried. That's all."

"Why is she worried? Did something happen?"

"No, no—nothing like that. She thinks what happened at the school is going to happen here. She keeps saying the subversives are back."

"She said that?" He rolls his eyes then hangs his head. "She can't get past it. How many times does she have to relive that? Over and over again. It's carved in stone, what can worrying do about it? I wish she could leave it there." He lifts his head—his thoughts waking him up enough to realize what he's said. "Sorry, I don't mean to bother you with our drama."

"That's all right, I don't mind."

"I know you don't, but it isn't your weight to carry. Have you eaten yet?"

"No, I haven't—I'm starved."

"I'll make us something to eat. Go ahead and take that mask off and come help me in the kitchen." He smiles.

"I'm not sure I should take it off." His face sours. "I'm not scared or anything, but Mother was so insistent that I wear it. I've never seen her that serious before."

"Is she forcing you to wear that thing?"

"Well, I guess you could say that. But it's only because she's worried. I'm sure she'll want you to wear yours as well."

"That's ridiculous. There is no need for that. Just take your mask off and have dinner with me."

"I really don't want to choose sides."

Father's response is cut off as Mother enters the room.

"I can't believe you, Allen! You're trying to put Evelyn at risk just so you can get at me! I know you won't listen to me, but clearly, Evelyn has. Even that idiot Standish listened to me. Is it so impossible to admit that I'm right?"

"Why are you talking to Standish?" There is a defensiveness in Father's voice I've never heard before.

"I ordered him to recheck all of the building's filtration systems of course. You think I can sit at home and hear about people sabotaging air filters without taking action? I think not."

"You told him to do what? This is insane, you're overreacting.

It only happened in that one school." Father shoves his index finger toward the ceiling for unnecessary emphasis. "We have nothing to worry about."

"You're always so blind to what's going on around you! The subversives are back, and they're coming after all of us!"

Pinching the bridge of his nose, Father bows his head. He seethes, then something shifts, and he brings his head back up with a goading laugh. "What you do is your business. If you want to keep reliving the past and ripping open old wounds, that's on you." All his kindness burns away. "But leave me and Evelyn out of this." His words roll around the room like a gauntlet thrown.

Tonight, like every night they fight, I feel the air crackle with tension before the storm hits. I've been out of this conversation for a while now, but now is the moment I need to get out of it completely. Wanting to be nowhere near them when it erupts, I make the all-too-familiar dash for my room.

The screams start as my door slams shut. Slipping under the covers, I press my pillows over my head. They, in combination with the mask, all but erase the fight. Hunger still gnawing at me, I linger on the edge of sleep. A maelstrom of white-hot emotions conducts my dreams.

CHAPTER NINE

MORNING COMES QUICKLY and in a bad way. My face is hot and sweaty from another night buried under pillows and trapped inside a rubber prison cell. Everything aches, consequence of sleeping on an empty stomach and troubled mind.

Sitting up, I glance at the clock. Seven forty-five. Just like every morning, even through my mask, the sound of Mother's shuffling feet is unmistakable. Her hand rattles the handle. A shock of electricity runs up my spine. Which Mother will I be greeted with today? The smiling and chipper one who wants to make me breakfast? Or the one with panic in her eyes and fear in her voice?

The door opens, and the terrified husk of my mother shuffles in. Her rhythmic, rasping breaths fill me with pity. I twist off my filter in preparation. She wastes no time approaching me with her hand outstretched—a new gleaming filter clutched in her fingers. I try to catch her eye and give her a smile, but she's a million miles away.

I take the filter and twist it into my mask. A faint click tells us it's secure. Wordlessly she turns and shuffles out, leaving the door open behind her. I watch her slowly cross the living room then disappear back into her bedroom. A moment later the blue-white flicker of the television appears under her door. Today is starting to be another terrible day.

Taking clean clothes with me, I leave my room, flicking off the light switch as I leave. Passing the couch on the way to the bathroom, I notice two pillows and a haphazardly folded blanket sitting on the arm. I've seen Father sleep on the couch before, but the pillows and blankets have always been put away in the morning. I wonder how long he'll be sleeping out here? Something has shifted in Mother's mind, and it's beginning to undermine the family.

Despite the brewing disaster at home, the questions and doubts I have about the world are so intense they push every-thing else aside. Mother's probably in the same headspace I am but instead of hope, she's driven by fear. I wish I could ask her why she's scared, but with the way she's been acting lately, I think that's probably just as dangerous as asking Speer.

The bathroom door clanks closed as the bolt slides into the wall. The bathroom is replacing the window as my sanc-tuary. Free from Mother's prying eyes, I pull off my mask. A nauseating stream of sweat pours out into the sink. It takes all my self-control to avoid vomiting. How can she stay in her mask all day? Left on for days it must become a sweltering cesspool of filth that is surely no healthier than the 'poisonous' air. Turning the shower knob, I step into the lukewarm water and start scrubbing my face with soap. I trace a line of painful acne bumps where the mask makes a seal.

Showered, my body and mind feel better. One look at the mask though and nausea stirs again. Going to the linen closet, I take out a clean wash rag and start scrubbing the inside of my mask. After several rinses in hot water, and a good five minutes of washing, it's clean enough. Wearing a knee-length, yellow cap-sleeved dress I look like the woman in the billboard when I put on my mask.

Stopping quickly in the kitchen, I open the refrigerator and peer inside. Four boxes of two-week-old take out and a gallon of curdling milk. Has it really been two weeks since Mother went shopping? I close the refrigerator door and move on to the pantry. Equally barren. I settle on a hard slice of bread. Stomach still grumbling, I put my trench coat on, sling my backpack over my shoulder, and walk out the door.

Stepping out of the airlock, I emerge onto the packed and filthy streets. Masses of masked people push and dart past each other seemingly all on some important errand. I pay no attention to them, placing my eyes on the school bus—bobbing and weaving until I get there. Taking my regular spot halfway down the bus, I settle in.

Closing my eyes, I think of that moment of calm before last night's fight. If I were back there again would I have been able to stop it if I had jumped up right then and there and interjected?

I doubt it, but it makes a comfortable distraction to kill time.

The bus slows. The change in momentum nudges me forward, waking me from my daydream. I take a second to reenter my surroundings. I survey the kids sitting in front of me and count them to know my place in line. Thirteenth. *Lucky me.*

Row after row in perfect order and wordless discipline we do what we're supposed to do. A fire of indignation erupts inside me. I sit at home, school, and here on the bus every day telling myself I will find the truth. That I won't put up with the way things are, but I never act. Enough is enough.

Student ten stands, enters the aisle, and turns to exit.

My turn.

Quickly, without the chance for anyone else—or myself—to lodge any protest, I spring from my seat. Taking large strides down the aisle—backpack banging on every seat—I reach the exit in an exhilarating blink of an eye. Hopping off the bus, I'm invigorated. The worries of the last few days melt away.

But no good thing lasts forever.

"You—stop!"

Two large monitors make their way toward me through the lines of students spilling out of the other transports. They must have figured out that Victoriana didn't type that search. I wonder how long they tortured her before they decided she didn't do it? I hope they didn't turn her into a potato.

Feeling like an animal in the zoo, my fists tighten—teeth clench. They picked the wrong day to bring me in. I won't go quietly. Not today. Not ever again.

"You. Are you a twelfth-year student?"

Expecting fighting words, I relax my guard. "Yes, I am a twelfth year."

"Report to the parade grounds immediately."

Both monitors point in unison to my left. A line of monitors is corralling the other twelfth years around the corner of the school out of sight. This could be a trap, a way of singling out who the real perpetrator is. Or maybe we're simply practicing for graduation? Too many uncertainties. I'll wait to run once I turn the corner. I'm not willing to comply, but I can't start running without knowing what I'm running from.

"Do you comply?"

I desperately desire to say no, but fear and complacency hold me back.

"Yes." The word sticks in my throat.

Not wanting to spend any more time under their gaze, I head toward the left-hand side of the school.

An iron gate that's normally locked stands open and flanked by monitors. I pass through it, holding my head high. The monitor on my left locks eyes with me. In no mood to look away, I stare right back.

I pass through the gate and continue the length of the school. I'm struck with the realization that nothing happened. All those years I sheepishly looked at my feet and answered their questions with ersatz zeal, I was bowing to authority they didn't possess. What would they have done? Beat me for looking them in the eyes? There is no rule saying you can't, no grounds for their power, it's just one of those things you pick from the other kids: "Never look them in the eye, or they'll beat you. Never back mouth, they'll crack you." A bunch of crap. One monitor, at one school—one time—must have beaten some poor kid into a pulp. By the time the tale made its rounds to all the schools it had turned into a full-blown myth. How much of our imprisonment is self-inflicted?

The corner of the concrete wall approaches. Muscles tensed, tendons loaded, I'm ready to bolt. But when I turn the corner there are no Peace Officers are waiting to grab me. Instead, a few dozen meters away a stage has been set up in the middle of the parade field. Most of the twelfth-year students have already arrived and are forming neat rows in front of the stage. A wide ring of monitors encircles the gathering students. Beyond the field, a ring of skyscrapers disappears into the soot-filled sky.

Nothing like this ever takes place without months of notice and I've never known the Authoritarian to give pleasant surprises. It can only mean trouble, but with no good options for escape, I cross the field leaving a trail of footprints in the layer of slag and soot covering the dead, yellow grass.

With each step, the fuzzy objects of the stage come into

focus. The Authoritarian is standing in the middle of the stage at a chrome microphone. Behind him is a sturdy steel table with a box draped in a mustard yellow cloth set squarely in the middle. Otherwise, the stage is empty. What could possibly be under that cloth that they couldn't show us in the auditorium? And why only the twelfth-year students? This has something to do with Victoriana—I can feel it—but it's so unprecedented I can't place my finger on it.

Reaching the gathering, I slip into the middle of a row, never taking my eyes off the Authoritarian. He's nearly motionless—soot builds on his wide shoulders.

The wait is agony not because of its length, but because of the uncertainty. Will they pull me up on stage and subject me, in front of the rest of the class, to whatever horrors lay hidden under the cloth? Or will they pull it back to reveal Victoriana's twisted and mangled corpse as a lesson in asking forbidden questions?

The anticipation turns my stomach into knots. My nerves reach a fever pitch. A desire to run overwhelms me. But that's exactly what they want. They don't know who did it. That's why we're here. They're looking for the first one to flinch. Delia's parting words echo in my head: *blend in, cover your tracks, and don't make waves.* They're waiting for me to break, but I won't give them the satisfaction. I steel my resolve. Prepared to wait until soot doesn't fall, I stand resolute and unwavering.

We linger in silence long after the final student arrives. Smog blows in on the wind, soot piles on our bodies. The

Authoritarian's will breaks first.

"You must all be wondering why I brought you out here. Recently, you were given the important lesson on how and why our Great Society came to be. You were witness to the sacrifices and many toils of our forbearers. You were shown the many ways through which you can contribute to the Great Society's legacy of peace and prosperity. Yet some among you spit on the graves of our patriots and snap at the hands of the Caretakers like rabid dogs! They would say this whole world is a lie! They demand proof that the outside air—that we ceaselessly guard you against—is truly poison. I do not bow to the whims of the weak and ignorant, and I am not doing this to satiate them. No, a mind that sees lies when staring at the truth can never be satisfied. I do this to protect you, to codify your own beliefs so you can stand vigilant against your subversive peers who would erode your faith in the Great Society. Bring up the girl."

Inspector Aldridge appears on stage—her white OSS uniform turning gray. Her sizeable hands wrap all the way around Victoriana's petite arms. Victoriana's face is hidden by her mask, but her clothes are tattered, and her body bruised. I can only imagine how deformed and swollen her face must be.

Aldridge drags Victoriana next to the Authoritarian then drops her. Victoriana falls like dead weight. A plume of ash billows up as she lands, momentarily blocking her from view.

"Stand! Face your peers. See condemnation in their eyes."

Victoriana attempts to stand. Her body is convulsing from

the effort. Halfway on one leg, she falls back into the accumulated ash on the stage.

"Do it! Not so defiant now are you?" The Authoritarian looms over her—his gleaming jackboot pressing on her back.

Trembling, Victoriana fights, but he keeps her down. A howling wind drives across the field filling the air with thick, black ash. Swirling around the stage, and among all the students—I can't see the end of my own filter the cloud is so thick. It passes as quickly as it arose, but it's left us covered in a thick layer of clinging filth. The world feels different now, and the exposed skin on my legs and neck are starting to itch.

"Now the moment I want you to take with you the rest of your lives." The Authoritarian stretches the moment to the breaking point. "Inspector Aldridge, remove the cloth."

Aldridge dutifully obeys. Pulling the cloth off sends another cloud of ash into the air. When it settles, the box is plain to see. Made of glass, the cube contains a small orange cat.

"Now witness what happens when you throw away all good advice and breathe poison."

The Authoritarian steps over Victoriana and positions himself on the opposite side of the table. He leans forward placing his hands flat on either side of the box.

"Cinnamon? What are you doing with my cat? Why are you doing this?"

Victoriana's words are distant and weak. They have no effect on the Authoritarian. Guilt erupts in my chest and threatens to topple me. With awesome speed, he lifts the box. Cinnamon's cries are immediate.

A terrible wail the likes of which I've never heard, and never wish to hear again, pierces my heart. Collapsing into convulsions, the poor cat thrashes about violently. The assembly wavers and the soft, whimpering cry of a hundred students fills the field. Victoriana scrambles to her knees. She wails, arms out begging for mercy.

"Cinnamon! No! Stop this! I'm sorry for whatever I did, I'm sorry, just please don't kill Cinnamon."

Victoriana's pleas fall deafly on the Authoritarian's pitiless ears. Cinnamon's eyes bulge. Bloody foam sprays from her mouth with each ever-more-shallow breath. I can't believe my eyes. I did this to her.

I wish I could take the beatings and bruises Victoriana received and transfer them to myself. How could I have done this? Because of what Delia said? Because she followed me? No amount of scrubbing will wash the blood from my hands.

Unable to look any longer, I turn away and stare off into the roots of the towering buildings. Parked next to the diner across the road—shimmering an eerie silver in a city of black and gray—a hulking truck ru¬mbles to life. Brushing off the lenses of my mask I look again to make sure I'm not seeing things.

The truck appears to be a large canister. With the distance, it's impossible to determine the symbol on its side, but it looks like the warning labels on the back of the cockroach poison Mother keeps under the kitchen sink. Walking out of the diner, I see the unmistakable profile of a Peace Officer bathed in blue. Carrying what must be leftovers in his hand, he hops into the idling truck. As it drives off, I'm left with a horrible sense of unease. I know what I just saw. There is no denying that Cinnamon is dead. But why beat Victoriana? Isn't killing her pet enough? They've had us for twelve years and only now do they feel it's necessary to give a demonstration? And for that matter why have they never done something like this on the news? You could get the whole city at once, not just a single twelfth-year class at a private school.

The Authoritarian's words echo painfully in my thoughts. *A mind that sees lies when staring at the truth can never be satisfied.* Is that me? Someone so convinced that what she sees isn't real that she tries to justify it to herself even when she's staring the gurgling, horrible truth straight in the face? No, it doesn't add up. That truck, the field, the news reports without photos. Something else is going on. I can see the soot, I understand that. But soot doesn't cause a cat to flatline in seconds. It doesn't necessitate beatings if you question its lethality.

My heart aches for Victoriana and Cinnamon, and if I could trade places, I would. But I can't, so I need to do what I can. Delia's words return to me: *what's hidden in the silver trucks?* A terrified shiver runs down my spine. She knew something, but

I don't think she knows how bad it really is. I'm not even sure I do. But I know what I can do. Find the answers. Find the truth.

I turn back to the stage. Monitors are dragging Victoriana away. Her cries are shrill and wheezing. A small black bag is brought up, and Cinnamon's remains are unceremoniously thrown inside. The Authoritarian retakes his place behind the microphone.

"That concludes your lessons for today. Fall out to your respective classrooms. You will spend the remainder of the day sitting in silence to contemplate what you have just seen."

Without visible protest, the traumatized twelfth-year students comply. I'm frozen—they move around me like water around a stone. They are all trembling and whimpering softly to themselves. The Authoritarian thinks he's won. He thinks he's stomped out the insurrection from his senior students, but he's mistaken. The fire he sought to quench within me has only grown stronger. I owe it to everyone to find the truth. I owe it to Victoriana, Delia, Mother, Father. I owe it to myself.

I won't find the truth today, but now I have somewhere to start, and I won't stop until I've found it.

Shaken but undeterred, I follow the other students back across the blackened field.

CHAPTER TEN

THE CLASSROOM IS A COFFIN. The first hour of sitting here after the Authoritarian's demonstration was filled with stifled sobs and the creaking noises of fidgeting students. But now a malaise has fallen over the class, and they sit staring at their desks unable to meet each other's eyes. Speer watches us over the top of his dog-eared copy of *Drumbeat*.

His eyes are obscured, but I'm sure they are twinkling with some kind of sick pleasure. One day he'll get what's coming to him along with the Authoritarian and Inspector Aldridge. How can they claim to be doing what is right and just when innocent blood stains their hands? The stillness they have dished out as punishment has given me the time I need to process the past few days. It seems every obstacle they place in my path to discourage me from finding the truth serves only to boost me up to another level of dedication and commitment.

I need to choose my path and choose it carefully. I've been lucky so far, but I'd be a fool to think that my luck will last forever. Tackling any of society's problems is beyond me. How does anyone, let alone a seventeen-year-old, challenge the establishment without falling victim to it?

The obvious place to start is my mask. Why is there no real explanation as to why we wear it? And why is that answer guarded so viciously? There is more here than meets the eye, that much is clear, but where to begin? Should I simply remove my mask and see what happens? The image of Cinnamon convulsing in the throes of an agonizing death tempers my enthusiasm for that plan in an instant. I wonder if Delia died in that alley, face down and covered in ash? I could have run right past her—her body left to rot entombed in the soot.

Indecision strangles me. It seems whatever course of action I take will lead me right back to capture or death. It's as if I'm already in prison—the mask my cell. I want to be free of it, but the un-caged world is full of too many unknowns, too many dangers.

It hits me. I feel stupid not to have seen it sooner. I'm approaching this problem like a free person. A person with options, allies, places to run. If I approach it this way, I'll never succeed. The way to get out of here is to think like a prisoner. Does an inmate ask the guard for the keys? Does she try to stroll out the front door? No. She burrows her way out. Piece by piece she moves the earth and stone that inters her. She does it alone, and she sticks to the plan. It takes diligence, patience, and a good deal of luck, but in the end, she's able to tunnel out, and no one's the wiser. I must embrace my status as a prisoner of society confined to cellblock me. So where to begin?

A filter a day keeps death at bay. Are these the words of a concerned friend or a guard? The billboards are my prison guards—the mere sight of them fills me with fear. But do guards tell you the truth or do they say what they must to keep you in your cage? There's only one way to find out.

Mother has bought into the guard's lies. Every day she obediently does what they ask of her. She changes her own filter and then watches me change mine. I have to put an end to this ritual.

Tomorrow, I'll begin a test dig. I'll prod the edges of the illusion and see what's true. When she hands me a new filter, I'll screw it into my mask without complaint or hesitation, but when she's gone back to her room, I'll pull my old filter out of the trash and put the new one there in its place. When I'm here at school, and she comes into my room, she'll still see a single filter sitting in the trash can.

It's a good plan. It doesn't leave behind anything out of the ordinary to pique her interest and start her snooping around. It also gives me a way to sample the outside air in a diluted and controlled manner. If one day I feel the telltale signs of burning or irritation I can return to a new filter the next day and lay my doubts to rest. I need to be careful though. I can't raise any suspicions. I have to keep this completely to myself. I can't step out of line or get into an altercation with anyone. A single misstep could be my last.

I feel my lips turn up in a smile. One day I'll be out of here, and they'll all be left scratching their heads as to where I went. Content on the solidity of my plan I close my eyes and drift off into a daydream of tunneling out of some ancient stone prison. Dwelling there until the end-of-day bell tolls, I feel a tiny bit of the weight that has been pressing on my chest pull away.

The bus ride home from school is uneventful. Some students in my class talk a little on the bus. It's too hard to pick up every word they are saying, but it's clear they are terrified and have no intention of ever taking their masks off. Earlier I would have felt uncomfortable with their willingness to comply and give up on finding the truth, but I have to admit, the Authoritarian's demonstration was pretty powerful. If I hadn't known the truth about Victoriana or seen the silver truck Delia warned me about, I think I would have given up too. Fear is powerful. Capable of forcing doubts even into someone's most fervent beliefs. If I were angry or disgusted at them, I wouldn't be any better than the Authoritarian.

I pass through the airlock into the lobby. I take this moment to pull off my mask and breathe in the clean, refreshing air of the building. Still filtered, it doesn't have the carbon taste or hot, uncomfortable humidity of my mask. Plus, the faint smell of lemon makes me feel at home.

I lose myself in the whirring gears and pulleys of the elevator ride. It's such a soft and peaceful noise that it's completely lost when I'm wearing the mask. It's a secret, beautiful song playing just for me.

I step out of the elevator and start down the long hallway to home. But instead of comfort, each step builds a sense of dread. Pausing at the door, I run my fingers over the 1745 engraved in silver on the plaque. My reflection stares back at me in the shining surface. Looking at myself in the warped reflection I gird myself, and with a quick motion, place the mask back over my face.

The door handle turns smoothly. The lights are off, and the house is still. The hunger I've been keeping with me for days now hits me. I go to the fridge. It's been cleaned and emptied of the Petri dishes masquerading as leftovers. Filling the shelves now are row upon row of instant prepackaged meals for one. If this is a sign of things to come, then I think it's safe to assume family dinners, and hot-and-ready breakfast, are out of the picture for the foreseeable future.

I take a box off the top without looking at the cover, rip open the package, and throw it into the microwave. Knowing what the meal is supposed to taste like only leads to bite after bite of disappointment.

Grabbing a fork from the drawer, I lean against the counter. Watching the food spin while I wait is hypnotic and oddly soothing. The microwave beeps loudly, disturbing the stillness of the house. The meal comes out steaming. I toss it on the table in the kitchen. Taking my ash-stained trench coat off, I hang it on the hook just inside the front door then go back to the table. The meal's steam beckons me back. I lift my mask up just enough to eat. I cut into the hunk of mystery meat with the side of my fork. It's gelatinous swimming in a viscous, overly salty, brown gravy. I force down four bites before the taste and texture become too much to stomach. I toss the rest away, rinse my fork, then pull my mask back down over my mouth.

Walking quietly so as not to disturb the stillness, I move to the living room windows. I see the blue-white flicker of the television under Mother's door. There is nothing I can do about it now. Maybe once I dig myself out, I can come back and bring her with me. But that's a long way off. In my regular spot, I focus in on the cheery dolled-up housewife. *Remember, a filter a day keeps death at bay!*

"We'll see about that," I whisper.

Tomorrow is a big day, and the excitement is going to keep me wired. A quick shower then I'll go to bed. I probably won't sleep, but I have to try.

Tomorrow the tunneling starts, and there is no going back.

CHAPTER ELEVEN

HOURS OF LUCID DREAMING leave me disoriented for a few minutes after I wake. I dreamt of the Authoritarian's cruel display in horrifying detail. Trapped in a loop, I was forced to watch from Victoriana's perspective as the glass box was lifted, and the poison gas killed her beloved cat. It was terrible and seemingly without end.

Shaking the dream from my head, I rest on the edge of the bed. The dream is gone, but I can't stop wondering where Victoriana is now. I hope they've let her go home. I hope her parents never make her go back to Neptus Memorial again.

The light of the clock grabs my attention away from my thoughts. Seven thirty-two. I don't normally wake up early, but then again, I don't normally dream of being trapped in an infinite loop where I'm forced to watch my worst mistake over and over. I still have thirteen minutes to wait before Mother enters the room, shuffling and wheezing. I need to concentrate. I can't let my past failures interfere with my plan. I will make it up to Victoriana one day, but that day requires that I get through this one.

I fill my lungs to bursting. The taste of charcoal is over-whelming and helps refocus my attention on the task at hand. Closing my eyes, I wait—my palms grow sweaty. My leg starts bouncing of its own volition.

The digital numbers on the clock shine seven forty-five. Predictably, the sound of Mother's shuffles builds. A nervous sigh falls from my lips. I wish I could tell her. I wish she were someone I could trust.

She turns the handle and opens the door. One look at her and I know she can't be any of the things I need her to be. Her frame is already withering, no doubt from malnourishment and confinement. She shuffles over, her hand quivering ever so slightly as she extends the new filter toward me. Taking it from her, I replace it swiftly. The old one plunks loudly into the bottom of the can. Satisfied, she turns and shuffles away. Her rasping, distorted breaths grow softer until they finally disappear behind the faint click of her door. The blue-white flicker begins almost immediately.

Standing, I wipe my sweaty hands on my legs. It's such a simple thing. Pull the old filter from the can. I turn it over and over in my hands. *Mountain Air* is stamped into the metal on the inside lip. Underneath it is a sticker with the model and unit numbers: *CFC-4811 MA-YS-12936*. I line up threads and twist—the magnitude of the task slows my hand. I let out another anxious sigh.

"Here it goes."

Slow and quiet, I close my bedroom door. Walking on tip-toes, I move back to the can. Plucking the filter from the trash, I become keenly aware of its weight. Before I can hesitate or second guess myself, I twist off the new filter and toss it on the bed. Clicking the old filter into place a wave of accomplishment splashes over me. Picking the new filter up one last time, I lower it gently into the trashcan to avoid any unusual sounds. This was the first and most important step in my plan, and now it's done. This won't be the most difficult part of my journey, but the success or failure of my plan depends on this first step. I've dug out the first rock from my tunnel so to speak, and I'm ecstatic. Piece-by-piece, day-by-day, I'll pull back the curtain on this charade. With purpose I move to start my day.

I fall into the routine with ease. Making each day its own little victory, my spirits remain high. Mother shuffles into my room each morning looking more withered and sullen than the day before. Once she's returned herself to the binding vortex of her television, I close my bedroom door and exchange my filter with her new one. Slowly lowering each new filter into the trashcan builds my confidence and extends my imaginary tunnel.

Father has taken permanent residence on the couch. For a week or so after he was exiled to the living room, he would fold his blanket and stack his pillow neatly, but now he leaves them as he left them. He's working later and later, most likely to avoid having to interact with Mother, but consequently, I hardly see him anymore. I rarely stay awake late enough to see him stumble through the door, take a *Meal for One* from the refrigerator, then plop himself in front of the television. He has taken to falling asleep with it on so its light shines under my door now as another reminder that our family is falling apart.

But not everything is looking grim—I won a small victory over Mother. She can't dispute me having my mask off in the kitchen when I eat a few bites of a *Meal for One* before I give up on it.

As soon as the front door closes behind me, I pull off my mask and relish in the few minutes of my day without its restricting presence. Once I'm through the lobby, the airlock, and onto the bus, I mold myself into a perfect student. I do as I'm told. Sit or stand, walk, or wait. I'm the definition of a model prisoner.

Victoriana still hasn't returned to school. The looming presence of extra monitors drives that point home with every step I take within Neptus Memorial's halls. The faculty have started calling it the 'Zarrov Incident,' and in that first week after the nightmare on the parade grounds, they were surprisingly lax about students crying or mumbling things in the hallway. But at the start of week two, Britney had a breakdown in the cafeteria.

Weeping, she climbed up onto a table and demanded to know what happened to Victoriana. Monitors struggled in vain to bring her off the table and for a moment it seemed like my fantasy uprising was imminent. But Inspector Aldridge burst into the room, grabbed Britney by the hair, and dragged her out screaming. When Britney returned to class, she was a wafer-thin reflection of the gregarious girl that had gathered the courage to take a stand in the cafeteria. Aldridge only let her go because she didn't have anything on her. I can't make the same mistake.

The two weeks came and went for the air filtrations systems to be upgraded yet still we wear our masks inside and watch the endless volumes of Caretaker films. Each day I sit and nod diligently to Speer's endless ramblings about the importance of what we are about to see and how we should take these lessons to heart.

At lunch, I sit alone, eat quickly, and never speak. I haven't done a single thing, for even a single moment, to give Speer, Inspector Aldridge, or the swarms of watchful monitors, a reason to suspect me of anything.

I've taken to lingering in the lobby to absorb the unrestricted feeling of breathing without a mask. I never stop or loiter too long, but I walk slow enough to drink in as much freedom as possible.

Making the trek down the hallway, I prepare myself to re-enter the farce. I put on my mask, then step inside the apartment. Normally Mother is locked in her room. Whatever mystical power the television has over her keeps her enthralled, but occasionally she's released from her cell to do a few aimless laps around the yard. I keep my mask on prepared for those rare moments she emerges.

After I eat a few more bites of the processed slop in a box, I spend a few hours looking through the window at the city below. Watching the swirling clouds of ash and the hectic push and shove of the people on the street from the calmness and objectivity of my vantage gives me infinite fuel for thought and contemplation.

The routine normally ends after sundown. Alone in my room, I read. I read whatever I can get my hands on, but mostly it's the drivel they put out in the *Drumbeat* or *Caretaker's Quarterly*. They don't provide me with the stimulation needed to create new thoughts, but they do give me a sense of the depth and complexity of the grand illusion the Great Society weaves.

Each night I dream of Victoriana. I dream of escape. I dream of a better tomorrow.

Day after day I breathe through the same old filter and day after day I make it through. I haven't experienced a single symptom like the ones I observed in Cinnamon. Soon my tunnel will be complete, and I'll be a fugitive on the run searching for the one thing that can clear my name: the truth.

CHAPTER TWELVE

I HAVE FALLEN so lockstep into my routine that Speer's words take me by surprise as the end-of-day bell tolls.

"It has been a pleasure exposing you all to the wonders of our Great Society. Heed my lessons and those of the Caretaker's films, and you will go far. It is a shame our graduation ceremonies have been postponed." Speer places his hand to his heart in a gesture vacillating between mocking and sincere.

Is this it? All these years of school, all the pressure to excel—no room for second place, top marks or bust—and when the finish line comes, we get a half-assed, "thanks for showing up have a nice life." It feels like an organ was ripped from my belly leaving behind a nagging, gnawing cavity.

I had no intention of walking through that ashy field. There is no way I could have stood on stage with the Authoritarian after what he did to Victoriana. But there was supposed to be some revelation at the end. Graduation was supposed to mark a turning point, but it's turned out to be just like any other uneventful Friday. Was I so focused on getting through each day without detection that I failed to notice my sudden catapulting into adulthood? I certainly don't feel any different. Maybe there is a mark on me now? A tattoo only visible to the others in the adult club. Another illusion. No, a lie.

Adulthood peers into me with swollen, void-black eyes. Will I go to university? Will I get a government job like Father? Will I spiral into a blue, blinking vortex like Mother and ooze through life as a husk? Before I can fall any deeper, Speer resumes his speech.

"As you leave these protective halls and venture out into the workforce, take a moment and ask yourself: How best can I serve our Great Society? Not how can the Great Society best serve *me*," he thrusts an accusatory finger—Hector lurches back in his seat. "I'm sure you will all have—" he mumbles something, "productive lives. Wouldn't want to end up like that poor girl… what was her name? No matter. Enjoy your adult lives. And if you ever see me at a bar and want to talk, walk the other way and spare yourself the insults I'll hurl at you."

A stewpot of fermented emotions burbles in my guts. How dare he so flippantly cast-off Victoriana. How dare he make light of the irreparable nightmare they performed on Cinnamon. I'm trembling. My armpits are soaking through. Then guilt squashes my anger. Chain's cinch around my heart.

Chairs squeal. Excited chatter fills the room. Students file passed Speer shaking his hand, perfusing gratitude. The walls are spinning—there's too much to process. *Guilty, guilty, guilty!*

I sling my bag over one shoulder then slip out of the room avoiding any final awkwardness with Speer.

I pass half my classmates on my race to the exit. With each step down the hall, the crushing weight of the future and the snaring hooks of the past sublimate from me. The caldera cools allowing a new emotion to take center stage: excitement.

I'm finally finished. I'm free. Who cares for how long? For the first time in my life, I'm stepping into a day that hasn't already been planned for me. I'm so close to enacting my escape plan I'm buzzing—a smile wrenches up my trembling lips. I entertain a moment of gratitude for my mask concealing the kaleidoscope of expressions on my face.

The bus ride home is full of joyous excitement. None of the other students can keep their enthusiasm in check. The gaunt bus driver, normally so keen to keep the noise down and keep us in our seats, seems to be turning a blind eye. It's a refreshing change. Having no one to share in the revelry, I assume my normal position at the window staring out into the swirling shapes passing by. Today, though, I listen to the delight and happiness pouring out of the other students. They lay out detailed summer agendas or weigh the pros and cons of various universities. This is the single most enjoyable bus ride I can recall. An ember of hope sparks to life.

Perhaps this world is not totally grim and gray? The Great Society could be remade to radiate with freedom and joy instead of oppression and fear if only I can figure out how to pull down the veil smothering us all.

The bus slows then squeals to a stop. All good things must come to an end.

The streets are teeming. Pushing my way toward the airlock, I find a place in line and wait patiently for my turn to enter. Stepping into the cylinder, air whooshes over me knocking loose some of the ash clinging to my hair. Hidden systems grind and hiss. The doors open on the lobby and clean, lemon-tinged air rushes in. I pull off my mask making no effort to hide my smile. I mosey to the elevator—mopbots zip around in my wake. My smile finds its way onto a few morose faces going past.

The soft whirring of the elevator is music to my ears, but when the doors open my smile fades. My feet grow heavy, and the hallway seems to be crushing in around me. By the time I reach door *1745*, I've replaced the smile with stone.

The apartment is quiet and calm. Mother is in her room and Father is off at work or wherever he disappears to. I take off my ash-covered trench coat and hang it on the hook by the door.

Starting my routine, I throw a *Meal for One* into the microwave then go to my room to gather night clothes while it cooks.

The microwave's beeping brings me back into the kitchen. I take my mask off and set it down on the marble countertop. I take several bites of the hot mash then toss what I can't stomach in the trash.

A quick shower washes the last bits of Neptus Memorial off me for good. Watching the water swirl down the drain, I imagine the entire school being sucked into a mighty whirlpool and pulled down to the depths of the ocean never to inter students again.

Changed and dry, I spend a few hours watching the city through the windows. Everyone is busying about down there fast and frantic. It stands in stark contrast to the apartment's, and my own, stillness. I watch them buzz about until the glow of the sun fades away and the red tinge of neon lights up the city.

Retiring to my room, I look past the magazines for tonight's reading. Hidden in the back of my closet, underneath a box of toys I don't think I ever unpacked, I dig out a small newspaper clipping I found when we moved in. It must have fallen out of one of the boxes, and it's so small no one noticed it missing. *Has it really been ten years already?* I can still recall it so vividly.

Closing my eyes, I drift back to that day. Empty rooms. Boxes stacked and labeled in Mother's beautiful script. The Mountain Air billboard. Mother's tears—her burning eyes. I try to dig deeper looking for a happier memory from where we lived before, but I can dredge up only emptiness—as if all the paint has been scraped away from the canvas. I push and tug at the void and immediately regret it. A searing pain races from my temples to the bridge of my nose. I squint hard and rub my temples—silver tendrils dance behind my eyes. Teeth clenched I breathe through it. *Just breathe, Evelyn. Just breathe.*

The pain dissolves. Blinking myself back to my surroundings, I return my attention to the delicate clipping. The words are unimportant. The back side has a fragment of a headline: *Dissent crushed*. Nothing special about that.

Flipping it over there is an ad for *Amano air purifiers, air so clear you'll gasp!* A garish cartoon shrimp is greedily sucking in clouds of fly ash. I cover up the crustacean with my thumbs and narrow my gaze on the tiny halftone photo above it.

A soaring snowcapped mountain frames a dense grove of full-leafed trees. Puffy white clouds linger in front of a clear, radiant sun. I've never left the city, so I can't say for sure, but I know unpolluted vistas are few and far between—if there are any left at all. I know—it's an ad. But even the promise that places like this—somewhere free from soot and ash and the claustrophobic confines of Einsam—could still exist fills me with hope. Projecting myself into that wilderness, I sink into sleep.

I wake up on the floor. I blink until I can focus on the clock. Ten forty-seven. I'm unaccustomed to naps, but I thought they were supposed to make you feel better—I feel stretched thin like saltwater taffy.

Taking my mask off, I rub my cheeks and jaw both. I have to remember not to fall asleep in that stupid thing. I hide the article, being careful with its fragile edges, back in the corner of my closet. Stretching a little, I look at the clock again. It's late, and I should rest for my big day tomorrow, but I can't sleep now. Wired and apprehensive, I'll lay on the bed for hours. I might as well not waste this moment. Going out into the living room, I take my spot against the window.

The city is more interesting at night. The ghastly red glow of neon gives the bustling crowds and swerving automobiles a magical, abstract quality. Following the sweeping red lines of taillights, I fall under the city's nightly spell.

Father opens the door. The flood of light from the hallway breaks the enchantment. So, this is how late he's been coming home from work. He wastes no time and has already planted himself in front of the screen by the time I turn to look at him. This is a rare opportunity. I'm glad now for the nap, even with its grogginess. I walk over to him, lift my mask up, and kiss him on the cheek.

"I love you, darling," he says.

"I love you too, Dad. There is plenty of food in the fridge."

"Thank you, sweetie. I'll get some later."

His voice aches of exhaustion. I guess that's what passes as a good conversation as of late. *How long have we been drifting away from each other?* He's already starting to nod off—the television lighting up his eyelids. I linger next to the couch just beyond the invisible barrier that keeps the grunts and crunches of the Brawl Ball game from assaulting me.

This could be the last time I see him. Our last conversation.

If I die tomorrow will his last words to me rattle around in his head forever? *I'll get some later.* Why can't he just get up and go to the kitchen? We could joke about how bad the *Meals for One* are. He'd ask me about school, I'd dodge asking him about work. He'd deflect telling me, "You know I can't tell you anything. Besides, it's boring—paperwork, paperwork, paperwork. It'll be the death of me." Then he'd pretend to choke to death. We'd laugh. Then he'd kiss me on the cheek and tell me to get to sleep like I'm still seven and not seventeen.

He's slumped over now fast asleep. I wave my hands through the television control console, and the sea of neon red outside washes in to replace the momentary darkness. *Nature abhors a vacuum.* Speer's words echo between my ears. I throw the blanket draped on the arm of the couch over him then move back to my place at the window.

I push Father from my mind and start thinking about tomorrow. I try to recall how many days have passed since I started throwing away my new filters. *Remember, a filter a day keeps death at bay!* If the billboard housewife is correct, I should have died months ago. That's one lie down. It's time to move on to the next phase of the escape.

I fixate on the interwoven neon letters of the *Wear Your Mask* billboard. I think I'm finally ready to take it on. I've tunneled under the prison walls, and I'm anxious for a taste of the sweet air of freedom. Eyes darting between the couch and the master bedroom, I wonder if I can get them out of their prisons too. Or have they been in them so long they wouldn't want to leave?

Excited by my escape attempt tomorrow, sleep won't come easy, but I need to try. I make sure to close my bedroom door softly, so I don't wake him.

Staring at the ceiling, my mind's eye fills with the image of the dead girl on the billboard and the blaring neon words: *Wear Your Mask*. Her twisted shape is replaced by Delia's. That image is haunting enough, but soon the image of Cinnamon rasping with bloody breaths takes hold of me and won't let go.

Nightmares consume me. They force me to watch myself choking on polluted air. Then the Mountain Air housewife cartoon climbs off the billboard, saunters over to me, and leans in close. I clutch at her. "Help me" forms on my silent lips. She swats my hands away.

"I told you so," she says as I gargle out my final breath. Then the stage resets, and the vision plays again.

CHAPTER THIRTEEN

EVEN WITH MY EYES SHUT and a pillow over my head, Mother's presence is palpable. Whirr pause, whirr pause—her rhythmic breaths boil me up out of sleep. Pulling my pillow shield off, her vacant eyes confront me from behind the glass disks of her plastic prison cell. Obediently I pull the covers back and sit on the edge of the bed. She places the filter in my outstretched hand. I've done this so many times that it's second nature. The dead filter plunks into the trash.

I am unable to gauge any emotion on her concealed face as she turns and begins her tedious shuffle back to the vortex in her bedroom. I hope it still makes her happy to know I'm not going to die. I wish I could tell her what I've been doing, but the shock alone might kill her in the state she's in. I'm not sure if I'll ever be able to tell her. Even if I took her out to the street and took my mask off right in front of her—assuming I don't instantly crumble down and die—I doubt she would be convinced. I'm still struggling to believe Delia did it. I hope, one day, I can figure out how to tell her what I've seen.

I'm getting ahead of myself. I haven't even broken free yet. And there is still the chance the posters, the news anchors, instructors, and my imprisoned mother are all correct, and the instant I take my mask off I'll fall to the street writhing in pain for a few agonizing moments of burning, acrid breaths before my eyes gloss over, and I exit this world.

Either way, I'm content with the outcome. If I live, then I can begin to tear down the lies of our Great Society. If I die, well, then at least I will serve as a warning to anyone who has their own doubts. I wonder what it would be like for a camera crew, so used to sporting events and fluff pieces, to film a *real* dead body? I'm sure they could handle it, they do it every day, right?

I pick the filter from the trash. I run my finger over the sticker on the back and read the number to myself. The sticker is yellowing. Its glossy plastic film is starting to peel back on the edges. I swap today's filter for *MA-YS-12936* and take care to set it in the trash without a sound.

I wait until Mother's door closes then I slip out of my room and head to the bathroom. I take a quick glance over at the couch. Empty.

I shower quickly—nervous excitement buzzing in my stomach. Towel-dried, I put on my outfit. Black leather boots, jeans, purple stain-resistant blouse, and my ankle-length synthwool trench coat. I grab my backpack and unceremoniously dump its contents onto the bed. I throw my mask into the bag then turn the lights off and exit the room. *Will this be the last time?*

Taking my usual spot at the window, I scrutinize the poster one last time. My fear manifests itself onto the face of the cartoon girl and I take her place in death. I look away and head to the kitchen. I can't back out now.

Nothing in the fridge looks good. Going to the pantry, the shelves are loaded with dozens of boxes of Mother's *Smoothies on the Go*. Curious, I grab one then head to the door. One deep breath, then out into the hall.

I sip the smoothie on the way to the elevator. It tastes all right, I suppose, but it's a bit too sweet almost like it's hiding something, and the primary flavor can only be described as *blue*. I don't think I could stomach drinking it every day.

Reaching the elevator, I tap the call button a few times. Leaned up against the wall, I finish the smoothie just as the bell dings and the elevator doors open. I look around for a trash can. Finding none, I toss the empty pouch onto the plush cerulean and silver carpet.

As the doors close, a brushbot darts out of its concealed port in the baseboards and gobbles up the garbage. I shut my eyes and listen to the familiar whir.

The elevator jolts to a stop. *Ding.*

The lobby is packed. People are rushing out of other elevators and queuing up at the airlocks. I wade through the crowd and secure a spot in line. Waiting my turn, I let routine take over and turn my attention elsewhere. Muzak plays from hidden speakers in the lobby's vaulted ceiling. The musicians' lack of enthusiasm for the piece is palpable in their sloppy tones and poor timing. I want to criticize them—how could you play this crap if you don't like it? But then I think of myself sitting obediently in school these past few months, doing everything exactly as I was told. Meanwhile, I was plotting my escape. Perhaps every sloppy note is a hidden message for people like me. *Keep your head down, we're in this together.*

I'm up next for the turnstile. I unzip my pack, grab my mask, and slip it on. Giving the straps a few quick tugs, I step inside the open airlock. As the doors close behind me, the bustle of the lobby fades away and for a few moments while the door seals behind me, I am alone with the sound of the rhythmic rasps of my filtered breath.

Smog hisses past me as I'm spat out onto the sidewalk. I push my way into the crush of foot traffic so packed it's spilling onto the road. I hate how the city looks from the street. Crowded, loud, and impossible to navigate, Einsam is a hard city to love. The streets seem wider from the penthouse and the pollution—so surreal, almost magical looking, from up high—is smothering down here.

Visibility during the day is far worse than at night. The sun reflects off the smog creating a dull glow that obscures anything farther away than your outstretched arm. But there is no way you could ever even see that far with all the people and cars clogging everything up.

From above I would know exactly where I was, but down here it takes me forever to get my bearings. I've decided that I should test my hypothesis somewhere where no one can see me—I don't want to be arrested—plus I really don't want to scar someone with the sight of my corpse if I'm wrong. On the other hand, I don't want to go somewhere so hidden only the rats will find me. I shudder at the thought of thousands of tiny rat teeth ripping into me. I'll have to find someplace that's not too busy and just wait for a clearing. Walking from street to street, it's clear that this will be harder than I thought.

The streets never seem to empty. I wander awash in a sea of trench-coat-wearing, mask-concealed nobodies. If it weren't for the rainbow of hues available for coats—except for Peace-Officer brown, there's an ordinance against that—people would have no identity on the street. An endless procession of aimless ants.

I didn't put on a watch, and unable to see the position of the sun in the glowing slivers between skyscrapers, I have no way of telling time. Judging from the hot throbbing in my heels, hours have passed since I began my search. My aching feet and a rumbling stomach persuade me with little resistance to take a break.

There are cafés on nearly every corner, so it doesn't take long to find a place with a short queue to get inside and grab a quick bite to eat. The line for the airlock moves quickly, and I soon find myself inside.

The café is somber with dashes of neon bombast. *Welcome!*

Rusting pipes cover the walls like lacework. *Art or neglect?*

I grab a pre-made turkey sandwich and a bottle of *Cava* berry medley seltzer from the illuminated open-faced refrigerator running the length of the bar.

The transaction is quick and wordless—the curly-haired barista never even lifts her eyes from her terminal. Swipe, approved, receipt, next.

I take a seat by the window. Observing the throng of multi-colored ants, I chew slowly giving myself more time to watch. A gasp at the airlock pulls my attention away from my sandwich.

"I'm sorry miss, I mean-er-ma'am." A grungy man—threadbare coat, matted hair, ancient cracking mask—is apologizing to a middle-aged socialite in line for the airlock. She turns away from him. I catch a glimpse of disgust before she slips on her mask and exits. I sip my seltzer, following him with my eyes. He waits his turn in line appearing not to notice the scrunch-nosed faces and rude retching sounds those around him are making. He plucks a sandwich from the display.

The airlock hisses open. Two Peace Officers enter. Air catches in my throat—all the oxygen has been sucked out of the room. Electric tension fizzles on rising hackles around the café.

The grungy man places an egg salad sandwich on the counter. The display lights up: $11.59. The barista's nose twinges. She steps back. The Peace Officers swivel in unison. The grungy man is fishing coins out of darned pockets. His eyes fix on the Peace Officers and balloon.

Hands trembling, he spills a handful of coins onto the counter. They scatter and bounce. He scrambles to the ground trying to collect them. Every eye in the café is on him now. The Peace Officers step forward. He looks up at them—his eyes are gleaming black disks.

"I-er-uh…" he gulps hard—his eyes dart to the door. The taller Peace Officer reaches for his baton.

He bolts for the airlock.

"Halt!"

My spine stiffens. He shoves a couple out of the way and narrowly squeezes into the airlock before the doors seal shut. The Peace Officers hurdle the splayed-out couple. Batons in hand, and champing at the bit, they're forced to wait as the cylinder recycles.

They jam into the airlock together as soon as it's ready and rush after him blowing their whistles—pedestrians scatter like fish darting out of the path of a barracuda.

Heart racing, I keep my eyes low and pick up my sandwich—my hands are trembling. A piece of turkey bounces out from between the bread onto the table. My stomach is a rock. Tears well in my eyes. I squint hard to keep them from falling. He was just trying to buy a sandwich. So what if he was dirty, he had money like the rest of us. The reality of what could await the outcome of my little experiment hits me square in the face. I gulp down the last of my seltzer to alleviate the dryness cloying at my tongue. I've always known the stakes were high, but I've been able to float above it all—those are someone else's problems, someone else's reality. But that delusion is crumbling before my eyes and there is no going back now. What am I supposed to do, go home and sit in my mask staring blankly into a television like Mother?

I scan the street through the grime-stained windows. The chase has scared people off the streets. I may never get another chance like this. It's now or never. I put my mask back on and give it a few tugs to tighten it up.

There is a cluster of people prattling by the door with the couple the man knocked over. I push past them—I'm bouncing, coiled like a spring.

The streets have cleared up significantly. Everyone still out has a head-down-staring-at-their-feet busyness. Morning rush hour has cleared, and only a few cars join the omnipresent street sweepers to slosh through the soot. Across the road, the connecting street appears promisingly empty.

Looking both ways for traffic, I dash across. The street bends off around the corner into a dense mixed-use megaplex. Drawn to its stillness, I jog along the curve keeping my eyes peeled for a discrete place.

A few hundred meters down, the street curves again in the opposite direction. In the space between, I stand alone. I glance back and forth. The street is empty and filled only by the low bass rumble of the city and the shimmering of slowly falling ash. I empty my lungs to dissipate some of the nervous electricity dancing on my skin. I'm actually going to do this.

My fingers run along my neck, stopping on the pressed-tight rubber of my mask. Nervous, I look around again. There's no one in sight, and the windows are blackened with filth. But I can't shake the feeling of invisible eyes, flesh or mechanical, zooming in on me. I look harder for a more concealed spot. I spot a narrow alley a few meters away and dash into it. My heart gives me a drumroll. A final look. Alone.

Retracing their path, my fingers press under the rubber seal.

I rip my mask off.

My chest seizes up. My throat constricts. Panic sets in. What the hell am I doing? How stupid am I? Of course, the advertisement lied to me, why would I change my filter every day if they lasted a long time? A filter a day is good for business, but what reason does the government have to flat-out lie to millions of people? Fumbling with the mask, I attempt to loosen it enough to slide it back on.

"Stop!" The ferocity of the command pricks every nerve in my body. The Peace Officers from the café have turned the corner. Their batons are still in their hands—crimson ribbons drip from the ends. They're sprinting toward me shouting—their voices mechanized by the synthesizers in their mirror-black rebreathers. Conscious thought melts to static. I'm running.

Holding onto my mask with a death grip, I tear down the claustrophobic alley. My narrow frame lets me pass through at full speed. Chancing a glance back, I see that they have had no such luck. With their broad shoulders and thick coats, they are struggling to push their way between the constricted brick walls. I'm heaving unfiltered air. It has a tart, sulfur taste that lingers and prickles at the back of my throat, but I'm not dead.

Free from the mask, I breathe deeper than I ever have before. I feel my muscles working harder and springing back faster than I thought they could.

The gap between us widens significantly with my new-found energy. The alley is beginning to open up. Once it widens enough for them to run, their longer legs will eradicate my lead. I have to lose them somehow. I glimpse a perpendicular alley. Attempting the turn, my feet shoot out from under me on the oil-slick stone. I crash down hard on my left knee. Searing tendrils radiate through my leg, but adrenalin blunts the edges of the pain.

I clamber to my feet—damp ash clings to my palms. I chance a glance back. They're bearing down on me. Stomach lurching, I turn the corner and take off at full speed. Thankfully this alley is narrower than the first which should buy me a few precious seconds. I scan my surroundings desperate for another inter-section. I spot one with plenty of time to prepare for the turn. I make it effortlessly. I hope they didn't see me make it, but I can't stop to find out.

Their footsteps reverberate behind me like approaching thunder. I need to find another alley. My eyes dart back and forth searching for another path, but none appears. Their splashing steps echo against the narrow alley walls. They're still on my tail. Fear slithers through me like fishing hooks. *Will my blood drip from their batons too?*

Frantic now, my eyes search ceaselessly for a way out. *There!*

A few more seconds of sprinting and I make the turn. I turn too fast and slip and fall again slamming into the alley floor. Having lost my momentum and my wind, I barely manage to pull myself up into a stoop. I pause for lack of breath—white-hot pain radiates in my chest. Bruised, winded, and covered in muck, escape seems hopeless.

I open my eyes—tears fall—and there it is, my way out.

That fall was fortuitous; without it I would have run right past my salvation. Only inches above the alley floor a wide transom window, scarcely large enough to squeeze through, stands open. Without thought, I leap through the tiny opening. The window seal scrapes along my chest and back. Tucking in to try to save my head, my shoulder bears the full impact of the fall onto the concrete floor.

Ignoring the hammering pain, I jump up and slam the window down and throw the latch. Collapsing against the wall, I squeeze my eyes shut and hold my breath. Time slows. The loudness of their footfalls swells with each agonizing instant—*kur-splunch kur-splash*. Petrified, I pull myself into a ball.

Landing in a puddle outside the small window, their feet shower the glass with muck. Even with my eyes closed, I can sense the drastic drop in light. They don't stop. Their stomping splashes fade then disappear below the sound of blood pulsing in my temples—*kertoosh, kertoosh*. Finally, a break. Even if they had stopped to look through the window, the soot would render me invisible.

I linger frozen until I'm convinced they're actually gone. I crack open my lips and draw in a breath. Air never felt so good.

I keep my eyes closed—the surge of survival hormones coursing through my body is fading away. Like wiping Vaseline off a mirror, I can see my thoughts clearly now. My mind seems to think that now is a great time to try to process everything that's just happened. I just want to linger here in the cool, quiet stillness but that train has already left the station. In a matter of months, my life has flipped upside down. How can everyone wear their masks without question? Is this some big joke no one remembered to fill me in on? Seventeen years of wearing masks, of fearing for my life, for what? So filter companies can rake in profits with the market up or down? No, this is beyond that, and, I fear, far more nefarious.

If it were up to my head, I could sit here in the dark pondering for eternity, but with the pain-numbing effects of adrenaline fading fast, a laundry list of aches and pains jostles for my attention. I turn to my knee first feeling around the patella for a break. It's tender, but it bends okay without too much pain. I lift my shirt and check the scrapes on my stomach. Their superficial but they sting like an insult. As I'm pulling a piece of gravel out of my palm, the room explodes with light.

Positive that this is the end, I slam my eyes shut. I don't want to see the batons.

Nothing happens. I dare a peek. A middle-aged woman is standing in the doorway across the storage room. Smoking a long cigarette, she doesn't seem the least bit shocked to see me.

"I was wondering how long it would take you to look."

"It was an accident. I slipped and fell through."

"Then why'd you close the window instead of just crawling right back out? And where's your mask? Was taking it off an accident too?"

Unable to think of a response I break down. The game is up.

"I… my mask," tears spill down my cheeks.

She takes a long drag from her cigarette.

"Don't worry honey. I think I know exactly what happened. You aren't the first one to find yourself in such a jam. Your secret is safe with me."

Is she trying to trick me into revealing something incriminating? Best to play dumb.

"What secret? I'm not hiding anything. I slipped and fell that's all. I'll go now." I wipe my tears away with the one clean patch on the back of my hand.

She drops her cigarette. It smolders on the concrete while she crosses the room. I stand up and back away, but I run out of space and slam against the wall. She stops an arm's length away.

"You just discovered the big joke. Why do you think that window was open? Because I'm terrified of the air?" Her face twists up in a smile—deep laugh lines fractal out from the corner of her eyes.

"You're not going to turn me in, are you? I won't tell anyone you had the window open I swear."

The woman's expression is inscrutable. The room is crushing down on me, and at any moment I might melt into soup and splash onto the floor. There's no way out of this.

"I'll go quietly. Just, please, don't tell my mother."

Sticking my wrists together, I shove my hands toward her in surrender. Her smile morphs into a smirk. She takes my hands in hers and leans in close. Her sage eyes are speckled with umber and ringed in muted gold.

"You're just shaken up honey—I'm not going to turn you in. Your secret is my secret." Her eyes are trusting and her words soothing.

"Come on—I'll make you some tea, and you can tell me all about what you've been up to."

She turns to lead me by the hand.

"Ouch." My left knee yowls with pain. I'm hopping on my

right leg, so she swoops around to support me under the arm.

"Oh honey, we need to get you off that knee. Come on, let me help you to the couch."

"Thank you."

We hobble across the room and pass into a bright, multi-colored kitchen. The cabinets are yellow with blue, green, and red trim. No two knobs are the same, and no pot, pan, or dish matches any other. Pain and relief turn me in circles—I'm about to lose my lunch.

A pot is whistling on the stovetop. The living room lies just beyond the kitchen in the same long rectangular room. She bends down to push aside the coffee table then lowers me down onto the plush yellow, velvet sofa. I use my elbows to straighten myself out resting my head on the armrest.

"Here let me help you with your shoes." She starts on my laces. I follow the murky slug trail from the storage room, across the kitchen tiles, and up onto the couch.

"I'm so sorry."

"Don't you worry about it, honey. It's just a mess." She pulls off my shoes. My leg is thrumming and hot. She pulls on my leg straightening it out. I wince while she rummages her hands around my knee.

"Well, the good news is I don't think it's broken. Just sore. You're tougher than you look. Here, sit up. I'll put a pillow under your head. That arm's more lump than stuffing these days." I sit up to let her slide a plump knit pillow under my head—the cuts on my stomach hiss. She straightens up and looks me over.

"Are you hurt anywhere else?"

"Just some scrapes. Nothing too serious."

"Let me get you some tea then I'll see what I can do to clean up those cuts."

She smiles then heads to the kitchen. She fills two mugs with hot water, scoops three heaping spoons of loose-leaf tea into two diffusers, then plunks them into the water.

"I'll be back in a second honey, just need to pop in the back and find my first aid kit."

She disappears through the only other door, halfway between where I'm lying and the kitchen. Everything is swirling. I feel a dopey smile work its way over my face. Sleep pulls at me lulling me to close my eyes and sink into the couch. *What are you doing?*

I sit up in a lurch. Holding my stomach and suppressing a wince, I shuffle forward looking for my shoes. How can I be this stupid? She's going into the other room to call Peace Officers. She's making the tea to lower my guard. I let her take my shoes off! What am I thinking?

Too late—her rummaging sounds have stopped, and she's headed back. I throw myself back and try to put a smile on my face, but it quivers at the edges.

"Here it is," she says emerging with an *All Better* brand first aid kit.

She places the kit on the table then perks up like she just remembered she made tea.

"The tea should be about ready. I don't like mine very strong. You?" She expertly navigates over to the coffee table with the two steaming cups and sets them down. I twist myself up doing my best to keep from grimacing too much. She takes a seat in the floral-patterned armchair to my right.

"Thank you." The mug's thick walls keep it from being too hot to hold, but I know if I try to drink it now, I'll melt my tongue right out of my head.

I draw in the steam—its warmth soothes my lungs, and the pleasant aroma of elderberry and hibiscus blunt the edges of my apprehension. I take a scolding sip and decide to trust her.

CHAPTER FOURTEEN

WE SIP OUR TEA IN SILENCE. After a few minutes of nothing but the *tick, tick, tick* of the clock over the fireplace, the woman gets up and rummages through the built-ins across from me. She rifles through a box of old, square tape disks, selects one from the back, and feeds it into the aging player. The room fills with the jaunty crackling of last century jazz. It washes over me like rain.

Retreating into myself, I try to mesh the pleasant oddness of this living room with the frantic chaos of the chase. By the time there is nothing in my mug but the bottom bitters, I've made no headway in the attempt. It feels like instead of falling through a window I fell into another world.

She takes our mugs over to the sink then turns her attention to patching me up. I pop a few *Ache Busters* and away we go. She helps me out of my shirt and sets about cleaning the soot from my cuts. A thick layer of *Kill All Anti-Bac* and a half dozen bandages later, I'm starting to feel like myself again. Packing up the first aid kit she disappears again into her room reappearing a minute later with a crimson tee-shirt and an oversized molted-gray trench coat.

"Best not to look the same when you head home."

I nod in agreement and slip on the red shirt.

"You're not kicking me out, are you?"

She smiles. "Not yet—you still haven't told me your story."

Taking a deep breath, I lean forward and start from the beginning.

She listens intently, nodding her head the whole time but giving little away. When I'm nearly up to the present, I come to the grungy man and the blood-soaked batons. Her composure cracks, and she turns away—tears well in her eyes. Before I can say anything to bring her back, the tape stops. She ejects it and returns it to its box.

"Sorry for interrupting you. Your story started to land a little too close to home." She returns to the armchair absently rubbing the side of her head. "I was much like you when I was your age. All fire and vinegar. I didn't like the way things were going. I thought I could make things better. But I didn't get as lucky as you when you fell through my window. They caught up to me—bloody Peace Officers. I blacked out when they smashed a baton into the side of my head. Next thing I knew, I was waking up in a prison cell."

"I'm so sorry."

"Ten years… long years. When I finally got out, they made sure I knew that repeat offenders don't get a second chance at prison. Next time it would be the gallows or worse."

"I'm so sorry," I say unable to think of anything else.

"It's all in the past. I'm not hung up on what happened. Even in my jail cell, I knew I was freer than any bird. They can cage you up, but freedom is in here." She taps on her heart—a triplet of tears splashes on the rug.

I start to stand, but she waves me down. She laughs as she wipes away the tears, "I'm just so happy to see that there are still people out there asking tough questions."

"Like why we wear our masks?"

"Exactly honey. Why do we wear our masks?" She chews on the phrase like burnt caramel.

"How do you go on from that? I mean, once you know it's all a lie what do you do? Do you hide inside, or do you still put on a mask and go places?"

"I need to eat, make money, and pay the bills—I got to live. Can't stand being cooped up for too long—I need to stretch my legs. And everything out there—well you already know— necessitates a mask. Thankfully, I've discovered ways to get by with what I need without having to wear one too often."

"Are you still trying to change things? Make things better?" I find myself teetering on the edge of the couch.

"I did for a long time, but I settled into the life I have now. There's too much to risk at my age—I couldn't go through it again. You can understand—surely. The last time I spoke up..." Her words trail off as she walks over to the shelf. I follow her with my eyes. Words tumble on the tip of my tongue—a thousand questions fighting to escape at once. She moves aside books and boxes, presses on a false panel, and reveals a hidden compartment. My heart races. My fingers twist on the welting. She reaches in and pulls out a dog-eared magazine.

"It's not the newest copy—I haven't been able to get my hands on one—but I think this can do a better job of answering your questions than I can." She offers it to me, and I pluck it from her with trembling fingers. It's a thin magazine of typical shape, but instead of the glossy plastic pages of glamor mags or *Drumbeat*, its pages are pulpy and matte. The title jumps off the page at me in bold, all caps lettering: *Nightingale*. I nearly rip the cover in my haste to get to the first page.

"Who writes this? Are there more people like you? Like us? Do the Caretakers know about this? How do they print it without getting caught? How do you get one? I can't imagine you can subscribe to it like a normal magazine—is there a secret password?" Once I opened my mouth, the torrent of questions couldn't be stopped.

"Sing sweet."

"What?"

"The password. Once you identify a distributor that's how

you let 'em know you aren't some OSS spook."

"Really?" I'm so wound up my eyes race over the headlines, but I can't make out the words.

"Yeah, well at least that's how I got them for a while. They must have changed the password on me because I haven't had luck in months. Most of the stuff in that is out of date, but by the looks of it I don't think you mind."

Here in my hands is a portal to the world I want to live in. Delia's world, her world, and now I suppose it's my world too.

I try to force myself to focus. *Resistance in the workplace. The art of sabotage. What to do if you're caught. How to check your home for surveillance. Your neighbor, your informant.* So many articles, each more intriguing than the last. I drag my eyes away from the page to the woman. She's still standing—my mask and the new trench coat in her outstretched hands.

"I'm sorry to kick you out like this, but you caught me on a busy day. I've got some errands to run, and I think it's best you run along home before PO's come knocking."

Deflated, I clutch *Nightingale* to my chest.

"Please—keep it. I've read through it a dozen times."

"So," I start to say before emotion gums up my throat. "So is this goodbye?"

"Only if you want it to be. I would like it very much if you came back to visit. You've taken a very important first step today, but your journey is just getting started. I'd love to be there for you, help you navigate it."

"Really? Can I come back tomorrow?"

"You read through those articles and bring me your questions, and I'll have a cup of tea waiting for you."

"Deal." I bounce to my feet and take the overcoat and mask from her shuffling *Nightingale* from hand to hand as I pull them on.

"Come on, I'll walk you out. Best tuck that away though—you never know who's watching."

I nod then follow her out through the front airlock. I'm practically hovering I'm so high.

<hr>

I follow behind her no closer than three paces, just like she instructed. I feel like a spy passing through the crowd like a ghost—no one the wiser to my forbidden cargo. But I also feel like a flashing bright-red neon sign. *Subversive! Guilty!* I keep my eyes low and press forward.

Our paths diverge at Victory Boulevard. She veers off toward the industrial park, and I make a right and head toward City Centrum and home. I can just make out the shape and glow of familiar billboards.

Alone with my thoughts, I have too much time to think—to

regret. Delia chose this path, the woman too, and for better or worse so have I. I should have reacted better to so many things. I should never have been so cruel to Victoriana, I should have prepared more, learned more. But it's over now, and I'm still here. I may be battered, but I'm alive. And now I have something concrete—a path forward that can only lead to the truth. Fear and doubt fester in the dark corners of my mind, but that only means I'm human—they don't control me.

The lobby is empty apart from Mr. Standish who's sitting at the front desk absently flipping the pages of a *Caretaker's Quarterly*. I pull off my mask with the aching knowledge that I'll never want to put in on again. He notices me and straightens up quick—his cheeks go pale. He flashes a toothy grin while tentatively raising his hand to wave. *Why's he being so weird?* I wave at him and keep on—my boot heel's clack and echo on the mirror-like marble. As the elevator doors close me in, it's impossible to shake the feeling of being constantly trapped. One prison to the next. Trapped in a mask, an elevator, a city—what's the difference?

By the time I reach the apartment, the electricity that had given me wings is little more than distant static. The reality of Mother on the other side of the door, the tender bruises on my legs, and my many itching scrapes all work together to pull me back into my regular morass.

Just breathe, Evelyn.

I take a deep breath, force myself back into my mask, and

press inside.

I hang my coat up and slip off my filthy boots. Gooseflesh prickles up my legs. On the kitchen counter, a *Meal for One* sits in the puddle formed as it thawed. I keep the handle twisted as I close the door trying to keep the latch from clanking.

Thunk.

"Shit."

Before I've even had time to turn all the way around Mother is in the hallway.

"Evelyn, is everything all right? I was so worried—you just took off this morning." She's twisted herself around me.

"Yes Mother, everything is fine. I just wanted to get out early, enjoy the day."

She pulls back, her eyes are a mess of conflicting messages warped through glass.

"Yes, of course. But you can't just leave without saying where you're going. There are bad people in the world—"

I roll my eyes so far back it hurts. Her fingers sink into my biceps like talons.

"I'm serious Evelyn. You must be careful. There are people who want to kill you—kill people like us."

"You're paranoid."

"No, I'm right."

"So I should just stay home then?"

"Where is this tone coming from? Your father?"

She releases me and slinks into the kitchen. I follow her like an out-of-sync shadow.

"I'm not your enemy Evelyn. I just want you to be safe. I need you to be safe."

"I am."

She picks up the *Meal for One*—no doubt it was well on its way to being a paradise for botulism—and holds it over the trashcan.

"I noticed you didn't change your filter this morning."

Fire darts down my spine. "They last a week—that's what it says—"

"I know what it says!" The soupy *Meal for One* hits the lip of the trash can, tears open, and spews across the kitchen floor. Frozen, I watch her weep. Mopbots are already on the scene lapping up the mess. I pull her head into my chest and wrap my arms around her. Her wheezing is strained by her mask.

"I was thinking of going to the cinema tomorrow. Catch a few shows. Maybe do a little shopping. I won't leave so early tomorrow—I'll change my filter." Her grip tightens. Her hands dangerously close to discovering the

Nightingale tucked into my waistband.

I push her away and try to convey a smile as best as my mask will allow.

"Are you hungry? I can heat you up a different one."

"No, that's okay. I was thinking of taking a shower and calling it an early night."

Her brows droop. "Oh, okay." Her hands fall away from me. "Goodnight then. Oh, and congratulations. I'm very proud of you."

"Thanks. It's nothing really."

Silence gnaws the space between us.

Moving only my eyes, I follow her silhouette until it disappears. A heavy sigh garbles out through my mask.

I pick the *Meal for One* container up off the floor and toss it in the garbage—the floor around it already squeegeed clean and perfect like nothing ever happened.

I navigate the shower as best I can. I try to clean up without taking off the bandages, but it's no use and I have to pull them off. A dozen new cuts announce themselves. My knee is a wilting plumb. I focus on removing the grime, scrubbing vigorously until it's gone or I'm too raw to endure it anymore.

I can't shake Mother from my thoughts, but I must. What can I do for her? She's just proved to me that she is in no way capable of handling my new reality. "You won't die, Mother. How do I know? Like this." I imagine myself pulling off my mask in front of her—her fingers claw at my face to put it back on.

No, I'm not far enough along into my escape. I'll come back for her when I'm safely outside.

I finish up and grab a towel. *Nightingale* is perched on the bathroom sink demanding I hurry up and dive into it.

"I can't help you if I don't help myself." Hiding the magazine under my towel wrap, I hobble into my room and lock the door. I slip into a tee-shirt and head over to my desk to crank some synthpop. Lying on top of the desk is a thick white envelope with my name on it written in Father's secretary's flourished script. I set *Nightingale* down and crack open the envelope. *Congratulations!* exclaims the generic corner store card. A one-hundred Mark bill falls out as I open it. I collect it and set it on the desk before I read the inscription.

My Dearest Evelyn,

I'm so very proud of your determination and resilience. Graduation is no small feat. Here's a little something to enjoy your summer with.

With Love, Always,

Dad

P.S. Don't worry about University right now. You can stay at home as long as you like. Tomorrow comes for us whether we want it to or not. There's no reason to rush into it.

I put the letter back into the envelope and look around the room for a pair of pants to shove the cash into. Why can't Mother just do something like this? No, don't think about her. Focus.

I turn on the stereo and crank whatever synthpop disk happens to be inside. It's way louder than I'd typically listen to it, but it should convey the message quite clearly: stay out. Bouncing on my good leg, I scoop up *Nightingale*, grab blankets and a pillow from my bed, and hunker down in the closet.

Every page is jammed so full of subversive and unorthodox words and phrases that I'm spinning. I devour it front to back. *Kill or be killed. Fight. Resist. Sabotage. Undermine. Infiltrate. Assassinate.* I come up gasping for air.

I toss the magazine into the corner, lean back, and try to catch my breath. What have I gotten myself into? If these articles are to be believed, the escape I've been attempting has been futile from the onset—there is no escape only life-long struggle. Fingers trembling, I hunt for the newspaper clipping. The sight of it provides momentary release. There are no bombs in those mountains. No blood-gorged rivers. But I can't keep messages from the Caretaker's films and the *Nightingale* from sliding over each other in my mind. They seem to diverge only in the overlap—mirror images blurring where the edges align. I shudder. There has to be another path. The circle of violence is just another cage—another veil separating us from freedom.

But perhaps I've got it all wrong, and the only illusion is

the serenity of mythic mountain air.

Bile builds in my throat.

I slip the magazine into the box of old toys, turn off the music, and make the bed. I'm walking a razor's edge with Mother, and I can't afford to have anything out of place. My aching body yearns for rest but my mind struggles, lashing out against the encroaching dark.

I find myself back at the café. Trying to buy a sandwich, only this time I'm the grungy man. As Peace Officers beat me unconscious in the street, I turn back and see myself watching disinterestedly as I sip down the last of my seltzer.

Everything is as she would want it. Bed made, today's clothes neatly steamed and ready. She arrives right on cue fresh filter in hand. I play along with added gusto even attempting a smile so wide she'd have to notice it despite my mask.

"Going to the cinema today?" Her eyes are bloodshot. Did she get any sleep? Has she been crying?

"Yeah. There's a ton of summer blockbusters out. I haven't picked one yet—I might see two."

"And you'll be home before dark?" She's turned away from me looking at the door like she can't wait to leave.

"Yeah."

She nods and starts her exit shuffle. "Be safe."

When she's safely sealed in her room, I take a deep breath through the new filter. I'd forgotten how sterile they smell when they're new. I'm careful not to put all my weight on my bruised knee while I get ready, then I'm out the door. It's too late to go back.

The cineplex is already packed when I arrive. School's out, so Centrum is teeming with kids. Waiting in line to buy a movie ticket, I study the central geodesic glass dome. Twenty stories above me, the concentric floors—each bursting with neon storefronts, projected light advertisements, and costumed employees beckoning shoppers inside—seem to retreat into infinity. Normally everyone would have their masks off—Centrum has only the best airlock and filtration systems money can buy according to the signs plastered at every entrance—but then again nothing has been normal in months.

Do Not Remove Your Mask barks at you from graphic posters glued everywhere. Cutting through the crowds are triple the regular patrols of Blue Coat security and Peace Officers. When their patrols draw close to me, it's all I can do to keep from running. *Keep your head down, don't make waves.*

I fixate on the marquee. What film should I not see today? A romantic comedy? A spy thriller? A two-hour firehose of explosions and gore? Or maybe the biggest film out right now:

Citizen Zero. It's got it all, war, love, a plucky sidekick and of course the greatest hero there ever was or ever will be again, our great first High Caretaker Antonius Neptus. The documentary laid out the facts, but here on the silver screen mega-star director Hunter Maxwell gives us the emotions, the heartbreak, and the triumph in hyper-real simulacrum. Judging by the poster, Maxwell has taken some liberties—I don't remember Neptus being an early thirties beefcake with a chin that cuts through helmet straps—but the history books can't get it all right, can they? More importantly, this is the film nearly everyone here is going to see. If I pick an obscure film, or something I'd actually watch, I would have no cover, no way to explain the film. But I could tell you everything about *Citizen Zero* this instant and get nothing wrong. Plus, the theater will be so packed I'll just get lost in the shuffle.

"Next," commands the tele-linked display. The attendants are safely inside a sealed glass tube. How do they get in and out? Or do they just live in there?

"One for the first showing of *Citizen Zero*."

The cash slot clanks open—its hungry rollers thrum. I feed it the hundred Mark bill, and it spits me back ninety-five Marks and a ticket.

"Enjoy the show. Next!"

I pass through the cinema's airlocks, let the masked attendant tear my ticket. I linger inside just long enough for the pungent aroma of popcorn, artificial butter, sugar, and vomit to make my eyes water, then I duck behind a group exiting the theater and leave. Skin prickling, I keep my eyes straight ahead, hands shoved in my pockets, and head for the woman's house.

———

"I see you found it all right. How are you holding up?" She takes my overcoat and beckons me to the table where two steaming mugs of tea are waiting.

"Yes, thank you. It was much easier than yesterday." I take a seat, and my knee sings in relief. "Physically, I'm a little sore. You were right, nothing's broken but—"

"But what you read has you all shaken up."

I bring the tea to my lips and blow on the edge—its heat dances through my fingers. I try a sip, but it's still much too hot. I set it down and sigh.

"I don't know what to make of it. I love it—there are other people out there asking questions. People who won't settle for what they're told. But the means... The vision... It's all bleak and blood. There's no escape."

"Is that what you're really looking for? Escape?"

"Maybe? I'm not sure. I guess... I just wanted to know the truth, but now—"

"The truth's uglier than you thought."

Flashes of Cinnamon, of Victoriana weeping on the stage,

of Aldridge dragging Britney by the hair, the chase and bloody batons.

"No, no that's not quite it. I knew that. I thought maybe there'd be people offering a different world, one without the lies, without the violence. *Nightingale* doesn't offer an escape from all of this, it embraces it, accepts it. I can't do that. There has to be a different world out there somewhere."

She takes a long gulp. Her finger twirls on the edge of her cup—her eyes fix on me unmoving.

"What if this is all there is? And the only two choices are kill or be killed?"

"Then I'll make a different way."

She pushes her tea aside and leans closer—her arms bent at the elbow supporting her chin. "What if I could help you? Show you a different path—a better path."

I mirror her and lean in, "Show me."

Her expression cracks and a smile sweeps her face. I pick up the cup and take a solid swig. My chest blooms with fire lifting me up even as it smolders away. She scoots her chair back, pushing on the edge of the table, and hops up. She disappears into her room. I start to get up, but she re-emerges before I can.

"No need to get up, I've brought it here." She waves me down.

She's holding an old leather-bound book. The binding is

coming apart and the yellow pages look like they've been rifled through a thousand times.

"I think this may be more to your liking." She hands me the book then retakes her seat.

I turn it over and run my finger along the title: *The Long Path Forward.*

"I should have trusted my gut. I've met a few young people, pushing the curtain back like you. I tried starting them out on stuff like this—the good stuff—but they are always clamoring for action." Her face sours and her attention shifts to the front door. She lets out a sigh then turns back smiling. "I had a feeling you were cut from a different cloth." She takes a sip of her tea. "That expression makes me sound like an old lady, doesn't it?" She winks and we share a laugh.

I lay the book down with care, then pick up my tea. "I had a good feeling about you too." We raise our mugs and sip together.

A volcano of excitement is erupting inside me and it's all I can do to stay in my seat. It'll be slow going, but for the first time it really feels like there may be a way out.

***

The next two weeks pass in a blur. Every morning I give Mother the performance I know she needs to hold herself together. I keep our interactions light and brief. I make sure to say goodbye and give her an itinerary that won't raise any alarms.

I've found five different routes to the woman's house and I never use the same one twice in a row. I stop along the way and choose a store or café at random to buy something that way I always have a time-stamped alibi.

Her door is always open, and the tea is always ready. She seems to have an inexhaustible supply of books and recorded speeches. Each of them champions different, but ultimately similar, plans for nonviolent revolution. They argue that the use of force can only ever replace one oppressor with another. That the Caretakers have a monopoly on violence and every drop of blood spilled—especially their own—erodes your position and reinforces their own.

As radical and appealing as they are, the words of these men and women have me tied in knots. *Nightingale* was alarming, and certainly new to me, but its message was easy to swallow. It was written in the same language as everything else in the Great Society: conflict. But these people are saying things that I'm struggling to even comprehend. When they beat you, stand resolute, when they kill you, persevere. Your weapons—I have no word for something that cleaves without killing—should never be bullets and bombs, but truth, virtue, and kindness. Each individual unborn from violence tips the scale toward victory.

It sounds great, and I want it to be true, but I'm struggling to buy in. How can you overthrow the Caretakers with ideas when they have poisoned all the places they can grow? How can your movement stay together when they start gunning you down in the streets?

She guides me with limitless patience. Probing me to look deeper, but never pushing me beyond where I'm ready to go.

I smuggle something back each night. Books are too hard, but pamphlets and audio disks are easy to hide discretely in my waistband. I get home before dark and sit down to dinner with Mother. She's thrown everything out but the *Smoothies on the Go*. Slurping them through the liquid ports on our masks, we dine in near total silence. Father's been working so much I catch him only as a shadow slipping out the door.

Tonight's no different and after dinner Mother seems content to return to her room. I shower as fast as possible scrubbing the soot out of my hair until the water stops running black. When I'm finally alone in my room, I lock the door, throw my mask on the bed and take in an exaggerated lungful of air—holding it until I nearly burst. I change into a sleeping shirt and sweats, turn on some music then curl up in the closet to pore over today's pamphlet: *The Declaration of Workers' Rights*.

The pages crackle open filling the closet with the pungent aroma of decades-old mildew. I sneeze hard into my elbow then open the closet door a crack to let in some fresh air.

At the top the first page is a bold proclamation. "We, the workers and downtrodden of the Great Society, declare open rebellion upon the system we find ourselves currently oppressed. We will not yield until every citizen has a voice in their own governance. Until human interests are risen above corporate ones. Until the levers of power are uncoupled from oppression, wealth, and cronyism. We are building a better tomorrow and there will be no room for Caretakers." Below it are nearly one hundred, hand-signed signatures. Squeezed onto the pocket-sized page, there is more faded black ink than paper. The date scrawled in the corner will be ninety-one-years ago next month. It grips me in the chest to think that for nearly one hundred years—and undoubtedly longer—people have been fighting for a better world. It dawns on me that I may never reach the end of this road—that I am only one of many on the long path to freedom. I'm filled with a competing mixture of hopelessness and pride.

I thumb through their demands, but the weight of history has dragged me leagues away from where I'm sitting. I look over at the stack of pamphlets and audio disks that have built up behind my box of old toys over the last two weeks—their collective subversion could send me to the gallows if they're found. How many people have been where I am, searching for a way to rebuild society? What were their dreams? Fears? How did they make it through? And did they ever find peace?

The optimism I had only moments ago has blown away on the wind. It feels like an elephant just sat on my chest. I could lose myself in my music, or find something mind-numbing to watch on television, but sleep is the only thing that will do.

I stand and put my hand on the closet door ready to slide it open the rest of the way. Approaching feet obliterate the sliver of light under my bedroom door.

Knock, knock.

I sober up fast. I race to the bed and throw my mask on. Hairs yank from their roots.

Knock, knock.

"Just a second." Hopefully the distortion in my voice hides my panic. I tap the input panel on the speakers cutting the music off with a static pop. I start back for the door—a metal rod shoved down my back. I flick the lock open. In that moment I realize that the pamphlet is still in my other hand.

Fire washes over me. I hurl the pamphlet behind me hoping to make it to the other side of the bed. Mother pushes open the door.

"Do you have a minute to talk?"

I swallow hard trying to dislodge the lump in my throat. "Yeah, sure. Of course. I was just listening to music."

Inscrutable concealed behind her mask, she pushes past me. Turning with her, my heart jumps. My throw was crap—the pamphlet is teetering on the edge of the bed.

I surge past her and sit next to it. She shuffles to the other side and sits. I swivel around to look at her using the movement to conceal my sleight of hand as I push the pamphlet under my folded leg.

She's staring at the open closet. Everything succumbs to the whooshing of blood in my head.

"You know I'm very proud you," she turns to me, her eyes shimmering behind the glass.

"I know." I fight to keep my attention on her and not let my eyes dart over to the closet.

"I wanted to give you some space. I hated the way my parents forced me into the academy. You know I never wanted to study neuroscience. Did I ever tell you that? I wanted to be an astronomer. There is something so reassuring about the stars—once you know their orbits you always know exactly where they'll be."

"No, I never knew that."

"But what does that matter? You can't see them anymore anyway." She sighs, her shoulders slump forward. "I'm not going to pressure you now, I just wanted to see what you're thinking. Have you started to make any plans?"

Everything is swirling and I want to puke. I have a plan for my future, but I could never tell her. "I… No, I guess not. Nothing concrete."

She puts a clammy hand on my knee. "That's okay. We're here for you, you know? Your father and I love you very much." She retracts her hand—her voice stretches thin. "Maybe it's for the best the way things are going, keep you close to home."

The pamphlet feels like it's about to ignite—cold sweat is beading on my neck. She stands, taking a step toward the closet. I scoot to the edge, ready to pounce.

"I was thinking about…" she stops, faint sobs seep through the mask. "Sorry. I was thinking about when… you… were a little girl."

In single fluid motion, I stand, drop the pamphlet behind my foot, and kick it under the bed. I embrace her, my body vibrating uncontrollably.

She squeezes my hand. Her eyes are swirling brown oceans. "I was just thinking that maybe it's time to start a new chapter—put your childhood behind us."

I push back cocking my head. "What were thinking exactly?"

She points to my box of toys. "I was thinking, maybe its time we let go of some things. I wanted to see what you thought about donating these old toys?"

It's out of my lips before I can stop myself. "Sure, sounds good to me." Her cheeks lift around her eyes in what must be a smile under there.

"Great. That's great. I'll put them by the door and have someone come pick them up." She's halfway there, her arms stretched out to grab the box, and when she does the tower of illegal contraband will come toppling down.

"Oh, no—let me." I swoop in, getting my hands around the box just as she does.

"All right." She straightens up and steps back. I could really use a falling star right now to put me out of my misery.

I lift the box slowly trying not to upset the delicate balance of the pile behind it. My shoulders are twitching—it's a lot heavier than I remember. Pivoting around, I keep my body in the opening.

"Could you get the door for me?" It's still ajar—I could easily shoulder it open—but I'm out of cards to play.

She nods and moves to the door. As soon as her back is turned, I take one hand off the box—lifting my knee to take its place—and pull a shirt from its hanger. It plops to the floor draping over the pile. A weight lifts off me and I practically float past her.

She lingers in the hallway wanting to talk—I'm vibrating out of my skin. Picking up on my discomfort, she bows her head and says goodnight.

"I love you, Evelyn."

I search for a hiding place for my contraband until I'm on the edge of collapse. Under the mattress, behind the desk, the back of the closet—each spot is worse than the last. I stuff them into my backpack and contemplate taking them all back at once, but one misstep and I'd be screwed. I'll come up with a better solution tomorrow, but I need sleep.

Apprehensive, I pull out my dresser drawers and tape as many books and pamphlets as I can to the back of each one and still have them close.

I float on the edge of sleep—my head just above the lapping waves trying to pull me under.

Every eye sees my guilt. Every slow-moving car an informant calling me in. Convinced I can't take any of my regular routes, I take unfamiliar streets searching for a sixth. It takes me an extra hour to get to her house and it's nearly noon when I finally get to her street.

A few houses down the block, I notice a hulking man stomp out of her door. He's well over six feet tall. The top half of his head is uncovered, and the bottom is shrouded by a stiff cowl. His trench coat doesn't sway like cloth it swings like steel. The light around him seems to dim—alarm bells clang in my head.

He stops on the curb and starts scanning the street. I have only a split second to avoid being seen.

I reach into my pocket, throw a few coins behind a row of parked cars, and duck down to pick them up—my pitiful task should divert passing suspicion. I paw aimlessly for the coins, my attention fixed on him through the gap between bumpers.

A drab gray saloon—painstakingly configured to be as ordinary and featureless as possible—pulls up. The door swings open and he steps in. The car glides away.

I watch it turn the corner then pop back up and start

walking, careful to keep my pace from morphing into a jog.

"Hey!" My heart seizes.

I turn, ready for a baton. A woman in a well-worn coverall hurries up to me holding a fifty-cent piece.

"You missed this one." She hands it to me.

"Thank you." She tips her head then walks on.

I take a moment to compose myself—you can't be this careless—then pocket the coin.

I walk slowly to keep from drawing any more attention to myself, but it only gives the tension in my stomach more time to build.

Finger shaking, I press the call button and the airlock buzzes open.

As soon as the door slides open, I know something's wrong. She's standing in the doorway to the storeroom. When she spots me, she takes one last drag of her cigarette then flicks it onto the concrete.

"I'm sorry honey, I'll put the kettle on." She fumbles with everything, searching through the wrong cabinets, and misplacing things right in front of her.

I approach the table with caution. The air is charged—my hairs prickle.

"Oh honey," she plops a mug down in front of me sloshing

some over the lip. "There's no need for that face—everything is fine."

"That man. I couldn't see him clearly, but he seemed dangerous."

She sits across from me and chews on her thoughts. "Don't worry yourself about him. He's just a ghost stirring things up, that's all. I'll be fine here in just a minute." She takes a long sip of the piping hot tea. "Now what did you think of *The Declaration of Workers' Rights?*"

She brightens up as the day goes on, but her eyes can't stop flicking back to her room like she's expecting a monster to leap out.

I leave early and with nothing to take home.

I take an aimless path back, stopping only to get a coffee in a shop so narrow there's nowhere to sit.

———

Mother is more talkative than normal today barraging me with a single question. "Did you have a good day?"

I lie in bed thinking of a thousand scenarios for her interaction with the man and they all come to the same conclusion: trouble.

———

She's sitting on the couch when I arrive—her hands clenched around something so tight her knuckles are white.

"I've got the tea ready today." She smiles lifting the dark bags under her eyes. She moves to the table. I follow, skin itching.

She waits silently while I settle in and get in a few sips of tea. She hasn't touched her own. With great care, she lowers her fist to the table and unfurls her fingers. She pulls her hand away revealing a translucent blue sphere. It looks like a jeweled robin's egg. Foggy memories cloud up my head—it looks like the spheres they feed into the imprint cradles at school, but this one seems different and I can't quite put my finger on it.

"Go ahead, pick it up."

I reach out for it cautiously—the infinite possibilities lurking inside it give me pause. It's incredibly heavy for its diminutive size and surprisingly warm like there is a fire trapped inside. I bring it close for inspection. The sphere isn't really a sphere at all but a geodesic with thousands of tiny facets. At its core is a suspended metallic tangle. I twist it around and around trying to make out its shape, but its color and content morph with even the slightest shift in perspective.

"Is this—" I pause, combing my memories for the right word. "Is this an impress?" Her eyes light up, and she nods enthusiastically.

"Yes—yes, it is. But it's no ordinary impress. No, what you have in your hand is quite special—this is the cause of all that unpleasantness yesterday. It's the key to unlocking the truth. The truth of our Great Society."

My ears prickle. I was right, trouble.

"What's on it?" My incredulity is growing. Imprint devices are seriously impressive pieces of tech, but they have considerable limitations. They can impart simple concepts like one plus one is two, but they can't make you a rocket scientist with a press of a button. If you try to put too much in at once, it turns your brain into gravy or something. I've never seen it happen, but I've heard the stories. Feeling myself spiral into examining the veracity of everything I've ever assumed to be true, I force myself out of my head and back into the moment.

She extends a hand palm up. I pass her the sphere—my fingers spring back as it drops away.

"I can't say for certain. But I do know Domhnall wants it back—and he's willing to kill for it. Remember the first day we met? I got a call from a friend of a friend. He handed it off to me for safekeeping. I didn't want to get you messed up in this, but it's too late, and it's best you know what's going on."

I'm on the edge of the chair.

"Nightingale broke into the Presidium and made off with two dozen of these. This is the only one they haven't recovered. They've mobilized everyone. The OSS have been working around the clock to find it. Whatever's on here, the Caretakers have made it their mission in life to get it back."

My heartbeat is throbbing in my neck. "Why show me? What can I do?"

"I want you to access it."

The room shrinks and contracts. I clutch at my chair to keep steady. I'm diving into something I don't understand, and I have no way of knowing if I'm a player or if I'm being played.

"This is a lot honey, I know. But believe me," she presses the sphere back into my palm cupping her hands around mine. "This opportunity has fallen into both of our laps, and we can't pass it up. You can help tear down the Caretakers. Not with guns and bombs, but with knowledge."

I rip my hands free—the sphere thuds to the table. "Why not just do it yourself? You don't know me that well—maybe I'll take this straight to the Halls of Justice—turn it over to them." She's shaking her head.

"You're scared, I understand. But it's the only way. I can't explain it easily, but I won't be able to get past security."

"Security where? And I will?" My knee catches the underside of the table as I stand. The table jerks and what's left of my tea splatters everywhere. The sound of dripping fuels the tension. She looks away from me to the abstract painting hanging over the couch. Tears brim on her lashes.

Holding the sphere up between us, her face turns somber— her tone drops its sweetness. "We each have our roles to play. Mine is giving this to you. This is about more than me, more than you, more than the bloody Caretakers."

"What's it about then?"

"The truth." The dam bursts. Tears flow down her cheeks joining the tea pooling on the floor. Pinching the bridge of my nose, I slam my eyes shut and shake my head. What is going on here? Is she crazy? Is this some sort of trap? She's talking about the truth, but she can't even be straight with me. I could have kept myself out of this if I had just gone to the stupid movie. Sat there with my popcorn like everyone else, unplugged and checked out. But I didn't do that, did I? I came back. I knew what kind of person she was the moment she didn't turn me in. And ready or not, I'd be lying if I said I didn't want to be that kind of person too.

"Okay," I say breathlessly. "Tell me what I need to do."

She's up and over to me in a blink. Her arms are around me. Her hug is strong but gentle. I melt. She pulls away, picks up the sphere, and offers it to me again. This time I take it without trepidation.

"This won't work in any ordinary imprint device. You'll need to use one that can handle this much information without frying you into a limp vegetable. Imprint devices that powerful are strictly controlled, and under normal circumstances, we'd never be able to get you into one. But there is one they've forgotten about, the original. It's called the Oracle Device. It was built long before you were born. Hell, long before I was born. A moth-balled relic, it's been buried and forgotten. Through a friend of a friend, I can get you access to it. I know I'm sounding crazy but hear me out. You'll go to the Societal Archive and hand the receptionist this note." She rushes into the kitchen and rummages through the drawers. Producing a notepad and pen, she scribbles a hasty note, rips it from the pad, and folds it into a square.

Numb, I take it and start to unfold it. She clamps her hands around mine to stop me.

"The receptionist is a cute young fellow, dark complexion curly hair. Hand him this, and he'll know what to do." I nod, too dumbstruck to do anything else, and shove the note into my pocket.

"I wish it didn't have to be this way—I wish I didn't have to thrust this tremendous burden on you. But I knew the moment I laid eyes on you that you were special. Strong." She clasps my deltoids. Drunk on her words, I stay transfixed on her eyes. "When you've accessed it, come back here. Make sure to use a different route in case you're followed. I'll figure out our next move."

The fluttering in my guts has me teetering on the edge. Is this the point of no return or did I cross that when I fell through the window?

"I can do this."

"I know you can, honey." Nestling the sphere next to the note, I scoop up my backpack and make for the airlock. As I'm stepping into the cylinder, she grabs my shoulder. I jump and spin around. She's holding my mask. Panic flushes down my neck. I'm rushing everything, but I don't know how to stop. I take it from her and pull it on.

"Thank you."

"Of course, honey. Be safe."

CHAPTER FIFTEEN

THE STREETS ARE FILLING UP as the veiled sun comes into view in the gaps overhead. I've made quick time across the city. The cocktail of competing chemicals surging in my brain have kept my aches in check. But turning the corner, the archive comes into view and dread burns through me. The massive stone building—built ages ago in a time before plate glass, steel, and machines—looms out of place among monoliths lusting for the sky. It has no external airlocks—its stone façade and sweeping buttresses make it look straight out of a horror film. I climb the marble entry steps and grab the elaborate brass handles. Pausing to collect my courage, I shove my way inside.

The once vaulted entrance hall has been retrofitted with squat, modern airlocks. The steel and glass structure looks like cancer on the intricately carved wood and stone. The airlock's mechanisms are slower than I am used to, and I nearly walk into still-closed doors they opened so slowly. Equally as slow to seal me in I have too much time to worry—nervous sprites flutter in my stomach. When it does finally open, I impatiently rip off my mask and jump out.

Rows of chestnut bookshelves fill the cavernous structure. The smell of moldering books is pungent. Its unfamiliarity is beautiful. Approaching the front desk, I reach around and stuff my mask back into my backpack. I rest my hands on the aged wood of the counter. It feels foreign to my concrete-and-steel-accustomed fingers—it's glorious. The librarian looks up from his computer screen with a mild look of surprise.

"Do you need directions?"

By the tone in his voice, it's clear he isn't asking for directions within the archive. She wasn't wrong, he's pretty cute. His eyes are bright, and his curly hair moves just a little slower than he does giving him a puppy dog quality.

"I do in fact. I was hoping you could help me find where I'm going." Fishing the note out of my pocket I press it onto the counter and slide it over to him.

His eyes grow wide as he pops up out of his chair to grab the note. He unfolds it, reads it, then starts searching his desk for something. I shift my weight off my right leg—my nails dig into the counter.

He produces a silver lighter, flicks it open, and torches the edge of the note. It burns nearly to his fingertips before he shakes the fire out and tosses the charred corner on the floor.

"Were you followed?"

I gulp hard. "No. I mean, I don't think so."

He looks me over, sussing me out. I stiffen at his lingering eyes, and it breaks him out of his trance.

"Right. Well then," he points to the last row of books on his right. "Follow that row all the way back to the staircase, take the door marked Special Collections, then simply follow the path until, well, there's nowhere left to go. Look for the end—that'll take you where you want to go." He taps the side of his nose.

Not entirely sure what he means, but convinced I'll figure it out when I get there, I give him a resolved nod. With business out of the way, his expression lightens.

"Sorry for the look of surprise earlier. You aren't the usual type—I was sure you were lost."

I cross my arms and squint at him.

"No, no I didn't mean it like that. You just seem nice is all."

He's struggling a little too much, and it's making me uncomfortable, so I loosen my guard.

"Well, it is my first time here, so you weren't too far off." Distant coughing breaks up the awkward tension. "Breathtaking building," I say.

"Isn't it? We've lost this in architecture." His eyes drift into the ribbed vaults and grow distant. He snaps out of his admiration, "Anyways, welcome. I hope you find what you're searching for."

"So do I."

I give him a smile then follow his directions down the long row of encyclopedias to the staircase. Its wide stone wedges spiral down and out of sight. I keep my hand on the rail during the descent to steady my building nerves.

Forty steps down I round the final corner to find a small landing. A lone door adorned with a plaque reads *Special Collections*. I step inside.

The door closes automatically behind me, and the room falls to near darkness. I linger on the threshold waiting for my eyes to adjust to the scant, amber light. Nervous, I move my feet in short, cautious steps.

Rows of books line a long central corridor with branches that lead off to oblong reading rooms crammed floor to ceiling with oversized leather-bound books. Making my way down the hallway, I stop and peer into the many glass cases filled with remnants and scrolls—their hidden climate control units softly humming.

He wasn't joking and soon enough, emerging from the shadows is a dead end. It's an oblong reading room just like the others only perpendicular to the hallway cutting it off like a capital T. This can't be it, can it?

My knee is starting to act up, so I plop into one of the overstuffed leather chairs. Fine dust plumes up to greet me sending me into a coughing fit. I wipe the tears away from the corners of my eyes. I relax into the chair and pull the impress from my pocket. I turn it around in my hand. The amber light glistens along its facets. It contains something specific and finite. I know that rationally, but looking at its iridescent shimmering depths, I can't help but see infinity. I let myself spiral down that rabbit hole longer than I should. As I'm returning the sphere to my pocket, a faint amber glow coming from a sliver in the bookshelf draws my attention.

Rushing over to the shelf, I run my fingers along the supple spines and smooth walnut cabinetry scanning the titles for anything that jumps out at me. The subjects vary wildly and whatever order they are in escapes me. *Coal and the Ideal Self. The Airlock Compendium. Counter Insurgency protocols Volume II.*

Thump.

My finger snags on a false book's spine. I tap it again to be sure then read the title. *The End by Yelena Orlov*—his nose tapping suddenly obvious.

Vigor renewed, I grab hold of the book with one hand and, steadying myself against the shelf with the other, pull it back.

The hidden door's mechanisms operate to perfection. The shelf slides noiselessly into the wall revealing a cavity with a door at the back. The opening begins to recede the moment my fingers lift from the false book. Moving faster than I thought I could, I dive into the hidden chamber.

Sprawled out on the floor, I tuck my feet in just as it presses closed. I hop to my feet and brush myself off. The walls are lined with rich mahogany that seems to drink in the light. The door is illuminated by an elegant silver fixture resembling a rising sun—its concentrated beam casting the rest of the room in shadow. Anticipation skitters into my fingers as I twist the handle.

A wall of heat and smell and sound rushes at me. Crossing the threshold, I enter a cavernous stone vault. A mechanical device crafted from seemingly every metal fills the massive space. Pistons and gears race beneath its glass and steel skin. Jets of steam sporadically shoot from decorative pipes. I plug my fingers into my ears, but the machine's roar is inescapable. My heart swells in disbelief. A host of smaller machines, fed by thick braided cables that snake up through the ribbed arches, circle it blinking and whirring. Tidal waves of air surge and recede from the machine like the heaving lungs of a dragon.

A set of ornate brass stairs leads to a small landing and what appears to be a human-shaped cavity in the machine. This is it. This has to be the Oracle Device.

Each step across the room is electric. The radiant heat from the device is stifling. The smell of burnt matches intensifies as I approach. My heart races and my lips curl up in a grin.

This is impossible. I wipe the sweat from my eyes and take the last step up the stair to the platform. *This is amazing.*

Across from the cavity is a command module. Its buttons and dials are foreign to me, but they are clearly labeled. The controllers are solid and cold. They turn only with effort, unlike the projected light interfaces I'm used to.

I follow the instructions written on the panel and the machine bursts to life. Startled but excited, I twist the last few knobs into place and throw the final switch. Anxiety constricts my chest as I grow weightless. I embrace the swirling contradictions and press on.

The center of the module opens revealing a spherical opening roughly the size of my palm. *The sphere!* I nearly drop it pulling it from my pocket my fingers are jittering so much. It snaps perfectly into place. A rush of energy springs my step, popping me up onto my tiptoes. Everything she's said has been true so far, so what's hidden in this impress?

The Oracle Device releases a thundering bellow of steam. Turning around, the glass panel shielding the cavity rises on gleaming hydraulic arms. Vapor swirls in vortices around it.

When the steam clears, I stand facing the impression. Comprised of innumerable metallic prongs, it appears to have only one way to enter it.

Trusting my instincts, I press my back into the millions of tiny metal fingers. They're ice-cold. I shudder and go to recoil, but it's too late, they have me in their embrace. I struggle in vain as they pull me in until only my nose and mouth are uncovered.

The shield door closes, and the thundering of the machine disappears behind the glass. The grip of the metallic fingers is writing and alive. A fire burns hot in my mind. This was a mistake. The helplessness of claustrophobia overtakes reason. Thrashing about, I struggle to free myself from the ocean of wriggling mechanical fingers.

Hyperventilating, I realize, despite my best efforts, it's far too late for me to escape the otherworldly embrace of this machine. I focus on each breath to turn my mind away from the ceaseless frozen slithering.

Blinding pain consumes me for an instant as millions of tiny needles emerge from the ends of the fingers and punch through my skin.

As suddenly as the pain appears it vanishes. In its wake, the world begins to swirl.

In the needles' embrace, the ache and anxiety of the last few months leaches from me.

The calm is fleeting.

Electricity floods into every pore. My teeth clench down on the edge of my tongue as My spine seizes stiff. Creeping tendrils work their way through my veins. I'm slipping away, and the machine is forcing its way in.

Tremendous flashes of light pierce my clamped eyelids. Trillions of colors—beyond the scope of normal perception— explode in my eyes. My body boils up to fever heat and down to hypothermia cold. I am as immobile as stone and fluid like water both. My mind rages against this supernatural assault.

Fully engulfed in the machine, I suffer its every will and whim whether I struggle or not. Deciding to let go, to stop fighting, is herculean. But the only way out is through.

"Is fighting more important than discovering the truth?" I ask myself.

"No, nothing is more important," we—mind and machine—answer back.

The moment I relinquish control, the Oracle Device seizes it.

The journey begins—I am a puppet on a string. The world I know drops away. Floating in the emptiness of space, I can no longer tell where I end, and the machine begins.

Rocketing off at unachievable speeds I cross over solar and systems galaxies, too quickly and too many to count. I can only revel in the scope of the universe. Far in the distance, a tiny blue speck appears. Hurtling toward it, it continues to grow until I can see nothing else.

A blinding light pulls me from the universe, and I hang for a time in limbo. As the light recedes and I regain my sight, I know I have arrived.

Experiencing everything, I delve into the vision, and my first step toward the truth.

CHAPTER SIXTEEN

THE THUNDEROUS ROAR OF ROCKETS overhead drops me to my knees. Holding onto the steel helmet on my head, I become aware I'm not just somewhere else, I'm *someone* else.

Looking around the small one-room shack I'm in, I see radios and maps set up on collapsible wood tables. The walls of the cramped shack are made of sandbags. The roof looks to be made of heavy, rough-hewn lumber. I'm not alone in this shack either. Huddling like myself are four men wearing brown uniforms and steel helmets. The sound of the rockets passing overhead disappears. Moments later the rumble of their distant explosions reaches me. I stand up, reflexively dusting off my highly ornamented uniform. Looking down at my chest I see all manner of ribbons and pins and know with certainty how each one ended up there—the memories of how I earned them drown me in flashes of horrific violence, sacrifice, and paperwork. I shake my head to snap myself out of those spiraling thoughts. The four men have returned to their positions behind the radios. Words form in my mind moments before they exit my mouth.

"How is the assault going corporal?"

One of the men turns to face me. He's just a kid—he's no more than twenty. His eyes are soft brown and innocent.

"The barrage has broken their last line of defense surrounding the perimeter of the parliament."

"Order all units to fix bayonets and charge. I'll personally give two weeks' pay to the unit that captures the Prime Minister!"

"Yes, sir!"

The young corporal eagerly relays my message into his headset. The chirping of units acknowledging the orders blares through each of the shack's four radios.

Moving with the bearing of a person devoid of self-doubt, I stride to the table next to the doorway and pick up a collapsed field telescope. Moving to the embrasure, I extend the telescope with a satisfying *schlik* and survey the battlefield.

Before me lie the outskirts of a devastated city with its many buildings smoldering and shattered. Pillars of dense smoke billow high into the sky and make it difficult to discern much detail. Despite the smoke, I can make out several columns of tanks being followed by cautious brown-uniformed soldiers. They all appear to be heading toward the center of the rubble. Looking at their most likely destination, I see only black smoke.

I watch it for minutes hoping to see through a break in the dense haze, but I have no such luck. Trying to find the soldiers again, I spot the tail end of a column just as it slips beyond sight.

The telescope collapses smoothly, and I place it back on the table. Walking to the back of the shack with the same bravado, I take a seat on a small wooden chair.

Next to me is a squat, drop-leaf table scattered with maps but only the beautiful hardwood humidor grabs my attention. My fingers roll over a few of the fine cigars before finally settling on one second from the end. I slide the silver-clad guillotine shaped like a radiating star from its velvet slot. It's cool and heavy in my battered and aged hands. Looking into the reflective silver of the guillotine I see my face for the first time. A serpentine nose anchors my wizened face. Dark blue eyes set into a thick brow stare back at me. My new reality sinks in. Whoever I am, I'm living these memories through his eyes. For the rest of this journey, I'm going to be a passenger. Judging by how it began, this is looking to be an unpleasant trip. Knowing I can't change or interact here definitely doesn't help.

I light up the cigar and take a deep drag. Holding it in my lungs, I feel its warmth and every taste bud in my mouth dances in delight to the familiar flavor. It billows from my thin lips in a gray, swirling cloud.

Chatter squawks over the comms. The corporal presses his hands over his headphones straining to get it right. Nodding, he swivels around. He pulls his headset off and offers it to me.

"Sir, our men have reached the parliament building. The Prime Minister has surrendered, and the remaining Republican troops have laid down their weapons."

I rise and take two massive strides stopping at the corporal's side. Patting him on the back, I take the headset.

"All units, this is Commanding General Antonius Neptus. The parliament is ours, and the Prime Minister is in our custody! We've come a long way men, but here today, on this cold fall morning, the blood and toil of the last ten years have come due! Victory is ours, long live the Great Society!"

I return the headset to the corporal without enthusiasm.

"Corporal, get me transport to the parliament."

"Yes, sir."

He dutifully obeys, sending the call out over the radio as soon as he can get his headset back on. Returning to the embrasure, I look out over the ruins of the city. Taking deep draws from the cigar, I keep my eyes fixed on the fires. A malicious smile curls on my lips.

Dropping the smoldering butt of the cigar to the dirt floor of the shack I snub it out with my highly polished black boots.

"Transport is waiting outside sir."

"Carry on, corporal." My response the automatic reflex of a life spent in uniform.

I exit the shack stooping through the short, wooden door. Stepping out into the trench, frigid wind cuts me to the bone.

The sun's rays don't reach down here making the wind feel colder than it is. Reaching the light at ground level, relief washes over my old frame.

A column of armored cars is lined up on the road headed into the city. In the middle of the column is an open-topped car fitted with small, deep blue flags. In the driver's seat is a soldier wearing goggles. Beside him is another goggle-wearing soldier and sitting in the backseat is an officer. I advance toward the car, and the soldier in the passenger seat gets out. His pressed, brown uniform makes him look out of place on the battlefield. He opens the door for me. Taking my goggles down from my helmet I position them over my eyes. I slide into the back seat—its supple leather is much more enjoyable than the hard stool in the shack. The car's engine roars to life in chorus with the convoy.

Progress through the rubble is slow. The road has ceased to exist as a straight line and is now a labyrinth of craters, shattered homes, and smoking wreckage. When I turn my attention to the officer sitting next to me, I recognize him immediately.

"Nice of you to join us at the front, Daedalus."

"You know me, General, I'm always around when there's glory to be had."

"So, you've heard the news already then?"

"Why else do you think I left my drawing room?"

I pause for a moment. This colonel is astute in the art of

war, but when it comes to politicking and subterfuge, he has no equal. He is a powerful ally and not a man I care to cross, but his sardonic comments are almost too much to bear. In no mood to lecture him, I divert the subject.

"What are the initial casualty reports?"

"Better than predicted, but still pretty grim. Most units are at seventy percent strength. However, many of the vanguard units have been wiped out."

"Well, I wouldn't have expected them to go down without a fight."

Wanting to speak on other matters, I hesitate and look at the soldiers in the front seat. Pointing a finger at the two soldiers, I make unblinking eye contact with Daedalus.

"Colonel, can these soldiers be trusted?"

He smiles and nods. "They've been handpicked. Both men have sworn their allegiance to you and the army."

"Excellent." I turn away from Daedalus. My eyes linger on a cluster of dead civilians near a smoking ruin.

"I'm glad the day has gone so well but what's troubling me is why they surrendered at the last minute? Doesn't Abernathy realize we are going to execute him? He'll be dead either way, so why go out like a coward? What is he hoping to gain? What's his play here?"

Daedalus takes a moment to answer. His eyes dance between

the bodies littering the rubble.

"He must hope that now that the war is over, the soft civilian wing of our revolution will take pity on him. If Cornelius gets his way, I'm sure he'll be right. With peace at hand, Cornelius will more than likely spare his life as a sign of good faith."

"I'll be damned if Cornelius oversteps my authority. He may be the face of this revolution, but I'm the one who slogged through the trenches—ten years—while he gave speeches! This is my victory, my revolution, and I want Abernathy's head on a spike."

"I couldn't agree more sir, but we must choose our steps carefully. If you make Cornelius your enemy now, it will wash away all your victories. We both know he's too radical—his delusions of utopia are hard to listen to. But he's not too far gone. We can steer him to our way of thinking."

"And how do you suppose we do that? I've tried to get through to that man until I was blue in the face. He doesn't see reality. He's hell-bent on his fantasies. The people don't want fantasies. They want stability, they want normalcy after all the bloodshed."

The convoy swerves around a crater swimming with gore.

"We'll make him see it one way or another. Leave the details to me, but we'll either convince him or eliminate him."

"Eliminate him? How? He still has the public's support and the damned foreigners think he's some kind of messiah. If we killed him…"

"Who said we would kill him? We'll talk to him first, but if, and when, he decides to start the implementation of *his* Great Society, we'll get another player to take him out. Why send your knight to take the queen when a pawn can do it?"

"And we'll emerge from all of this with clean hands?"

"We'll emerge as saviors! Trust me, when this is all over with, the people will throw themselves at your feet."

"You better be right Daedalus, or it'll be our heads on spikes."

Looking at the soldiers in front of me, I make a mental note to have them killed. Loose ends, even loyal ones, need to be clipped.

Closing in on the city center, progress slows to a crawl. Every few minutes the convoy must stop to clear a path through the rubble. Block after block once magnificent buildings lie in burning heaps. How does Cornelius believe he can create his utopia from this wasteland? People don't want promises that tomorrow will be better. They want their due today.

I'll rebuild their homes and put them back to work. Perhaps they'll lose a few liberties along the way, but they're inconsequential to the comfort and stability I will provide. Maybe if Cornelius had succeeded with his plans for a peaceful transition, but that moment is too far gone. Dreams cannot grow in blood-soaked soil.

Looking around erases any doubts. Bodies litter the ruins in every form. The faces of the dead locked in eternal agony.

Impenetrable black smoke envelopes us as we reach today's battlefield. Pulling a thick cloth from my pocket, I press it over my face to avoid inhaling the noxious fumes. The smoke is so dense, visibility has dropped to almost nothing.

We creep through the smoke until it clears. Dropping the cloth from my face, I pull in a deep breath of clean air. The bittersweet smell of death is pungent.

With the veil of smoke behind us, the marred outline of the once glorious parliament building comes into view. The massive stones supporting the roof have been shattered in a few places causing portions of the rotunda to collapse, but for the most part, it looks able to stand, if just barely. Lines of trenches crisscross the crater-filled field surrounding the parliament. The burning hulks of tanks dot the field and bodies of innumerable soldiers litter the ground. The convoy comes to a halt. The driver turns around.

"This is as far as we can go, General."

"Very good, soldier. Carry on."

The soldier with the finely pressed uniform opens my door. I step out—the ground squashes underfoot. Daedalus joins me behind the car. Leading the way, I walk with slow, cautious steps across the still-smoldering battlefield. The moans of dying soldiers hit me as I step over corpses so caked with gore and mud it's impossible to tell which side they died for. Once we are out of earshot of the car, I stop and turn to Daedalus.

"I want those soldiers relieved of duty."

"Already on it sir, I'll make sure their bodies are mingled in with the casualties out here. Great patriots sacrificing themselves for the revolution—you do them a great honor."

"I'm glad you see it that way."

His twisted smile disgusts me but I have no doubt he'll get it done.

Crossing the battlefield is arduous, but we emerge unscathed on the parliament's white marble steps. Revolutionary soldiers have taken positions around the building. They salute us excitedly as we pass. With many eyes watching, I make sure to take each large step in full stride, shoulders back and chest held high.

Cresting the top of the stairs, the once magnificently carved double doors that lead into the main foyer have been blown open. Only a few slivers of wood still cling to the hinges. Inside is a bustle of activity. Soldiers are hastily assembling a temporary command-and-control center. With the roof knocked in, the vast open-air hall dwarfs the small shack. *Now this is a space befitting a general.*

Noticing our arrival, a mud-covered captain rushes over to greet us. He snaps a sharp salute. I return it reflexively.

"Afternoon, General. I trust your ride over was smooth?"

"It was, Captain. Now tell me, where is the Prime Minister being held?"

"In the lower halls sir. Most of the building below ground is intact."

"Take us there."

"Straight away, sir."

Following the captain, we quickly exit the main hall and descend the narrow staircase to the basement level. The marble-lined passageway is illuminated by amber lights strung along the ceiling.

"Where is the power coming from, Captain?"

"Generators in the basement."

"What about water?"

"Plumbing is working in a few areas of the building, but most of it is destroyed."

Reaching the bottom of the stair we enter another hall. This one is a shoebox compared to the great hall above complete with claustrophobia-inducing low ceilings. The weak yellow light amplifies the discomfort and strains my old eyes.

"Through the double doors at the end is a holding cell," the Captain says pointing his arm down the short hallway. "The Prime Minister and the surviving members of his cabinet are in there."

"Thank you for the tour, Captain."

Snapping another salute, the captain turns and leaves.

Walking into the room, the soldiers flanking the double doors pull them open letting us glide inside without missing a step.

The Prime Minister and his cabinet look battered and broken behind the cell's steel bars. I remove my helmet, handing it to one of the soldiers standing inside. Daedalus does the same then joins me next to the bars. Abernathy and his cabinet sit in silence. Their suits are ripped and filthy.

I bang on the bars with my fist to grab their attention. Looking up at me, the graying Abernathy makes eye contact. His green eyes are bloodshot, and his hair is disheveled. Standing shakily, a younger cabinet member jumps up to help him to his feet.

"Antonius, I cannot say it is a pleasure to see you again."

"If our circumstances were reversed Preston, I'm sure I'd say the same. But standing on this side of the bars," I clang them again, "is exhilarating."

"Scum like you always find pleasure in the suffering of others. Whatever you hoped to gain through your treachery and rebellion is beyond me. If it is power you're after, I'm afraid latching onto some radical's coat tails is no different than when you took orders from me. You're still someone's lackey."

"I prefer to call it a revolution. Rebellion leaves such an unpleasant taste in my mouth. And I assure you, I am no man's lackey. Cornelius is not the one running this show. I am."

"I wouldn't be so sure about that. The people rally at his

side and not ten minutes ago I received news that I am to be granted a full pardon." He smiles at the discomfort on my face. "I know how desperately you wanted to see my head roll, but it appears your superiors have a much better understanding of what it takes to lay the foundations for peace."

"You think you're a free man? You're living on borrowed time. We'll see who's right."

"You're at the end of your leash general—I look forward to proving you wrong."

I turn away from the cage and stride out of the room. Daedalus shadows me.

"What does Cornelius think he's doing pardoning that man? And how dare he do so without consulting me?"

Daedalus' eyes twinkle as he turns to the door guard. "Soldier, where is a private room the general and I can go without interruption?"

The soldier snaps to attention then points off to his left. "Through that door, there is a sitting room sir."

"Very good, make sure we are not disturbed."

"Yes, sir."

Following Daedalus in, I close the door behind us. This room is small but well furnished. Polished oak bookshelves line the walls. Two doors on the opposite wall lead off to other rooms. Daedalus walks over to them and with a quick motion locks them. In the middle of the room is a round table surrounded by four high-backed leather chairs. I take the seat that allows me to see all three doors. Daedalus moves to sit then stops, a small smile on his face.

"Care for a drink?"

He motions to the bar cart against the wall.

"Sure. Make it strong."

Daedalus pours an expensive-looking bottle of brandy into two tumblers nearly to the top. Handing me one he takes the seat across from me. I take a sip—it's turpentine with end notes of tobacco. After it has a minute to snake through my veins, the bubbling rage in my chest simmers. Daedalus takes his own small sip before he sets the glass down on the table. Leaning back in his chair, he crosses his legs.

"I think this business with the pardon will actually work in our favor."

"Is that so?" His tone makes my fingers ache for my pistol.

"All we need to do is frame it properly. We've been fighting to overthrow the corrupt republic. To build the Great Society. All those years Cornelius gave speech after speech about how we needed to eradicate the old system to make way for the new. He has convinced the people that the Great Society can only be built on a clean slate. But now, when the fighting has stopped, he wishes to grant a full pardon to the very embodiment of the corrupt and immoral state he's been attempting to topple. He always wanted a peaceful revolution—I'm sure he never had any intention of actually killing off every single person who flew the republican flag. But his rhetoric, in the context of protracted and bloody civil war, can be easily misunderstood to imply that a clean slate means lots of headless bodies."

"So all we have to do is convince people that he's gone back on his pledge to clean the slate?"

"Exactly. People are expecting us to clean house and start anew, so when he calls for pardons and reconciliation, they'll be confused. The people want retribution for all the atrocities they've suffered. They want a return to normalcy, and you will give it to them. When he comes to pardon Abernathy, we will arrest him for treason against the revolution. He'll admit to wanting to peacefully integrate those still loyal to the republic, and when he does, he'll sign his own death warrant."

"How certain are you that this will work?"

"I'm more than positive. We just need to make it showy, twist his words for full effect, and broadcast it for everyone to hear. When you kill Cornelius and take the reins of power, it will be to the sounds of jubilation." Daedalus' mouth curves up in a cruel smile.

"Now all we need to do is wait for him to arrive," I say.

"And with this fine brandy, I don't think that will be too hard."

Daedalus tops off our glasses.

We toast in unison. "To the Great Society."

Daedalus and I spend a few hours sipping on the brandy. The bottle is mostly empty when we decide to retire for the night. We find the captain, and he leads us to a remarkably undamaged wing of parliament.

"There are rooms set up for each of you. I apologize in advance for their crudeness, but much of the finer linens were destroyed in the assault."

"Nothing you can do about that, Captain," I say.

"If there's anything else you may need, let me know."

"Actually, there is one thing. The command-and-control station you are setting up in the entry hall, does that have the power to broadcast to the nearest civilian relays?"

"I suppose we could manage that, it would require reallocating some of the building's power away from lights and other utilities."

"Make it so," I say. "Try and get as many repeater stations in range as you can. I want to be able to broadcast to the whole nation."

"I'll make the proper calls and make sure the civilian stations are standing by to retransmit your message."

"Very good, Captain."

"Good night, sir."

The captain turns and walks away. I wait until his footsteps fade into the ceaseless rumble emanating from the beehive of activity in the roofless entry hall before turning to Daedalus.

"This is going to be easy Antonius. The pieces are starting to fall into place."

"Make sure they do."

We exchange a hard look. I maintain eye contact with him, unwilling to blink. Tense seconds tick by, but his will breaks first. With a curt smile, he disappears behind the door to his quarters. I stand alone in the dark hallway for a minute more then enter my own room.

The room is paneled in walnut with well-built, but simple, furniture filling the space. The bed is small, but it looks clean and more than comfortable enough. There is a wash basin on the nightstand. A large glass carafe filled with clear water sits next to it on the dresser. Across from the bed is a narrow roll-top desk with a lamp.

I remove my belt and set it on the bed's banister. The weight of my pistol and ammunition lifting off comes as a relief. Removing my jacket and boots next, I pull the chair back, sit in it, then place my aching feet up on the desk.

After ten long years of fighting and positioning to get where I am, my moment to finally seize total control is within grasp. Daedalus' plan seems sound enough. No doubt Cornelius will arrive tomorrow to give a heartfelt victory speech and pardon the Prime Minister in person. If our plan works, I'll be head of state before the sun sets.

Yet, Daedalus' duplicitousness gives me pause. A man like him will not be content to dance while I pull the strings forever. He probably won't try to take my power immediately—he'll wait until I've let my guard down. That could be a month from now or a year, but one day he'll undermine me. You can always trust a snake to be a snake. I need to eliminate him, and I know the best way to do it.

Tomorrow when the world comes crashing down around Cornelius's revolution, Daedalus will be his unwitting accomplice and share his fate on the gallows.

Excited about tomorrow's prospects, I get up from the chair and lay on top of the linens. My eyes close, and I drift off into a restful and dreamless sleep.

CHAPTER SEVENTEEN

STILL LIVING GENERAL NEPTUS' MEMORIES, my eyes open at four in the morning sharp, a consequence of living a soldier's life. The sun will not rise for a few hours, so I prepare for the day in the dim yellow light of the room. Stepping out of bed, I smooth out the few wrinkles on the clean white sheets. Moving to the washbasin, I strip off my undergarments and give myself a quick rinse with the cool water from the carafe. I tremble from the chill of the water and the nipping pre-dawn air.

Conditions for shaving are less than ideal, but I manage to clean up my white stubble with minimal nicks. No one objects to a little blood on a general.

Clean, I move to the small chest of drawers. Inside, I find a fresh, neatly folded uniform jacket. I remove it and set it on the expertly made bed. I rummage around and find the rest of the pieces. Pulling on starched clothes reminds me of the academy.

I complete my uniform by returning my gun belt to my waist. The buckles snap splitting the quiet. Running my hand over my holster, I get the feeling it will come out of retirement today.

As I exit the room, the stillness fades. The hall is bustling with soldiers. The swarm pauses to stand at attention and throw me a salute. In my wake, they return to their myriad tasks as quickly as they stopped them.

A gust of icy morning air rushes through the cavernous opening in the main hall dropping the temperature dramatically. Keeping my bearing in front of the soldiers, I suppress the shiver.

The communications center appears to be fully connected and established. The captain is standing in the middle of the room checking over a list in his hand.

"Good morning, Captain. I see you've set up the communications array."

"Yes, sir, my men had that done a few hours ago. Now we're trying to get the place cleaned up for when Cornelius arrives."

"What time do you think his convoy will get here?"

"I'm being told noon."

"Typical civilian—the day is already half over by then. Have a phone brought down to the sitting room next to the holding cell. I will wait for him there."

"Very good sir, I'll have that done right away."

The captain disappears into the swarming soldiers to carry out my task. Impatient, but powerless to do anything until

Cornelius arrives with his entourage, I make my way back to the sitting room.

Sipping on brandy, I light a cigar. Leaned into the high-backed leather chair, I fill the room with gray smoke.

Not long after I arrive, soldiers bring down the phone I requested. It starts ringing the instant they connect the wires.

Consumed in the details of troop movements and crushing the remaining pockets of resistance, hours pass. Ashtray on the verge of overflowing, Daedalus walks through the door.

Setting the receiver on the handle, I sit up tracking his movements with my eyes.

"Seems you got an early start this morning, General. I haven't had a chance to speak with you yet, but I went ahead and took care of those soldiers from yesterday."

"How?"

"I ordered them to follow me out into the rubble. I told them we were looking for a lost encrypted radio. They ate it up. No one should ever find the bodies, and if they do there won't be anything suspicious about finding two dead soldiers on a battlefield."

"What were their names?"

"What does that matter?"

"What were their names?"

"With all due respect, I don't see why…"

I rise from the chair with ferocity. The table topples over. The phone crashes with an ear-splitting clang. Cigar ash litters the floor.

"Answer the damn question, Colonel! Or have you forgotten that you are speaking to a superior officer?"

Daedalus is taken aback, but his indignant tone remains the same.

"Of course not, sir. Their names were Private Graffe and Corporal King. They shouldn't be missed. I took the liberty and assigned them to one of the units sweeping for resistance. Even if somebody follows the paper trail, it won't lead back to you."

"You'd better damned hope so," I growl—heart pounding.

Daedalus pours himself a brandy then works his way over to the fallen telephone. Setting it and the table upright, he sits down across from me.

"The preparations for Cornelius's arrival are almost complete. He should be here within the hour. We should talk about our game plan."

"Our game plan? You do realize that if this goes south, the ax will fall on my head?" I jab my thumb at my chest. "You'll get off on the defense that you were just following orders. I don't have that luxury. I've thought through my course of action. Thank you for helping me get to this point, but these last steps are mine, and mine alone."

"Then where do I end up when this all shakes out?" Daedalus says looking more earnest than he's been since he pulled up yesterday.

"If everything goes to plan, you'll end up ahead—don't worry about that."

Silence turns the space between us into a briar patch. The phone rings. I stare at him until it stops.

"Well then." Daedalus stands abruptly. "Best of luck to you sir."

He knocks back the rest of his brandy then slams the tumbler down on the table. "Come on sir, your moment awaits."

———

The entrance foyer has been swept and polished. Large blue banners of the Great Society hang around the room attempting to cover the blast holes and scorch marks. Nothing has been done to hide the large stones from the roof that crashed to the floor. Too little time, I suppose.

Stepping through the entryway, I see the battlefield in front of the steps has been significantly cleaned up. The hulking wrecks of tanks have been dragged away. The many craters surrounding the parliament have been filled in. The bodies must have been piled into the trenches and covered over. Revolutionary and Republican soldiers mounded on top of each other. If the city encircling the field were not a smoldering ruin, and the parliament building itself not gaping from fresh wounds, it would be hard to tell a battle took place here less than a day ago.

The soldiers, finished with their cleaning, have washed the blood and dirt from their faces and now stand at attention throughout the entrance hall and on every step of the marble staircase leading up to it. In the middle of the wide landing, a wooden platform has been hastily assembled—a steel microphone its lone adornment. Connected to the communications setup inside and an array of hanging speakers in the parliament, the microphone hums with power. Whatever is said in that microphone will be heard across the nation.

A strong wind blows across the field. It carries with it the smell of burning and death. The wind blows past the parliament and through the thick black smoke still billowing from the city. Through the momentary clearing, Cornelius's revolutionary convoy—a full two dozen cars draped in cobalt banners—appears.

Camera crews have set themselves up in the field eager to snap a picture of the revolution's leader. Standing next to the microphone, I watch them pass through the smoke and roll slowly over the covered-up battlefield. Cornelius rides in the first car. Standing up so the photographers can better find him in their frames, he slows the convoy to allow the photographers time to swarm in. Ceaseless flashes add to the spectacle which continues for a few minutes until even at their snail's pace they reach parliament.

Cornelius steps out of his car. Followed by a dozen handlers and crony politicians, he reaches the base of the staircase. As his foot lands on the first step, I move to the microphone.

"How dare you stroll on this hallowed ground? You are nothing but a charlatan who walks on the graves of the revolution's true patriots."

Two soldiers standing by the door rush over to me, rifles leveled on my chest.

"You aim your weapons at the wrong man, soldiers. You should be aiming at the man who would derail our great revolution at the very moment our Great Society was to spring to life from the fires of war. Ask him yourself."

Shaking his head and cursing, Cornelius races up the stairs and takes position—uncomfortably—next to me at the podium.

"Stand down soldiers," Cornelius says directing his words into the microphone. "I would love to hear what General Neptus has to say. Please, General, tell me what proof do you have of these baseless accusations?"

Both soldiers lower their rifles and step back.

I take a deep breath and speak to the nation. "Cornelius, great scholar, the man who inspired us all to dream of a Great Society. For ten, hard-fought years, we have bled to bring about your vision. But I have come to see the truth. Through every victory and every defeat, you told us that in order to build the Great Society we would need a foundation free of the corrupting legacy of governments past. You promised the people—the beating heart of your revolution—that no supporter of the corrupt republic would live to enjoy the Great Society. You promised them, and you lied."

Disgust, confusion, and piqued interest ripple through the assembly of politicians, soldiers, and citizens.

I wait for the camera crews to press in closer. "Cornelius, the great revolutionary, is here today to give you a victory speech. But what he hasn't told you, is that he has pardoned—in secret—the Prime Minister and every surviving cabinet member of all their crimes. What do you have to say for yourself, Cornelius?"

Cornelius's face is soured, but his lips remain sealed. A few of the members of his entourage seem genuinely shocked and appalled by my allegation. Taking a deep breath, Cornelius steps closer to the platform and with practiced gravitas places his hand over his heart.

"Let us all take a moment and remember the many fallen patriots of the revolution. It is through their sacrifice that we stand here victorious today. I do not approve of the manner in which general Neptus has brought about this revelation, but it is one you all must be made aware of. What he says is true. I have already signed a full pardon for former Prime Minister Abernathy and the remaining thirteen members of his cabinet. I have done this not because I want to go back on my promises to you, but because I want to show you a better way." He shuffles liking, his lips. There isn't a single sympathetic eye on him. "We have emerged from a decade of bloodshed. Can we not start the next one with mercy and forgiveness?"

Shouts of "betrayer" and "liar" come from too many mouths to count. Carrying the momentum, I push Cornelius aside.

"Do you hear the way he's speaking to us now? As if we are children? He would free men who upheld a corrupt state with the edge of a sword. For our sacrifices, he offers *them* mercy. It is not forgiveness we demand, but retribution! He may have led us into the light all those years ago, but now he's leading us down the path of weakness, and he expects all of us to follow him. I, for one, will not follow this swindler any longer. I was once in servitude to Abernathy and his corrupt goons—I am all too familiar with being in the presence of snakes. Cornelius has revealed his true nature and it's time we cut the head off this serpent."

"This is preposterous," says Cornelius. "You are staging a coup in broad daylight without a cohort of supporters standing at your back? Soldiers, detain the general until we can provide him with a court-martial."

The soldiers lining the stair and standing guard in the hall fidget with uncertainty. Enlisted soldiers look to their officers, the officers look to each other and then to me.

"Arrest this man for treason at once!" Cornelius shouts, his calm façade crumbled away.

No soldier moves. The air is tense. The afterimage of a

thousand flashbulbs dances in my eyes. Cornelius glares at me—he trembles with rage.

I smile at him. "Soldiers of the Revolutionary Army, brave patriots of the Great Societal Revolution, mark my words. Abernathy will hang for the crimes he has committed against us. And I will personally lead the hunt for every last supporter of the corrupt republic. Nothing of the old order will stand. But first, we must rid ourselves of this traitorous backstabber!" With as much drama as I can muster, I turn my body and extend my arm and index finger like a sword thrust at Cornelius's heart.

Most of the soldiers and politicians are immobilized, but enough of them act to turn the tide.

A soldier rushes forward and grabs at Cornelius's arm. Cornelius pulls back in defense. The soldier reaches in again to grab him. Leaning back to avoid the grasp, Cornelius slips on the edge of the slick marble step.

A sickening crack issues from his neck as he lands on hard white stone. Seeing what he has done, the soldier freezes in panic. Politicians swarm around Cornelius's writhing body like vultures. Flashbulbs cut the air like an artillery barrage.

"Step aside!"

The politicians jump back at my command and the soldiers snap to attention. Head and shoulders held high, I descend the four steps to Cornelius with a slow methodic pace. Looking down on him, bewilderment has replaced the rage in his watery eyes.

All eyes are on me. No one dares breathe.

The snap on my holster pops open like a thunderclap in the stillness of the scene. In a fluid motion, I draw the pistol from my holster and level it at Cornelius's brow.

"Long live the revolution! Long live the Great Society!"

I squeeze the trigger.

The shot echoes over the freshly tilled field then bounces down the shattered corridors of parliament. For a moment all is still—every witness shocked into silence.

Stepping through the entryway, Colonel Daedalus strides to the microphone.

"Long live General Antonius Neptus, savior of the revolution!"

The gathered throng echo his rallying cry. Far off, in ten thousand homes, I can almost hear the people shouting it too.

CHAPTER EIGHTEEN

THE PARADE GROUNDS and the blood-covered steps of the parliament building fade away into a black mist. The sensation of weightlessness tingles through me. And I have the sense of falling through time and space.

The journey is short, however, and soon enough the vaporous black cloud reconstitutes itself. Taking in the new scene, I feel the passage of time in the worsening arthritis burning in every joint. Seated behind an imposing mahogany desk, I find myself in a lavishly decorated office with white marble floors, and deep-blue velvet curtains draped elegantly from the two-story windows. The light of the setting sun pours into the round office bathing the wood, steel, and stone in orange fire.

Propped open on the desk in front of me is a simple wooden case. Tied to the corner is a small ivory note.

Please accept this humble brandy as my way of saying congratulations for your victory over the corrupt Republic and the Cornelius loyalists. Long live the Great Society. Long live its High Caretaker! G.V. Haeger.

Inside is a bottle of incomparable brandy nestled in velvet. I pull it out and study the label. Against the sleek glass bottle and deep brown spirits, my hands are nearly translucent and pocked with liver marks.

I pull open the upper right desk drawer and pull out two crystal tumblers. They ting against the oak of the table as I set them down. Carefully removing the glass stopper, I pour a generous amount into both glasses. With controlled and deliberate actions, I replace the stopper, set the bottle back in its case, and push it next to the humidor on the left-hand side of the desk.

I lean back in my chair taking mouthfuls of the glorious, honey-brown liquor. Its aromas fill my nose and bathe my taste buds with spice and sweet. It chips away at the tension that hasn't left my shoulders in weeks.

Arduous months have passed since I squeezed the trigger that seized a revolution, but only now that power is firmly in my grasp can I revel in victory. Years of being in the background—years of obeying orders from idealists and incompetent revolutionaries—and the reins are finally mine. My lips curl and I take another sip.

The intercom buzzes like pestilence interrupting my thoughts.

"High Caretaker, sir, there is a General Daedalus here to see you. Should I let him in, sir?"

I sit up and set the tumbler and its few remaining drops of brandy down on the desk. Moving my hands along my collar and sash, I ensure the tidiness of my uniform.

"Send him in."

"At once, sir."

Across the expanse of marble floor, the two outsized steel doors open inwards—their greased hinges noiseless. General Daedalus, clad in his new uniform, enters the room in full stride. As he approaches the desk, the conniving look that never seems to be absent from his face comes into focus. Stopping a meter behind the chair across from me, Daedalus snaps a smart salute.

"High Caretaker," he pauses scanning the room with an approving nod. "This office suits you. Neptus."

"And those generals' bars suit you, Daedalus." I motion to the chair. "Sit, there is no need for formalities."

Daedalus complies without hesitation. After settling into the high-backed leather chair, he leans over and takes the still-full tumbler.

"You didn't just come here to drink my brandy, so what brings you here Daedalus?"

He takes an audible gulp of brandy then sets the now half-empty tumbler back on the desk.

"The brandy is secondary," he winces a little, its fire still worming through him. "But I think you are underestimating how special that brandy is." He grins. "I'm here about my uniform."

"You were always eying mine, so now that I have no use for it, I thought you might like it."

"I'm honored, truly, but I feel that perhaps I've misinterpreted our relationship. This morning I opened a package and knew it was going to explode and kill me. But much to my surprise, this fine uniform and letter of commission were all that were inside. I don't understand your move. You have the evidence you need to have me executed. And what a great story it would make too: 'Close confidant and friend of our dear leader aids Cornelius loyalists by murdering two members of his staff.' I've never seen you pass up an opportunity to eliminate a rival, so why now?"

"My dear Daedalus—you are more valuable to me alive then you are dead. You are right though, you do pose a threat. But I've given it a lot of thought and your talents have stayed the executioner's hand." His brow furrows. I lean forward on my elbows. "Don't fool yourself—I haven't spared you without purpose and conditions. The first thing you are going to do for me is keep the army in line. For what I've built to stand, I need the officer corps' unwavering support. If I so much as smell a coup brewing, I'll release the information about Private Graffe and Corporal King and I'll let the chips fall where they may."

An awkward silence fills the cavernous office. The final rays of light from the sun disappear beyond the horizon. Hidden bulbs crackle to life doing their best to imitate the faded sun.

Daedalus breaks the silence with the creaking of his leather chair. Reaching forward he takes the tumbler in hand and with one large gulp, finishes it off. He slams the empty tumbler down sending a piercing echo darting around the room.

"And the second thing?"

I suppress the urge to reach across the table and smash his teeth in. He squirms while I wait for my temper to pass. A grin sneaks onto my face. "That damned mouth of yours—if it didn't have a silver tongue in it, I'd sew it shut." I sigh, the image of sewing his mouth shut is pulling me off course. "No one else can ensure my plans come to fruition like you can. I need the landowners brought to heel and the industrialists in my pocket. Put my opponents on the battlefield and they're good as dead. Put them across from me at dinner…"

Daedalus chuckles. "You may not have the same mastery as you do on the battlefield, but don't kid yourself—you have a taste for the game. You've played your hand well today, sir. Although I am disappointed you thought you needed blackmail to keep me in line. I am quite fond of scheming, but I have no desire for your throne. Connected to you I retain a level of anonymity and freedom I would never have in your shoes. You need me, and I need you."

"I have no doubts about your loyalty—I've had none since your voice of approval on the parliament steps. But I'd be a fool not to keep you on a leash. Even a tame dog bites his master when he is hungry."

"Fair enough. So," he leans forward pouring himself another brandy. "What are these plans of yours that need my attention?"

"What I did to Cornelius cannot happen to me. The military, the gentry, industrialists, the plebs, no one can ever have the desire, intention, and opportunity to commit the act I did. Our revolution was won by a hair's breadth and keeping hold of that power will consume the rest of my life. But when I am gone, and my successor takes power, I want guarantees that what I have fought for, what I've bled for, will not crumble."

"That is a tall order, sir. Your actions stand as the example, and it will be hard to both give the Great Society credit for its birth while also discouraging its imitation."

"That's why I need you to change it. Give us the clean slate Cornelius never had. We can formulate a series of events that paint our revolution, our fallen soldiers, and our goals as the very ideals of lawfulness, justice, and righteousness. Once we've rewritten the past, we need to convince the people that matter to play along. Their collaboration is necessary, no matter the cost. You have my permission to do whatever it takes—government production contracts, appointments, assassinations, sex, drugs—anything required to purchase the lie is currency well spent for the future of the Great Society."

Daedalus' lips curl up into a devilish smile. "It would be my pleasure to be your accomplice in this sir. This is a challenge worthy of my skills. One hundred years from now our truth will be unchallenged, and we will have won a victory sweeter and more glorious than any in the revolution dreamed possible." He swigs emphatically.

"Getting us on the same sheet of music—where did you envision we'd start?"

I pluck the ivory note from the case and run my fingers across the letters.

"You should pay Mister G.V. Haeger at Personal Protection Supplies a visit and sincerely thank him for this bottle of brandy."

"His collaboration is required?"

"Whatever it takes."

<hr>

The world swirls into a dark cloud. For the briefest of moments, I am suspended in the timeless void before being exploded back through the veil of reality.

Ten thousand colors assault my eyes. A million smells overwhelm my olfactory sense. Innumerable sounds converge into an indiscernible, thunderous cacophony. Every nerve and cell explodes with pain as the Oracle Device rips its connection from me.

The cavity door opens. Unable to cope with the reemergence into my own body and mind, I collapse onto the hot metal landing. Eyes blurry from tears, I see only steam.

All at once I am more tired, hungry, happy, sad, hopeless, and hopeful than I've ever been.

The emotional and physical drain—coupled with the weight

of what I have just experienced—is too much to bear and I drift toward unconsciousness.

Just before my vision turns black, a pair of boots ascends the stairs toward me in the swirling steam.

CHAPTER NINETEEN

I WAKE IN A GROGGY HAZE. My body is heavy, my arms and legs lie helpless like wet sand. I blink my eyes open. It takes the world a moment to stop swirling and solidify into recognizable shapes. And when it does, I wish it hadn't.

I'm strapped to a hospital bed. My wrists and ankles are restrained with black straps. I try to struggle against them, but nothing moves. Twisting my head over to the left, I see a large silver needle haphazardly shoved into my arm. Blood pools under the tape securing it in place. A yellow rubber tube runs from the needle to a half-empty glass bottle of clear liquid dangling from a stand. Whatever is in that container can't be good—it's turned my body to mush. Whoever put me here has ensured I can't get up. Escape eclipses all other thought.

I lift my head off the bed as high as I can. My muscles seize and spasm. The drugs desperately try to keep me down, but I fight them with all my willpower. Even so, I can't hold myself up for very long. Frantic, I try to take it all in. My clothes have been removed and replaced by a gray jumpsuit. My bed is in the middle of the room. The silver stand holding the vial of drugs is off to my left. I crane my neck around to the right. There is a mobile impress machine. Its neural interface helmet is resting on its perch—data cables run out the back making it look like Medusa's severed head. The drugs are impairing my vision—everything looks like it has Vaseline smeared over it—so I can't make out the words on the device's projected light display, but it's red like it's in an error state. Otherwise, the room is empty, clinical. The walls are barren concrete, the floors overly waxed. On the wall in front of me is the outline of a door, but there is no handle.

Exhausted, I fall back. A witches' brew of drugs and aching muscles writhes in my gut. Panic creeps into my brain from the base of my neck flooding my mind with nightmare scenarios. That's what they want me to do, they want me to panic. These people have nothing good planned for me and will most likely kill me when they are done. I need to regain my composure and come up with a plan. I can't die here.

Just breathe, Evelyn. Listening to that inner voice, I reel my swirling thoughts back into place. As calm returns, I see my first hope for salvation. Directly above me on the ceiling is an exhaust vent held in place by four exposed screws. I'm still strapped to the bed, and immobile from the drugs, so the vent is a long way from being my avenue out of here, but that dull ember of hope has stoked a fire inside me. A smile creeps onto my face—I'm not going to die here today.

My celebration is short-lived. The door swings open, and

two people step through. The first is a woman dressed in the ink-black uniform of the Revolutionary Guard. Expertly tailored and adorned with gleaming silver stars, she carries herself with iron confidence. The ramifications of the memories I lived, Neptus's memories—the real origin story—dawn on me. If they know what I saw, I'll never leave this room. Her underlings must have tried to extract the memories from me already but when they failed she came down to clean up the mess. And by the vicious look on her face, I don't think she's happy about it.

The hulking man behind her is dressed in civilian clothes. His sable leather trench coat is buttoned to the top, concealing his face below his unnatural violet eyes. He stands without the rigid composure of Peace Officers or Guardians. He's bulky from muscle and what must be heavy steel plates sewn into his coat. Is he the man I saw coming out of her house? His presence sends me spiraling.

The woman crosses the short distance from the door, stopping next to my bed on the left. Her boot heels ring out with harsh clicks on the concrete floor. The man steps back into the hall and pulls the door shut. It's just her, me, and the panic gnawing at the base of my skull.

She scrutinizes me head to toe. Her face is angular and accentuated by thin age lines. Her eyes are deeply blue, almost black, like the flag.

"I'm going to cut to the chase, Miss Brennan, how did you get the storage sphere? Was it given to you by one Margaret Waters?"

My stomach flips. Trying to play it cool, I lock eyes with her.

"I don't know what you're talking about."

In an instant, her demeanor changes. She raises a rubber truncheon over her head ready to strike.

"One more chance." There is no asking in her voice, and I doubt she's ever made a threat she didn't keep.

I gulp hard. I can't give her anything. The woman, or rather Margaret, is sweet, and kind. These people will chew her up and spit her out. I can't let anything slip, I have to protect her.

"I don't know…"

Her arm whips down in a blur. The truncheon slams into my stomach knocking the wind out of me. I cough hard between desperate gasps. I struggle against the straps, trying to inch away.

"Liar!"

"I don't…"

Her face turns to steel. She raises the truncheon high and slams it into me again. Hot, stinging pain explodes through me. I whimper turning my face away from her, so she can't see my tears. Before I can think of words to speak another blow lands.

She unleashes a flurry of strikes. Her arms flailing, her brows are shiny with sweat. I lose count after a dozen. It's all I can do to keep from blacking out.

The pain is overwhelming. A pungent copper taste fills my

mouth. Hot tears stream down my cheeks. My mouth hangs open wanting to scream, but nothing escapes—there is too much that needs to spill out and not enough wind to take it.

She returns her hands to her sides. Straightening her uniform, she pulls a small white handkerchief from her breast pocket and wipes the sweat from her brow.

"I already know she gave you the sphere, and that she pointed you in the direction of the Oracle Device. I thought it seemed obvious that I already knew—I wanted to start with something simple. But clearly, you are too stubborn or stupid to understand the severity of the situation you are in, little girl. Now, answer my questions, and this whole process can be much easier on you. Why were you seeking information on the Caretakers? Who are you working for? I want names and locations."

I take a moment to breathe and hold my rising bile at bay. My stomach is on fire, and the pain is beginning to envelop me. If I don't answer her questions, she's going to keep beating me until I lose consciousness or worse. I could die from internal bleeding long before I have an opportunity to escape. I don't like it, but maybe the truth will get her to stop beating me. Maybe it'll give me a chance to escape before they murder me.

"I'm looking for myself. I'm not working with anyone—"

"Liar!"

The truncheon slams into the right side of my face. My jaw pops loose with a crunch. A piece of chipped tooth grates against my tongue. My head rings. Electric aching pulses dart across my face. I begin to sob. I'm going to die because nothing I say will satisfy her. She wants something specific, maybe something that confirms some suspicion she has. She wants her truth, but I don't have it to give to her. The only thing I can do is try to figure out what it is that she wants and give her the best lie I can.

"I…" I hesitate, wanting to make sure these words are good enough to stop her from hitting me again. "Speer. I work for Speer. He's been teaching us about the Caretaker's failures all year. He sent me to get hard evidence. We discovered that the woman, Margaret was it? She possessed the sphere, so I broke in and stole it. I took it to the device to make sure it was authentic before I took it back to Speer."

Her face is a frozen enigma. She stares at me for eternal moments. I fight with all the power I have left to keep my eyes open and unblinking. Doubt is building in her eyes. Her hands tighten around the truncheon. I have to really sell it, I have to really commit to this, it's the only chance I have.

"Just kill me. I can't go back to Speer now—he'll kill me if he finds out I was caught. I'm dead anyway, just finish me off. Just don't beat me anymore, what's the point now?"

She digests my words. Her face remains stone.

"Likely story."

She steps back from the bed. Hands clasped behind her back, she paces along the wall.

"A little farfetched don't you think? Well, maybe not." She smiles. "Speer is under investigation following the Zarrov incident. Your story could check out—I doubt it—but it could." She stops, examining the information blinking on the mobile imprint's screen. "But so eager for death? No, I don't think so."

"Do it! Kill me!" The words fly from my mouth. I wish I could reach out and grab them, but it's too late.

Her ears perk up. She's standing over me in a flash. In a single swift motion, she pulls a stiletto from a concealed pocket on her waist.

Pressing my head down with her left hand, she holds the blade against my neck.

"Tell me you want it now. Do it! Beg for it!"

The edge slices into my neck a little with every breath. Sharp, searing pain mingles with the dull electric throbbing in my jaw. Fresh tears fall down my cheeks. My mouth opens to form words, but only wheezing air passes through.

"No... please."

Her laughter sears into my bones. Removing the knife from my throat, she stands back up, staring down at me again.

"You people are all the same. All talk and no action. I'll let you stew with yourself for a while, and maybe when I get back, you'll be ready to die."

She slams the knife into the bed millimeters from my leg.

I let out an involuntary gasp. A wicked smile cracks her unyielding face.

"If your story checks out, I'll let you die quietly, painlessly." She flicks the glass container—its contents slosh silently. "But if your story doesn't check out. Well, I guess we'll have to see how many cuts from that knife it'll take before you bleed out. This is the time to get the story straight, your one last chance to die peacefully."

Any doubt about her intentions have vanished. I'm dead either way.

"I'll be waiting." The defiance in my voice startles me—my tongue the only part of me still itching for a fight.

She turns and raps on the door three times. The lock clicks open. In an instant, the door opens, she passes through it, and it closes again.

Straining against the ringing in my head, I overhear the faint conversation outside.

"No one can know we've had a breach and that she's here. The imprint technicians?"

"Already handled ma'am." The man's accent is a thick coastal brogue.

"Excellent. He put her up to this I know it, but what's his angle? Why would he risk her? I need to deal with this before everything unravels—this door opens for no one, understood?

"Yes, ma'am."

"Keep your radio on, and if the call comes in, don't hesitate."

"Of course, ma'am—your will, my action."

I don't have much time. If she doesn't like what she finds that man is going to come in here and finish me off. I can't be here, but with these drugs in my veins I can hardly move. I have to get that needle out of my arm.

Leaning forward, my stomach explodes in fresh pain. I suppress any noise—I can't alert her brute. The determination to live burns in the base of my skull beyond the reach of hurt or fear. Adrenaline is finally kicking in and is fighting against the drugs. My body is starting to wake up.

Pulling closer to the needle, I contort and strain to reach it with my mouth. My muscles and bones fight the contortion, but I push through their cries. Biting down on the base of the needle, I jerk my head back. Coming out sideways, the needle rips from my arm in a crimson arc. Biting my lip, I struggle to suppress a cry of pain. Hot blood streams from the wound.

With the needle out, and the drugs no longer pouring into my veins, a static I didn't realize was there dissolves.

What feels like hours pass while the room comes back into focus. As the grogginess dissipates, new layers of discomfort reveal themselves in my stomach, arm, and face. This new pain is intense, but if it's the price for returning control to my limbs, I pay it gladly.

I tug at the strap around my left wrist. It's tight, but I don't think it was meant to hold me on its own. I pull hard, and my hand bursts free.

Without hesitation, I pull the knife from the bed. Carefully, I slide it into the space between my right hand and the strap. The razor-sharp blade slashes through it like it wasn't even there. I sit up, and the world warps like a funhouse mirror. I wait for the world to stop wobbling, then I free my ankles.

Focused on the ventilation cover in the ceiling, I attempt to stand on the bed. Still a little woozy, it takes a few desperate attempts before I get upright. Stretched to the limit, I reach it.

Sticking the knife long ways into the small indentation on the head of the screw, I get sufficient leverage to loosen it enough for my finger to twist it the rest of the way out. The screw is still difficult to turn, but after a minute of hard twisting, it falls free into my aching hand. I set the screw down onto the bed, so it doesn't make a sound, then start on the other three. The work is tedious, but all the screws eventually give up their hold on the ventilation cover. Lowering the cover onto the bed, escape calls out to me from above.

I can just reach the inside edge on my tiptoes. I give it a test pull, and it feels more than solid enough to support me. Taking a deep breath, I give it a try. The edge is sharp, and with my body weight suspended on my fingers, it digs in. Blood trickles down my arms. I bite my now swelling lip to keep any sound from escaping.

I crouch back down on the bed and use the knife to cut a strip of fabric from the sheets. I hold the fabric against the cuts until the throbbing subsides and the blood coagulates—the white sheet now soaked red. I slide the knife into one of the jumpsuit's leg pockets. I peel the makeshift bandage back to check out the cut. It doesn't look too bad, but I know I won't have more than a few more tries before my fingers are hamburger meat. I need to make this next attempt count and avoid further injury. Studying the opening, it appears big enough that if I leap, I should be able to hook my elbow on the edge and then pull myself up. I inhale deeply and let the oxygen coat my muscles. Letting the air out slowly, I focus on the attempt.

I jump. *Fuck yeah.* Hooking my elbows over the sharp edge, I have the leverage I need to pull myself up. Confident I've succeeded, my concentration slips. My right foot swings wide and knocks over the medical stand. The glass vile vaporizes on impact with a loud pop.

"What's going on in there?" Even muffled through the door, his bark sets my arm hairs on end.

The lock clicks open.

Instinct picks flight. I'm up and crawling down the air duct.

"Stop!"

I drown out his commands with the loud clanking of my arms and legs against the steel duct.

Everything hurts. Every breath is agony, but I know he

won't rest until I'm dead.

Ten or twenty meters into the duct there is a split to the left and right. Both paths seem equally long and neither shows signs of additional branches. I don't have time to think about it. The guard and the woman's other lackeys are no doubt scouring the building for me. My first impulse is left. Having trusted my gut so far, I go with it.

The farther I travel this metal tunnel, the more proficient I become at making less of a racket. I don't think there is a way to move through an air duct without making any noise, but I have definitely mitigated it. Hopefully, that's enough so that the people looking for me down below cannot hear it. Whether it's audible or not is beyond my control, so I shove the thought from my mind.

After what seems like hours, but what is surely only minutes, a small gleam of light grows at the end of the duct. Feeling freedom close at hand, I swim with renewed vigor, and I make quick progress toward it.

The light is shining through a similar ventilation cover to the one I removed from the room. Holding my eye up to it, I see a street lamp and a soot-covered walking path. I can't help but smile. The "ventilation system" doesn't even have a filter. It just pumps outside air straight in. Now all that stands between me and freedom is a ventilation cover, but this is no simple obstacle to overcome in my position. There is no way I can reach through the small slits to remove the screws holding it in place. The only option I see is to spin around and kick it open. Two problems with that option give me pause. First, I'm barefoot, and there is no telling how much more running I will have to do before I'm safe, so I can't risk breaking a bone or tearing up my footpads so badly I can't walk. Second, banging against the cover will make a lot of noise, and if I'm not successful quickly, they'll be able to home in on my location. Reservations duly noted, and seeing no other option, I commit to the plan. I have to keep on until the bitter end.

Turning around is a precarious and awkward experience in the confined space, but I'm confident that I didn't make too much noise. In position, I place my feet on the cover and prepare. I pull my legs to my chest and then with as much force as I can muster, I shoot them out and hit the cover. To my surprise, my legs kick straight through the cover and into open air.

Bewildered, I shimmy out of the vent. With nothing to gain a footing, I fall hard to the sooty cobblestones below. My right elbow bears the brunt of the fall. I lay for a moment clutching at it—wheezing breaths through gritted teeth distort the path of falling flakes of ash. I shake off the particles clinging to my face and eyelashes. Fighting through the pain, I clamber to my feet. The ash is warm and rough underfoot. My heaving breaths bring in bits of the slag that deposit a foul, acrid taste in my mouth and burn my lungs. I look up and down the street—I have no idea where I am.

Trusting the same impulse I had in the air duct, I head to the left sprinting from shadow to shadow between the pools of light cast by the streetlamps. Every movement is an enemy—every footfall is an uncomfortable reality. I make it down six lights before I glance over my shoulder. A pair of headlights flick to life. The van's engine roars and it barrels down the alleyway toward me. I sprint flat out shadows be damned.

My arms pump, my lungs inflate to the breaking point. Muscles and tendons act without complaint. Despite my body's best efforts, the van is gaining on me fast. Its lights illuminate the path before me revealing the dead end I'm racing toward.

The wall at the end, cutting the path off, is only a few meters high. Knowing I can make it if I'm going full speed, I dump the last of my energy reserves into my legs and lungs. The wall looms before me, growing higher with each step.

At the point of no return, I spring from the ground. The wall is taller than expected, but my battered fingers still manage to latch onto the lip. I get my left and then my right elbow over the edge. I'm going to make it.

Thoughts of escape vaporize faster than they formed. Strong hands grab my ankles and, with a violent jerk, pull me from the wall.

My head cracks against the cobblestones. The world splits in three then crashes back together. I've bitten my tongue, and my mouth is filling with blood. A knot is already forming on my head. Flayed nerves have left me both disoriented and out of breath, but my fire to survive remains un-dwindled.

I flip over and push myself from the ground. I charge back the way I came. A pair of arms grasp around my middle. I throw my right elbow back. It connects solidly with my attacker's mask-covered face shattering their glass eye port. Their cries of agony are filtered through their mask. The strike loosens his grasp enough for me to twist my way out. Free, I bolt.

Beyond exhaustion, I tap into the deepest, most primordial parts of my brain and muster forth the desperate energy of an animal running for its life. My strides long, breaths deep. I pass the open ventilation duct and feel safety approaching.

Crack!

A thunderous roar barks out behind me and rumbles down the walls of the alley, stopping me dead in my tracks. I turn around raising my hands in surrender. Another man is aiming a rifle at me—smoke billows from the barrel.

"The next one won't miss!"

Despite the distortion of his mask, his threat is clear, and I'm in no condition to put it to the test.

"Get over here—quick!"

Out of moves, I do what the armed man says. I jog back toward him at a hesitant pace. He keeps his sleek, geometric gun leveled at my chest. Just before I reach him, his colleague—still clutching his face—rushes between us.

"Where'd you even get that thing? Put it away! She's not our enemy."

"It'd be better to shoot her than let her get away—she knows too much."

"What the hell's gotten into you—what are you even saying? We're not like them—we don't just shoot people. Lower the gun, Damian."

Damian's eyes keep their sinister glint behind the glass circles of his mask, but he lowers the rifle. The other man approaches me. His left eye is swollen and bloody.

"Please hear me out," he says holding his hands out to me. My heart swells but I hold my ground. "Peace Officers, or worse, heard that gunshot—we don't have much time. I'll try and explain in the van, but you have to come with us, and you have to trust me."

I hesitate. He's not wrong, we need to get out of here in a hurry, but I've handed out my trust too liberally lately, and look where that's gotten me: barefoot, exhausted, and bleeding. But it also started this journey. It led me to Delia—it brought me to Margaret and the Oracle Device. Despite what I've endured, I wouldn't trade any of it for my former ignorance.

In a heartbeat, I make my choice.

"I'll come with you, but before I get in that van, I need to know your names."

"I'm Victor, and he's Damian." Damian glares at him.

"Trust us, we're on your side."

I step past them and pull open the van's sliding door. I hop in and take a seat on the empty floor.

"I hope so."

CHAPTER TWENTY

THE VAN'S INTERIOR has been stripped of its seats and the cosmetic plastic panels that normally conceal the rat's nest of wires, bolts, and seams. A tool chest is bolted to the floor in the back. I nestle against the chest and grab hold of the straps on either side of the roof. I try to both relax and prepare myself for flight. A tricky task made nearly impossible because I'm flitting in an out of consciousness—I've emptied every reserve tank, and I think I'm on the verge of shutting down.

Damian and Victor don't dawdle. Damian takes the driver's position. He takes a moment to fold the rifle into an inconspicuous cylinder—each section folding effortlessly into the other. He shoves it into a gap in the center console then replaces a small panel concealing it. Victor latches his seatbelt then points to the hidden compartment.

"Were you planning on telling me about this? What else aren't you telling me?" Damian turns to Victor and locks eyes with him. Unblinking he kicks the idling van into gear.

Damian twists himself around and uses the back window to guide us in reverse out of the alley. His hyper-focused eyes send a river of ice pouring down my back—I've seen that look before staring back at me from the mirror on a battlefield long ago.

The world is a blur of yellow light and deep shadows. At the end of the path, the road widens into two lanes. Damian whips the van around. I hold on for dear life and avoid sliding across the van, but my stomach does a somersault, and I barely keep it down.

Regaining some semblance of stability, I look out the rear window. A dozen shadowy figures swarm the alley—the silhouettes of their rifles stretching out toward us. I may have no idea who Damian and Victor really are, but I think I've made the right decision to go with them.

"I think they've spotted us," Victor says. "Try and shake 'em."

"Already on it."

Victor's insight proves correct almost immediately. Two pairs of headlights kick on in the road behind us and begin pursuit. Pressing the accelerator to the floor, Damian pushes the van to the limits of its speed. A few short hammer blows in my chest later, it's clear this van doesn't have the horsepower to outrun our pursuers.

"You're going to have to lose them in the alleys." Victor's tone is shaky but clear—the headlights behind us swell in the rearview mirror.

"I'll take them down into the Under City."

Victor nods his approval.

With that Damian makes a hard left and the van whips around another corner. This time I've got a better idea of how to manage it. I lean into the turn and make it with little discomfort.

I scan our surroundings trying to make sense of where we are. Between the bright-yellow streetlamps and the pitch-black shadows, I can't make heads or tails of what's going on. I'm glad Damian is driving and knows what he's doing. There is no way I'd be able to find all the narrow paths or navigate the tight turns that he seems to know like the back of his hand.

Curve after curve, turn after turn, we race through the upper streets of the city. Our pursuers hot on our trail.

"Here it is! Hold on back there."

I'm already clutching the straps for dear life, but it isn't enough. He makes the turn at full speed, and on the slick, ash-covered streets the back end of the van swings out wide popping us up on three wheels. Sparks fly as we scrape along the wall of the narrow side street. Damian's lucky he didn't flip us.

Crashing back onto four wheels the van groans, then growls as Damian slams the throttle full-open.

Engine redlined and screaming, we make two more vertigo-inducing, hairpin turns. As I fight to keep what's still in my stomach where it's at, Damian mercifully eases off the throttle.

We scan the mirrors. There are no lights behind us except for the endless chain of receding streetlamps.

I realize I've been holding my breath and let it out in a long, relieved sigh. Damian heaves out a manic laugh.

"Damn, Damian. If you hadn't pulled that off," Victor shakes his head, "I'd be so pissed at you."

"You never have enough faith in me, Victor."

Victor's hand is still wrapped around the handle above the window. "Well, it's hard when you do shit like that."

Still laughing, Damian wrings his hands around the steering wheel—waning adrenaline rippling down his quivering arms.

Pulling down a steep ramp, the Under City comes into view. Colossal ribs of concrete and steel bear the weight of the streets of Einsam creating a cavernous labyrinth full of squat buildings barely visible in the gloom. An endless rain of ash spews from chutes in the ceiling fed by the tireless street sweepers roving unseen above us.

The road ahead is only wide enough for one car to pass through at a time. The buildings are built with only the narrowest of gaps between them and they reach all the way up to the ceiling ten meters above. What windows there are, are small and barred over. Each dim, soot-covered light sputters like a distant star.

Damian navigates us into an alley. He pulls the van into a

jet of venting steam then kills the engine. The foundations of skyscrapers moan. Steam hisses. The van's suspension squeals at our slightest movements.

"Not a sound." Damian pulls the rifle from its hiding place in the console. Unfolded, it locks into lethal form with a *click*. He clutches it, willing boogeymen to emerge through the mist.

Victor eyes the weapon in his friend's hands. His earlier fire replaced by a tortured look of sadness and concern.

Anxiety builds in the van like a dam ready to burst. None of us dare breathe. Did we lose them or are we trapped waiting to die?

Somewhere in the static the last of my energy reserves fizzles away, and I collapse into nightmare.

I am alone in the void. Time is infinite and unmoving. There is a complete absence of stimuli. Am I dreaming, or have I died? Without competition, my thoughts swell to fill the space.

A crackling fire starts in my feet and works its way up my spine. The void condenses as the fire nears my nape. All the possible lives I could have lived—patriotic citizen, party-line bureaucrat, obedient daughter—implode into a lump dark as coal. The collapsing void and the burning fuse meet at the base of my skull.

I explode from the darkness to the alley behind Margaret's.

My mask is already in my hands—even here that choice cannot be undone. Antonius Neptus approaches me through the haze. His eyes twinkle like sapphires.

I run.

I sprint faster than I ever have. I weave and dodge with superhuman precision. I could have outrun anyone alive. But you can't outrun the devil.

He's never more than a footstep behind me. I make one wrong move—was there anywhere else to turn?—and find myself trapped in a dead end. I run until I've got nowhere left to go and I'm backed up against the wall.

I move to defend myself, but it's no use. His hands twist around my neck. I'd scream but with no wind to carry them, my lips twist in silence. His face is different now—his gnarled leather features are morphing into mine. Only his piercing blue eyes remain unchanged.

Is he becoming me, or have I become him?

All hope is lost.

Bursting from the alley walls around us, thousands of delicate silver threads like vines lash out and ensnare the doppelganger. The dark reflection releases its hold on me. I dart away gasping in heaving lungfuls of air as sweet as any mountain meadow.

Breathe, Evelyn. Just breathe.

The silver strands ensnare the apparition. It struggles in vain as they constrict ever tighter—the alley echoes with the shrill moaning of an iron girder ready to snap.

The nightmare figure shatters with a bang—a jumbled chorus of human screams and shattered glass. Its pieces collapse into slag. The silver threads slither back into the concrete and cobblestones fading into the alley walls.

I plunge my hands into the slag and pull out two sapphire spheres. They are small enough to fit in the palm of my hand but I struggle to hold them as they fight to return to the slag as though magnetized to the earth. As I try to make sense of the patterns flashing on their shifting facets, the alley and everything in it melts away.

For a timeless moment, I'm suspended in nothingness anchored in place by the gravitational pull of the crystalline spheres before we too melt into the void.

"Where are we? What is this place?"

Victor turns to face me. Behind the shattered glass, his eye is swollen and purple. He pulls off his mask revealing angular features hidden under boyish cheeks.

"How are you feeling?"

I pull myself up on my elbows then immediately crash back down onto the bare metal floor of the van. Every inch of me is a bruise. A dehydration headache is pounding on my temples, and I'm ravenously hungry.

"How long was I out? On the bright side, we didn't get caught."

Victor cracks a smile.

"You were real touch and go there for a while. We were able to get you to swallow a couple painkillers—your fever broke just after daybreak."

It hurts to sit up, but I can't lay down anymore. Victor offers me a helping hand. The steam vent we hid in last night has shut off, so I can see out the windows, but if Victor hadn't told me it was a new day, there is no way I would have known. The Under City is just as dark as it was last night despite the added glow of a few more lamps.

"What is this place?"

"You don't know what the Under City is?" he asks—his face a study in confusion.

"Well…" It hits me square between the eyes—I haven't got a clue. I know I've heard Rourke mention it on the Nightly News, but I never paid attention to what he was saying—I was more concerned with the power struggle on the couch. Mother always wants to keep watching whenever anything like that comes on and dad always switches the channel. "There's got to be something else on?" The screen blinks over to something saturated and bubbly. "I was watching that Allen." He commits to the new show even when there's no hiding how much he hates it. "I get enough of that crap at work." His taboo trump card kills any hope Mother has of riposte.

"I know the name, but I assumed they were just talking about the streets. I live in a high rise—I assumed that was the lowest you could go."

Victor's expression morphs from curious to flabbergasted. Damian wrings his hands around the steering wheel filling the rising tension with a sticky, grating sound.

"You've never been here before?"

I shake my head no.

"Shocker." Damian eyes me in the rearview mirror. "What floor of that tower do you live on?"

Victor shoots Damian a reproachful look. "What does that have to do with anything?"

"I'm curious is all."

"I live in one of the penthouses."

Damian chuffs. "You're one of those private prep-school twits, aren't you? Future Caretakers and all that crap."

I bite my tongue trying to keep the warmth behind my ears from bursting into flames.

Victor dismisses him with a wave. "How did you get mixed up in all of this then?"

"It's a long story." The past few months flash through my mind so fast I can't find a good place to start. "I guess I just wanted to know the truth." The warmth behind my ears starts to sizzle. "Does it really matter where I'm from? Everyone in the Great Society is being lied to, rich and poor. We're all being deceived."

"Oh, really?" Damian contorts himself around to scowl at me. "You want the truth? Huh? I'll lay it out for you!"

Victor puts a hand on Damian's heaving chest. He snorts, retreating into his seat, crosses his arms, and turns his gaze to the vista of dilapidated buildings.

"What he's trying to say," Victor says, his eyes scouring Damian. "Is you've had clean food, clean air, good schools, good parents. Down here people don't have any of those things. I certainly didn't."

"Spoiled brat thinks she's suffered, ha!" Damian snaps.

Fire mixes with venom in my chest.

"I didn't choose to be born in the penthouse, and for your information, 'good' schools and 'good' parents aren't all they're cracked up to be. My father is never home. Mother is distant, cold, and paranoid. School was little more than propaganda, and for even the smallest missteps, punishments were draconian."

Damian whirls around so fast his seatbelt locks up. Cursing through gritted teeth, he yanks hard on his seatbelt strap giving himself the slack he needs to face me. Anger drips from his eyes and rumbles down his vibrating fingers itching to become fists.

"Well boohoo. Poor little rich girl. Give me a fucking break. People who live down here work sixteen hours a day making the clothes you wear, the filters you breathe through, and all that fancy tech you take for granted. When they get home, they're probably drunk—how else can you deal with this, huh? More often than not, kids get their parent's frustrations as a back-handed bedtime story." His words have turned me to stone, and I can't pull myself away from the pain in his eyes. "Every meal—no matter how hard you fucking try—is full of bits of ash. People down here can't afford new filters. We've got to breathe in all the filth you people dump on us. I'll be lucky to see thirty and that's better than most. You think you had it rough at school? Down here instructors use the lash more than the pen, and almost no one gets beyond their fourth or fifth year because they've got to work to afford hospital visits for their sick parents and siblings and maybe if there's anything left over, to keep a little food on the table. The Caretakers don't need to feed us propaganda to keep us under their boot." He lets out an exacerbated laugh—his eyes veiled behind the moisture clouding his mask. "There's no time to revolt, no money for bombs. It takes everything we've got just to survive." He pauses to breathe—his chest swells to bursting. "This," he jabs his finger at the suffering framed in the window—his voice a hair's breadth from breaking. "Not their propaganda, their POs, or Guardians high-stepping through Victory Square. This is it—the real truth of the Great Society."

Tears stream into my mouth through the corners of my trembling lips. The amorphous structures of reality solidify with razor-like edges. His words have burned through the fraying veil I thought I had already broken through.

I've been retreating from the world. Cocooning myself in a bubble, nourishing myself on the suffering of others while claiming it as my own. Everyone else's struggles were irrelevant. They were just ants, weren't they? Automatons not worth a second thought. Only I had the perspective, from my gleaming penthouse twenty stories above the smog, to see the truth they were too blind to see.

Ants gnaw on every inch of me. The desire to vomit myself out of my skin pounds on the inside of my skull. I can see now that the only automaton was me—my own cold, mechanical eyes stare back at me from the warped mirror in my mind.

Am I really a spoiled brat discontent with the riches at my feet? I push back at the rising waves of self-hatred threatening to drown me. No, that gets me off the hook too easy. My intentions have been innocent, but I'm not free from guilt. It's clear the ignorance I keep telling myself I have shucked off still clings to me like ash.

I've walked through life so myopically focused on my own path that I failed to notice the injustices literally beneath my feet. I never gave a second thought as to where my masks and filters came from. Or even considered the people who made them and the lives they've lived. Everything I consumed, the gleaming products lining the ever-full store shelves, were simply there. As if by magic. Deep down I've always known the magic would disappear if I dared to learn how the trick was done.

"I'm sorry that I didn't know," the words cling to my throat like tar. "But that's why I'm here. I'm not going to play along anymore. I've come here for the truth. No matter how unsettling or painful it may be."

"You hear that Victor? Five minutes in the UC and she's got the truth all figured out." The anger and sadness in his voice have drained out leaving nothing but the vinegar at the bottom.

Victor fidgets in his seat. His eyes dance in their sockets searching for the words that will let him jump back into the conversation. Damian locks eyes with me. I match his gaze.

Ice forms between us, but I fight through it, willing my resolve to slowly chip away at his contempt. After an excruciating fifteen seconds, the tension in his shoulders dips. He inhales sharply then lets it out slow.

"All right, I'll give you the benefit of the doubt. You've seen the underside of their boots firsthand," he points to my bloody feet then gestures vaguely at my medley of mottled bruises. "Now what?

"I want to change things—make life better for everyone." I slam my eyes closed regretting those words as soon as they leapt from my mouth. They may be true, but they're going to ring hollow. Shaking it off, I press on while I still have the floor. "We need to start fresh, rebuild society. The Caretakers, the Council of Industry, they're all corrupt. The world's broken and we need to fix it."

Damian shakes his head in languid disapproval. "Oh, I know all about people like you—you'll come down here and preach to us about how bad we've got it and why we need to stand up to the Caretakers. Then while we're getting the shit beat out of us for standing up for ourselves, you're back home in your penthouse tucked up tight in your spotless satin sheets."

"I'm not some self-righteous messiah—"

"Then prove it! And spare me another speech. Give me something concrete—a plan with meat on its bones. Are you ready to burn it all down? Bleed for it?" Damian's hands twist around the rifle. "Kill for it?"

Damian's words catalyze Victor into action. He takes Damian by the wrist wrenching his hand off the rifle. "Are you hearing yourself?"

Damian overpowers Victor and puts his hand back around the rifle grip. "How many times are we going to have this conversation? Are you listening to me? Damian, look at me." Turning his head to Victor, Damian unhooks his eyes from me relieving a lump of tension between my shoulder blades.

"We can't fix our problems by adding to them. If we go to war with the Caretakers, you'll get what you want, and the streets will run with blood. And sure, some of it will be theirs, but you know full well most of it will come from innocent people." Damian eases his grip on the rifle returning color to his hands.

"Once you start blowing things up and shooting people—you can't walk yourself back from that. Any chance of a peaceful way out, gone!"

"Spare me, Victor!" Damian slams his fists on the steering wheel. "We've been doing things the old man's way—he's got you bought into it hook line and sinker—and what have we accomplished? Nothing! Not a goddamn thing is any better than when we started. There's no negotiating with them. Every plea, every boot-licking request, gets the same response: violence." His hands return to the rifle—he's shaking so hard the barrel is clanging against the window. "We have to fight fire with fire. Show the people that the Caretakers can bleed too. String up a Guardian from every lamppost in the city and you'll watch the Caretaker's power slip away like that. You know I'm right. I want you backing me up on this. We can convince Herrington to join Nightingale—he'll listen to you. A war's coming, mark my words. We need to be on the right side of it."

Victor's turned completely red. He's gritting his teeth so hard they're squeaking. "I wish this wasn't making sense, but it's all starting to piece together." His head is whipping from side to side. "So, this is the crap you've been trying to get me to sneak off to? You think I'm wrapped around Mr. Herrington's little finger, look at yourself, Damian. You're spouting their garbage like you thought it up all by yourself. I bet when they gave you those bullets, their plan sounded better than good—glorious even," Victor drops his head—tears splash on his bouncing knee. "But it's all a lie. And you know it." He wipes the snot from his nose. "Violence begets violence—those aren't just Herrington's words, they're the truth. Starting a war won't bring you peace."

They've turned away from each other and are now staring out the front window at the wisps of steam rising up around the van. The air is thick. My heart races as beads of sweat run off my forehead and down my arms to splash on the floor. Chests heaving, noses sniffling, the silence is filled with the aftershocks of argument and the ceaseless rumble of the foundations of a city on the verge of collapse.

"We haven't exhausted every peaceful option available to us. We don't need Nightingale. We have to keep trying to do things the right way." Victor sounds exhausted.

"I'm sick of trying—sick of losing." All hint of emotion has been purged from Damian's words. He strokes the rifle in his lap. "You'll see, the group will stand with me—it's time to act."

"Is there anything I can say to change your mind? Damian? Please?" Victor's voice is a gossamer thread. "You mean everything to me, and you know I've always had your back, but I won't go down that road with you."

Damian peels off his mask. He's young, maybe twenty-five, but life has not been kind to him. His jaw and heavy brow look like they were plucked from a statue at a war memorial. The left side of his face is heavily scarred from what appear to be cigarette burns and deep gouges from a blade. His skin is leathery and wrinkled well beyond his years. Bottomless pools of sadness shimmer behind his walnut eyes.

Afraid of striking another spark, I hold myself as still as possible. I've popped into their lives and stepped straight into the minefield separating them.

"Let's get her back to Herrington's," Damian says. "I need to cool down before I do something I'll regret." His detached tone sends a jolt of electricity snaking down my spine.

Victor looks understandingly into Damian's eyes. They share a moment, then Victor looks away and places his broken mask back over his swollen face. Damian lingers, staring into his mask. Silent communion finished, he slips it on with practiced ease.

Back behind their masks, silence refills the space between them. All signs of their confrontation are bottled up and hidden away.

The van rumbles to life and we descend into the Under City.

CHAPTER TWENTY-ONE

WE DRIVE THROUGH THE UNDER CITY'S filth-choked streets at a crawl. Ash falls in a relentless flurry. Trying to unbury their cars, or clear off the entrances to their store-fronts, people frantically sweep at the piling ash with push brooms. Every drive of their brush yields a fleeting glimpse of the cracked concrete below.

Everyone is so covered in soot and ash that it's impossible to determine even the most superficial details about them. Are they young or old? Women or men? Their uniqueness, their identity, is buried beneath the grime.

The crooked shapes of soot-covered children buckle under the weight of chamber pots, on their way to dump them in open cesspits. The van filters the outside air but even so it can't keep the putrid smell from seeping in. Fresh tears well in my eyes. All the days I shook out my ash-covered overcoat and thought how dirty I was, the shower was always there to take it away. I've never eaten a meal where I had to endure the harsh, burning taste of ash. I've always had plumbing and clean air.

Their situation is worse than mine—I can't deceive myself of that—but we are both victims of the same injustice. Damian believes that because I have lived a comfortable life that I am less committed, or less able, to fight for change. Most of these people probably feel the way he does. It's up to me to convince them that I'm willing to stand with them—shoulder-to-shoulder. I have to prove to them that for there to be any hope of rebuilding society, we need to stand as one. Without unity, our cause will be as futile as pushing a broom at the falling ash.

The route is long and winding. Navigating hazards dictates our glacial pace. I stare unblinking at the misery of the Under City rolling past in framed tableau. Each scene builds on the last, and by the time we pull into their garage, and the door closes behind us, I'm as brittle as glass. Any moment I feel that I might shatter, and there would be no way to put the pieces together. We sit in silence listening to the engine moan as it cools—each of us dazed from the recent whirlwind. Victor's steady tone breaks the tension.

"Despite everything that just happened, and everything we've said," he faces Damian, his expression pained, "we are glad to have found you, and we look forward to getting to know you."

Damian avoids Victor's eyes. Victor keeps up his withering stare. Damian relents and grunts in agreement. Without another moment's pause, Damian steps out of the van. Victor watches him walk around the hood then unclicks his seatbelt and follows him. They walk through the only door in the cramped garage and disappear.

Alone, crushing static rings in my ears. My head feels like a lead weight and nausea builds with every slight movement. I focus on each breath to take my attention away from the building bile and my many throbbing wounds. Images of the Under City are burned into the backs of my eyes. More tears fall. Wiping my face with my jumper's soiled sleeve, I slide the van door open and step into the garage.

The stench hits me first. The garage is a rat's warren of moldering boxes, dust-covered miscellanea, and a car stripped down to its rusting frame. I gag reflexively. Bracing myself for what's to come, I enter the house.

Much to my relief, the house smells pleasantly of lavender, but it's a far cry from the penthouse. Each room off the narrow hallway is small. The floor is black from soot tracked in on soiled feet, but in a few places, the dull orange floral design of the linoleum peeks through like a ray of sun in a storm. The walls are covered in wallpaper not too dissimilar from the floor, but the colors have long since faded away leaving only gray. Hanging on the drab walls are elegantly framed black-and-white family portraits from a bygone era. I run my hand along their elaborate wooden frames. A large family poses together under a full-leafed oak tree. A boy of six or seven swings from a rope swing. None of them are wearing masks. My heart twists, my breath catches. *Are there still places like this? Or is this just a ghost hung here to haunt us?*

Voices at the end of the hall pull me from my thoughts. They grow louder as I approach the door then fall into silence after my knock. "Come on in—join us," Victor says opening the door.

Damian and Victor are in a compact kitchen, glasses of murky water in their hands. With them is a tall, lean man with a leathered and deeply wrinkled face. He's at the sink filling two glasses with the murky water flowing from the tap.

"Sorry, I'm going a little slow—this is a lot to take in." I try to mask the weariness in my voice.

"Don't sweat it, it was a rough night. Take as much time as you need."

The old man shuts off the tap then turns around full glasses in hand. "It's rude to invite guests into my house without introducing them, Victor."

"My apologies, Mr. Herrington. We found her crawling out of the subversive's indoctrination center."

"Did you? And what, may I ask, is her name?"

Victor lets out an embarrassed laugh.

"I never thought to ask—it was all kind of a blur. What is your name?" His face is turning every shade of red.

I step forward extending my hand. "Evelyn Brennan. Thank you for allowing me into your home, Mr. Herrington. If it weren't for Damian and Victor, I would be dead right now."

Mr. Herrington's eyes gleam. "In all the commotion she was able to learn both of your names—even my name for heaven's sake—and you couldn't manage to learn hers?"

Shaking his head at Victor, Mr. Herrington steps past him and offers me a glass of water.

"It's a pleasure to meet you, sir."

"The pleasure is all mine young lady. Please have a glass of water. To new friends," toasts Mr. Herrington.

"To new friends," we echo back.

I raise the murky water to my lips and take a gulp. It's acrid, almost sour, but borderline dehydrated I drink it down greedily. The water has an immediate rejuvenating effect. Despite the knot on my head, the gouges in my fingers, and the swelling bruises on my stomach, I almost feel good. Finishing his glass too, Mr. Herrington takes mine from me and sets it on the counter.

"How are you feeling young lady? You look as if you've been through the wringer twice."

"I'm fine—thank you. Just had a few unpleasant encounters is all."

Victor takes our empty glasses and puts them in the sink.

"She's tough, but she was in a real bad way when we picked her up last night."

"Perhaps, a few Ache Busters and some rest would do you good? You too Victor, looks like miss Brennan isn't the only one in need of some rest."

Victor covers his swollen eye. Damian snickers and clasps Mr. Herrington on the back.

"This one's got a mean elbow."

Mr. Herrington inspects me, his bushy eyebrows raised.

"I imagine if you'd properly introduced yourself that eye of yours would be a lot less purple."

We all laugh, well Victor doesn't. Karma pays me back quick though—the bruises on my stomach flare up. Mr. Herrington takes me under the arm.

"Come now miss Brennan, let's get you to the sitting room."

I nod in agreement then let him guide me out of the kitchen into the adjacent sitting room. The room is larger than the kitchen but still cramped. The wallpaper continues, along with the floor, giving the whole house a cohesive feel. Two burgundy velvet wing-backed chairs sit across from a gray couch. An iron-grated coal furnace in the corner fills the room with warmth and flickering orange light.

"Damian, could you kindly fetch us some pain pills and two more glasses of water?"

Damian nods then pops back into the kitchen.

Mr. Herrington helps me into one of the chairs then takes a seat with Victor on the couch. The chair is old, and the springs have long since stopped being supportive, but my tired body relishes the comfort. Damian is quick in his task and delivers

Victor and me a glass of water and two bright-red pain pills. I gulp them down without hesitation then set the glass down on the coffee table. Damian takes the empty chair across from me.

"So, Miss Brennan, how did you come to be in the unfortunate circumstances my two friends found you in?"

I lean back in my chair and stare into the water-stained plaster above me.

"Where do I begin…"

Over the next hour, I retell the events of the last few months. Beginning with the newscast, I spare no detail. When it came time to describe my experience in the Oracle Device I thought it would be the most difficult part but the images, sounds, and sensations I experienced returned to me with near-perfect clarity. But everything that came after is a swirling storm of needles. My words trail off, and I have to repeat myself frequently to get even the vaguest of pictures out. Only now is the full gravity of my situation sinking in.

Both Victor and Mr. Herrington's faces ebb and flow with emotion as I tell my story, but never once do I see even a glimmer of empathy on Damian's face.

Nearing the end of the story, I notice Victor and Damian's growing apprehension. Legs bouncing, eyes darting. I don't think they want Mr. Herrington to know about the gun. Not wanting to stir that hornet's nest up again, I truncate the ending.

"I kicked through the filtration grate, struggled with the

boys a bit until I figured out they were okay, then we jumped in the van and got out of there in a hurry."

Leaning forward I sink my head into my hands and sigh. The fact that all of it actually happened to me, and in such a short time, is overwhelming. Perhaps this has all been just some endless, vivid nightmare? My aching body snaps me out of it and reminds me that it was all too real. With the story over, Mr. Herrington leans forward resting his elbows on his knees.

"Thank you for being brave and sharing your story with us. I'm sorry you got caught up in all of this and that you had to endure so much."

Damian chuffs. Mr. Herrington's brow furrows. He shakes his head at Damian then refocuses on me.

"I wish I could take away the painful parts," he continues. "But I'm glad you're here. Whether you know it or not, you've helped me put together a few disparate pieces to the puzzle we're in. Thank you."

"I'm glad I can help—but none of this makes any sense to me."

Damian rolls his eyes. Mr. Herrington has turned his gaze into the coals and doesn't seem to notice.

"We've spent years trying to get our hands on those impresses. I still can't believe Margaret managed to get one." Mr. Herrington's eyes grow distant. "You remind me of her in our youth. Before they broke her."

Memories swell in Mr. Herrington's eyes as he recalls a young, vibrant Margaret.

"They let her live, but they killed her spirit. She was never the same after prison, and it didn't take them long to force her to be their lackey."

The ground falls away beneath me. I clutch at the armrests.

"Wait, what? Margaret was working with them, the Caretakers?"

"Correct." He pauses for a moment, his eyes turned down to his interlaced hands. "It's a bit of a tangle—bear with me. You know the subversives. You're warned about them from the moment you're born. But they don't really exist—well at least not how they're portrayed. In reality, they're part of the Caretaker's state apparatus. That woman who tortured you, she's undersecretary to High Caretaker Domhnall, Ursula Fowler."

I'm shaking my head.

"I'm sure of it—it matches her description and MO to the letter—you're not the first to testify to her torture. She oversaw the last cycle of violence, and I don't think this city can endure her brand of terror and bloodshed again. The Caretakers overlook her methods because her work never fails to swell Peace Bond sales. Each new High Caretaker becomes more and more comfortable spending human lives like currency—she's redefined a new normal."

My thoughts are being pulled in a thousand directions at

once. *Just breathe.* I focus in on the question with the best chance of a solid answer. "How close is she to activating the program? Is there anything we can do to stop it?"

"It's hard to tell. Our network has been trying to infiltrate Fowler's organization for years with little success. Victor and Damian have been working on opening some new avenues, but it could be months or tonight—it's too hard to tell."

The swirling fragments of information begin to coalesce. As they fall into place, recent events take on a more solid dimension. I turn to face Victor. His eye is slowly returning to its normal size.

"You were bugging them through that ventilation duct. That's why I was able to kick it free."

Victor nods. "With Margaret's help, we were able to track some of Fowler's recruits to that facility in the industrial park. We spent the last few nights scouting out a way in. We found that ventilation cover, the day before yesterday, but we only had time to remove the fasteners. Last night we were supposed to be putting a bug *in* so you can imagine our surprise when you fell *out*." He pauses for a breath. He looks at me so intently it's as if he's trying to look into me. "That was a stroke of luck for both of us." The corner of his mouth turns up into a mischievous hook. A flash of heat envelopes me—roses bloom on my cheeks.

"There is no doubt about that," Mr. Herrington adds with genuine warmth. His words cut the growing embarrassment between Victor and me.

Thankful for his intervention, I shift my focus to Mr. Herrington letting the rest of the room drop away.

"But I still don't understand where Nightingale fits into all this? Why did they give Margaret that impress and what were they hoping to get out of it?"

Sitting back on the couch, Mr. Herrington looks up at the ceiling. A pensive look on his face, he collects his thoughts for a laden minute before he speaks.

"I'm still not sure how—if at all—Nightingale fits into any of this. What's troubling me the most is the Oracle Device. Fowler's connection to it suggests that she's using it on the recruits for her subversive program. Peace Officers and Guardians go through a similar process, but in newer, less intrusive machines that are meant to reinforce loyalty to the Caretakers not create it. She would surely have access to those facilities so that begs the question: why is she using the Oracle Device?"

Damian stirs from his long silence. "She's reprogramming people into her own soldiers. It's the only thing that adds up. Only two reasons to use the Oracle Device. One, even the new fancy imprint devices can't reprogram someone without making their brains fizzle out their ears—not enough juice. The Oracle Device is rigged into the nuclear plants—that's how we first picked up their trail. That thing sucks down more power than half the city."

I scoot to the edge of my seat. "And the second reason?"

"The only other reason to use it is secrecy. It's not enmeshed with the intranet like the others. If she wanted to reprogram her recruits with something and not have the OSS catch her out, then she'd have no other option."

Mr. Herrington reaches his hand up enthusiastically. His knobby, arthritic fingers dance with excitement. "You may have hit upon something Damian. That may also be why Fowler is using Margaret to disperse the impresses. That way she can insulate herself were anyone to find out."

"Whatever she's up to, it isn't good," Victor says.

"We need to go talk to Margaret," I say. "She should be able to fill in the missing links—she can tell us where Nightingale fits in."

Mr. Herrington nods. "That seems our best course of action. Hopefully, Fowler has not done anything to her, and she's willing to talk."

Damian stands up abruptly. "I'll gas up the van and put the seats back in for you two."

"We'll head out as soon as you're done, Damian."

Damian nods to Mr. Herrington then leaves—his overcoat desperately trying to keep up with his long strides. Victor helps Mr. Herrington up, stabilizing him while he gains his legs.

"Wait here a moment, Miss Brennan, Victor and I will scrounge up a change of clothes, shoes, and a mask for you.

They'll be looking for you, but if you're dressed differently and wearing a mask, we should be able to pass through the city unnoticed."

I smile and nod. Before they are even out of the room my chin slumps to my chest. I teeter on the edge of sleep, but approaching footsteps bring me back. Victor has returned with a jumpsuit, underwear, overcoat, ankle boots, and gas mask neatly folded in a bundle.

He offers it to me. "I took my best guess."

I glance over everything. The jumpsuit should work no matter what—that's their one redeeming quality. The boots seem a little large but everything else looks close enough to work.

"Thanks—looks like you've measured me up about right." Our eyes meet and his face flushes.

"Uh, lucky guess. I mean, I've looked at you…" his words rattle around in his head—umber turns to scarlet. His hands fly up, "Not like that. You know, like normal looking. Just a glance. I'm surprised I guessed it right at all."

I can't help but snicker and it clenches him even tighter. Sweat beads on his forehead.

"Here we are Miss Brennan," Mr. Herrington's voice breaks Victor loose and we turn our attention to him. "I couldn't remember where I put my last can of Salamander gel. After you wash them out, put a dab of this on your feet and those nasty cuts on your hands. It's not magic, but it's pretty darn close."

I rise and, balancing the bundle of clothes in one hand, take the can from him. "Thank you, I really appreciate what you're doing for me."

"It's my pleasure young lady."

At the end of the hallway is the coffin-like bathroom. I lock the door behind me then set the bundle on the narrow counter. I try the tap. It runs a murky brown.

I unzip my jumpsuit and it falls to the floor—naked, the cold sends a shiver racing over my skin.

Clank!

I squat down and rummage through the jumpsuit's pocket. A jolt of pain runs up my arm as my fingers wrap around the blade's handle. Moving closer to the sink, I hold it up to the light and inspect it. It could come in handy—it's already gotten me out of one jam and the way things are going I don't think it will be my last. But it's not just a tool. It's a weapon.

The nick on my neck still stings—her cruel intentions glimmer along its edge. If I take it with me what kind of woman will I be?

My reflection startles me—I hardly recognize myself. My body is a meld of purple and yellow bruises. My stomach a swirl of indigo. A trickle of blood down my neck has dried black.

I open the medicine cabinet and shove the knife inside.

With no time for a full shower, I wash my cuts as quick as I can. The ivory soap stings like crazy but it has to be done.

I twist open the can and scoop out a glob of the translucent-peach gel and smear it over the cuts on my footpads. It starts as a sting, then swells into a roaring fire. But before I can cry out, the pain melts into a numb buzzing. I pull on fresh wool socks and my feet feel almost normal.

Despite the thick socks, the boots are still a size too large. The mask isn't as good as I'm used to, and it takes a great deal of effort to get a halfway decent seal. Good thing I don't actually need it. The idea of wearing a mask is repulsive, but it's a necessary disguise, so I tolerate its restricting presence on my face.

I dollop more Salamander gel on the palms of my hands. The ache busters are kicking in.

Changed, I rejoin them in the sitting room.

"I say," Mr. Herrington does a once over then nods in approval. "You look rather sharp. Now then, let's leave Miss Brennan to rest. We'll be just through the hall in the garage if you need anything."

"I should be all right here for a few minutes, thank you."

Mr. Herrington smiles and for the first time in a long while I smile too.

I shift in the chair to get comfortable, and it responds with a noisy groan. Looking into the coal fire smoldering in the furnace, I cling to the hope that Margaret is still okay.

CHAPTER TWENTY-TWO

EMERGING FROM THE UNDER CITY cuts a starker contrast than I imagined. The sun has risen lifting the shadows from oblivion to muddy haze. The buildings above are as tightly packed as ever, but with alleyways separating them, open space seems abundant in comparison. Ash still falls, but with the constant presence of street sweepers, it never accumulates more than a few centimeters before it's whisked away. Even the most rundown and poor neighborhoods have air filters and plumbing. It's hard to imagine that only a few hours ago there was a world beneath my feet that I had never known and that I had taken its hardships, and the efforts of its people, for granted.

Riding in the van is much more pleasant with a seat. Damian drives at a leisurely pace, following traffic laws to the letter. We do nothing to distinguish ourselves from the sea of other soot-covered vans obediently waiting in line.

The roads are congested, as usual, and what would have taken half an hour on foot takes twice as long in traffic. This lengthy rest is a welcome change from the running and constant physical exertion I've been doing lately, but it's nerve-wracking not knowing what may be happening to Margaret. I try not to think of the worst, but I can't imagine Fowler doing anything less. I sigh out loud, catching Mr. Herrington's attention.

Sitting right next to him, I see his warm, timeworn face in more detail. His nose shows signs of having been broken multiple times, and his right ear is missing a piece of the lobe. His eyes are a rich brown with speckles of green glimmering under salt-and-pepper caterpillar eyebrows.

"What's wrong, Miss Brennan? We should be there shortly." His words are calming like a salve.

"What if we're too late? I have a bad feeling that Fowler did something awful to her." Gingerly, I rub my battered stomach. "That woman is paranoid and sadistic, and she's capable of unspeakable things."

"I've had the same thoughts, but there was nothing we could have done earlier. Hopefully, she is still there, but if not, and if they've taken her, I know she would have left a note, a clue or something to let me know what happened."

"Do you know Margaret well?"

"Oh yes—I've known her most of my life. I was her first real boyfriend—schoolyard crushes don't count," he says winking. "We shared a fire, much like yours, that burned for the truth. We wrote pamphlets, hung up posters, and dreamed of the impact we'd have." His mood sours and the sparkle evaporates from his eyes. "That all fell apart when the Caretakers caught up with us. They destroyed our printing press, torched our apartment. They tortured us for weeks. There was a flame in Margaret, looking at her was like looking into the sun. They snuffed that out of her. When they let us go, she wanted to lay low, stay silent. But I was still full of fire." Mr. Herrington shakes his head. Tears rain on his twill pant legs. "We drifted apart. Not a day goes by that I don't regret walking away from her."

I place my hand on Mr. Herrington's knee. He smiles at me warmly—tears pool in his forest colored eyes. Damian's voice snaps us back to the present task.

"Pay attention, we're getting close. I'll make a pass before we commit to stopping. Look for Peace Officers, subversives, anyone out of place. If it looks too hot, we'll come back later."

Taking my eyes off Mr. Herrington, I scan the street. At first, everything seems normal. A never-ending throng of trench coat-wearing, mask-covered people, pushing and pulling past each other. Looking closer, between the momentary pauses in the stream, I see Peace Officers standing sentinel. They are perched against walls and behind lamp posts and are easily missed at first glance.

"I see at least three Peace Officers across the street from the front door," I say.

"They're watching this place too close. We'd never make it over the threshold," Damian says.

"Agreed," says Mr. Herrington. "I'm too old to run or fight. I say we wait until they leave."

"We can still make it in," I say. "If you drop me off up the street, I can find my way through the alley and slip through the window."

"I'm sure they've closed that by now. Besides, there are probably Peace Officers in the alley," Victor says.

"We can't risk you getting caught," says Mr. Herrington. "They already have you on their radar from earlier, and once Fowler finds out you're in custody, they'll either lock you away the rest of your life or execute you. I couldn't bear either scenario."

"We need to know what happened," I say. "We can't wait much longer. I'm willing to take the risk, and no disrespect, but I will do this with or without your permission."

Damian turns around from the driver's seat seething. "Damn it, girl! We're on your side. We want to find out what is going on just as badly as you do, but something has already happened to Margaret, and we can't afford to lose anyone else. There are so few of us."

"I understand your concern, but we can't play it safe. If you wanted to play it safe, we would have never left the house, you would never have tried to bug Fowler, and you certainly wouldn't have invited a complete stranger into your van."

"She has a point, Damian," says Victor. "We won't make any progress—we'll never find anything out—if we are afraid of getting caught. If Evelyn wants to try, we have to let her try. Besides, she's a fighter." Victor points a finger at his swollen eye.

Damian turns back to face the road. "We'll drop you off and then circle around. We'll wait near where we dropped you off, but we can't risk more than ten or fifteen minutes. If you don't make it back in time, we'll return to Mr. Herrington's until nightfall and then we'll try again."

"Understood. I'm ready when you are."

Mr. Herrington shakes his head but offers my hand a gentle squeeze.

Damian pulls the van along the curb a half block from Margaret's house. He puts the van in park and it jerks to a stop. I fumble with the new mask making sure it's sealed then I pull the door open and step out. Turing around to close the door, Mr. Herrington puts his hand up to stop me.

"Good luck, Miss Brennan."

I nod to him and then close the door. Moving to the alley, I hear the van pull off. I focus on the task ahead, trying to remember the path I took before. The chase was a blur, but it doesn't take long before the cragged stones and oddities in the alley's construction give me enough visual clues to find my way. Darting from cover to cover, I keep a constant lookout for Peace Officers. My feet splash in the puddles with soft plops that are deafening in the silence.

My worries don't come to fruition, and I find my way back

to the window with ease. During the chase, the distance from the street to the window had felt like miles and taken hours to traverse. In reality, the window is only a two-minute walk at a slow sneaking pace. It's amazing how circumstances can totally alter your perception. I only have eight minutes left, and I need two in order to get back to the street, so I waste no time on the window. It's closed like Victor thought it would be, but it isn't locked. It slides open on the first try.

Because I'm not being chased, I lower myself down feet first. Landing gracefully, I remain crouched and scan the room. They've ransacked the place. Every box has been busted open and their contents spilled across the floor. But after sweeping the storage room over twice, I see no evidence of movement. Keeping low, I creep toward the kitchen.

Stepping over strewn and broken things, I see Margaret's life in snippets. Pictures in the countryside, birthdays, happy moments intermingled with bright floral dresses, wide-brimmed hats, and high heel shoes. These must be the remnants of her life before prison, before torture. Reaching the door to the kitchen, I press my ear up to it and listen carefully for the distinctive sound of a Peace Officer's rebreather. I listen for as long as I dare with the clock ticking down on me. Satisfied with the lack of noise on the other side, I twist the handle. Halfway open, the door lets out a shrill creak.

I freeze.

Holding onto the door with crushing force, I listen for

anything suspicious.

Thud. Thud. Thud. My heart beats so hard I nearly mistake it for approaching footsteps. Running out of time, I can't wait to be certain. I push the door open the rest of the way and enter the kitchen.

The kitchen and adjacent living room have been completely scoured. Cabinet doors stand open or hang precariously from broken hinges. All the dishes have been pulled out, forming a pile of broken glasses and shattered ceramics on the floor. Stepping cautiously over the sharp pieces of broken glass, I move into the living room. The couch and chairs have been cut open—their stuffing covers everything like snowfall. The paintings have been sliced in half. The walls busted open with hammers.

I venture beyond into the bedroom and bathroom to find them in a similar state. Everything has been turned over, ripped open, or smashed. Margaret's once bright and inviting house is now ominous and foreboding. Margaret is nowhere to be seen. They must have carted her back to jail. That must have been horrible for her. Wherever she is, she doesn't deserve this.

With no evidence of Margaret or a note of any kind, I turn to leave. Passing back through the kitchen, I slow down to navigate the broken glass and see something out of place on the table. The table is the only piece of furniture in the state I saw it last. Probably because it stands bare except for a full cup of tea.

I rush to the table and topple the cup. The dark liquid pours out, spilling over the tabletop, revealing her hidden message. A common thumb-sized info disk. I snatch it out of the liquid. I rush back into the storage room and sprint to the window. Placing the info disk in my coat pocket, I jump up and grab the ledge. Injured and sapped, hoisting myself through the gap takes everything I've got.

In the alley, I cast two quick glances left and right to make sure I'm alone then push the window shut again as best as I can. I don't know how much time I've used up, but it feels like I'm cutting it close. Wanting to make up for lost time, I run as swiftly as my dwindling energy allows. After the repeated twists and turns, I emerge back at the street and slow to a walk. My mask conceals my heaving breaths.

The street was busy when they dropped me off, but it's now choked with pedestrians and soot-marred cars. I push through to the edge of the curb and look for the van. It's close, only ten meters away. The van comes to life, taillights glowing red. He's getting ready to leave. I could rush out into the street and wave them down, but that would draw too much attention. I push back into the crowd. I can make it if I hurry.

Going upstream I fight for every step. My shoulders are numb from being whacked by focused commuters. Nearly there, a glimmer of violet stops me dead. Only wearing a half mask, his violet eyes shine unfiltered from under his cowl. He locks eyes with me. My blood runs cold. He's closing in, the current hurrying him along. I stumble backward—I don't want to turn my back on him. The people between us part enough for me to catch a glint of the garrote pulled taut between his fists. If I don't make it to the van, I'm dead. There isn't enough time for me to make the distance before they drive off. I have to risk it.

I push the woman between us hard in the chest. She topples back into the violet-eyed assassin and I burst into the street.

Damian is cutting into traffic and is about to pull away from the curb.

Weaving through honking cars, I race to the van waving my arms. The van stops. The door opens as I run up. The instant my whole body is inside, Damian slams the gas. He swings the van into the opposite lane to break away from the traffic. I struggle to take a seat and buckle up while Mr. Herrington closes the door. As soon as the door slams shut, they start in on me.

"Are you crazy?" Damian says. "There is no way they didn't see that. We'll have to loop around the city for hours to lose them."

"Were you able to find anything?" asks Victor.

"What of Margaret—did you see her?" asks Mr. Herrington.

I gasp trying to catch my breath. The mask stifles ever gulp so I rip it off.

"I had to, he saw me. I was dead if he didn't." I pause, inhaling sharply through my nose.

"Wait, what? Peace Officers? Are you okay?" Mr. Herrington rests a gentle hand on my knee.

My heart is going a million miles a minute. *Just breathe, Evelyn.* I nod yes while I get ahold of myself.

"No, it was one of Fowler's men—his eyes. I recognized him from the room they tortured me in. And no, I didn't see Margaret. The house was torn apart, but I didn't see any evidence of violence."

"Let's be thankful for that at least," says Mr. Herrington.

"I did find this," I hold the info disk out for them to see. "She hid it for me in a cup of tea."

"Some good news is better than none," says Victor. "We'll have to stop by the Uptown safe house to view it. Mr. Herrington doesn't own a computer."

"Never trusted those damnable things," Mr. Herrington shakes his head. "They're built by the Caretakers after all—there is no telling what sorts of eavesdropping they're capable of."

"A valid point, but it's hard to live without them."

"I'll disagree with you there, Victor."

Damian clears his throat theatrically. "Regardless of how you feel about computers, we need one. I'll take us to the Uptown safe house, but I'm not even looking in that direction until I'm absolutely certain we aren't being followed. If you want to get some rest, this would be the time."

"Wise plan Damian. I think I might get a few winks. Car rides can be very relaxing. You should try and rest too, Evelyn.

CHAPTER TWENTY-TWO

You're recovering well, but you need rest to heal."

"I'll try."

Damian drives slow and steady. I drift off to sleep, but I find no rest. The suffering I've caused Victoriana and Margaret haunts me. In a twisted nightmare, I watch over and over as a sinister version of myself lashes them as they plead with me, "What did I do?" After witnessing this cruel illusion for an immeasurable span of time, the dream reforms and I am once again inhabiting the body of Antonius Neptus. My finger pulls the trigger that kills a revolution.

I wake suddenly. Mr. Herrington is shaking me softly by the shoulder.

"We're here, Miss Brennan."

Wiping away condensation on the window, I see the telltale signs of the setting sun just before we pass into a garage and concrete replaces the view. This garage is much larger than Mr. Herrington's. Wide enough for four vans, our footsteps echo in the vaulted space.

"How do you afford to pay for a place like this?"

"Our group is larger than the three of us. We have a few dozen members, and some of them can afford to pay the insane rent needed to have a place like this so close to Centrum," Mr. Herrington says.

Damian leads the way to the door at the other end of the

garage. He holds it open for us revealing a sparsely furnished loft. It was probably a warehouse or a factory then at some point someone turned it into living space. A compact, well-stocked kitchen sits off to the left. Along the far side are four sets of bunk beds made up with white sheets and tan blankets, and a row of dressers. Lockers, some with heavy padlocks, line the wall to the right and in the middle of the space is a computer terminal and a few mismatched chairs.

Mr. Herrington steps up to the wall of lockers, grabs a lock and drops it. The clang echoes in the cavernous room.

"Victor, Damian, what's going on here? Where did these come from?"

Damian pushes himself between Mr. Herrington and the lockers.

"Emergency supplies. Best to keep them locked up. Don't want them running off before we need them."

"What sort of emergency supplies?" Mr. Herrington turns to Victor. "Did you know about this?"

Victor shakes his head, "No. This is the first I'm hearing about it."

"Damian, I don't like the—"

"Ando helped me arrange it."

"That's fine, but I don't like there being secrets in the group. Open communication is key. I don't want you and Ando sneaking around making decisions that should be made by all of us."

"We did decide, just not with you." Damian steps past Mr. Herrington knocking him with his shoulder. Victor flinches. I try to melt into the wall. Mr. Herrington's composure is unflappable.

"We'll discuss it later, but right now I think we're all a bit hungry. How does chili sound?" Mr. Herrington pushes past Damian and heads to the kitchen. Damian fumes for a moment then makes for the garage. Victor holds a hand up to stop him, but he waves him off. Damian slams the door. Utensils clank in the kitchen. A wave of paprika and garlic hits my nose.

Victor is still stunned, so I try to break the tension.

"I guess he's grumpy when he's hungry?"

Victor cracks a smile and shakes his head.

"I don't know what's up with him lately. He's been on such a short fuse. I'd go check on him, but it'll just make things worse."

I put a hand on his shoulder. "I'm sorry."

"Thanks. But don't worry about it. Just the usual drama."

Victor lets out a heavy sigh. "It's going to take me a minute to see what's on that info disk. If you'd like to clean up, the bathroom is through that door." Victor gestures to the door marked W/C in the middle of the left-hand wall.

"Search through the first dressers—there should be some new clothes that fit you. By the time you shower and change,

I'll have the info disk ready to read."

"Thank you, Victor."

I pull the info disk from my pocket and hand it over. He takes it—his eyes lingering on mine. I stare back and his cheeks practically burst into flames. Twisting away he sprints over to the computer terminal. The terminal glows to life, and he sets to typing on the projected light keyboard.

I shake my head—*boys*.

In definite need of a little space, I follow Victor's suggestion and walk over to the first dresser. Inside are neatly stacked clean jumpsuits. *Great, more jumpsuits.* They're labeled by size descending from biggest to smallest. I find one my size then rummage through the other drawers until I've found a full complement of underwear.

The bathroom looks a lot like mine at home with a minimalist aesthetic of clean lines and glass. Hot water feels great against my aching muscles. But the instant I apply soap, I find a dozen cuts and scrapes I didn't realize I had. Their collective sting drowns out any relief. The water gurgling down the drain is a sickening mixture of black, brown, and red.

Looking down, my body is a kaleidoscope of yellow, green, and purple bruises. I lean against the wall and try to relax in the jet of steaming water. The tiredness I've been trying to suppress calls to me. I want desperately to curl up on the tile floor and fall asleep in the water's warm embrace. The only thing stopping me is the nagging at the back of my mind that I have more important things to do.

I turn the faucet, and the warm, comforting torrent of water ceases instantly. Without the heat and steam of the water, my skin turns to gooseflesh. Reality washes back over me. I dress quickly and return to the loft.

They're all seated around the table. I see none of the tension has cleared out. Each has a bowl of chili in front of them. An extra bowl sits waiting for me. I take the space they made for me and take a deep sniff of the chili. I've never been a huge fan of chili, but this smells amazing.

"Don't be shy," Mr. Herrington says smiling. "Dig in everyone." The room fills with the clanking of spoons. The chili is spicy, savory, and just a little bit sweet. It satisfies my hunger and blunts an edge I didn't realize I had. We all finish about the same time. I walk around, collect the bowls, and deposit them in the sink.

"Thank you, Mr. Herrington, I can't tell you how much I needed that."

"My pleasure, young lady. I think we all did."

Damian shoots Mr. Herrington a nasty look but holds his tongue. Victor jumps up from his seat and returns to the computer terminal.

"Okay, everyone, I'll play it if you're ready."

"Let's see it," Damian says pulling up a chair next to Victor.

Victor's fingers dance in the projected interface. Margaret's face shimmers to life in the display.

"I haven't much time. They're onto us. Hopefully, you got out of there in one piece. I'm sorry I had to put this on you, honey—truly I am. But if you're watching this, you must have seen what was stored inside the sphere. I hope it was as damning as we'd hoped."

Margaret looks to her left—her eyes wide with panic. There is a booming off camera. She turns back to the lens—all the blood has vanished from her face.

"They're at the door. I have information hidden on this disk. Bernie will know the password. Use it to take them…"

The screen fills with static. My heart races. Victor shuts off the recording. The desperation in her voice has stunned us into silence and it's a long while before anyone dares break the stillness.

"It looks like she made this just in time. I'll look for the hidden files right away," says Victor.

"Do any of you know who Bernie is?" I ask.

Mr. Herrington blushes. "I'm Bernie. I prefer Bernard, but Margaret always insists on calling me, Bernie."

Victor swivels around in his chair. "I think I've found the files. What do you think the password is?"

"It's a secret I vowed never to share with anyone but Margaret. If you don't mind, I'd like to keep it that way. I'll type it myself."

"As you wish," Victor throws his hands up in surrender. "Just fill in the open box and hit execute."

Victor steps back from the terminal. Mr. Herrington rises from his chair—a few joints crackle and pop—and takes over behind the command console. He looks lost for a moment then with slow, deliberate strikes against the projected input board he hammers out the password and strikes 'execute.' Victor, Damian, and I share an amused look. The file opens, and dozens of folders flood out.

"I'll sift through all of this and try and make heads or tails of it," Victor says. He waves Mr. Herrington away from the controls.

"I'll go call everyone in," says Damian. "This is big. Everyone needs to know what's going on."

Damian and Victor go straight away to their self-appointed tasks leaving Mr. Herrington and me with nothing to do but wait.

"I think I'm going to lie down for a while, Miss Brennan. A man my age can only handle so much excitement in one day. The cots are comfortable and clean if you're so inclined."

The thought of sleep is appealing, but the knowledge that I'll dream gives me pause.

"You go ahead, Mr. Herrington, I think I'll stay with Victor and help him look through the files."

"All right, but remember, you may be young but you're not a robot—you need to rest sometimes."

Mr. Herrington claps me on the shoulder then makes his way to one of the eight bunks. Pulling my chair next to Victor, I watch over his shoulder as he pores through spreadsheets and candid videos of Margaret speaking with Fowler. It doesn't take long for us to figure out something earthshattering is coming.

CHAPTER TWENTY-THREE

IT TAKES A FEW HOURS for the group to assemble. Observing from the far corner, I watch them come in ones and twos. Soon the group grows to thirty-two people. I study each of their faces as they come in. I don't recognize any of them. I could have passed these people a hundred times on the street, but with everyone always hiding behind their masks, it's impossible to know. They range from teenagers to middle age, but Mr. Herrington is the oldest member by far. Most of them are men. I count only five women besides myself. They each look poised and confident. Staring maybe a little too hard, I catch eyes with one of them. She's a stocky woman with silver-gray hair. Her forearms are covered in a swirl of bright multi-colored tattoos. She nods her head at me curtly. I nod back blushing.

Damian steps in front of the gathering. The murmuring stops—the woman breaks our staring contest. *I guess I win.* He waits until he has all eyes, even mine, on him before he begins.

"We are waiting on Charles," he says in a theatrical command voice, "then we can begin. What Victor, and our newest member—he aims a finger at me. Five dozen eyes turn on me sending my stomach into flips—Evelyn Brennan, have discovered is going to disturb you, so get a glass of water or whatever now, you may not feel like it after this."

The assembled group migrates to the kitchen. Their indistinct conversations swell to fill the vaulted room. With concerned faces and impassioned voices, they speculate wildly. Seeing me alone in the corner, Victor walks over to me.

"Doing the meet and greet with thirty-odd people can be a nightmare. Don't worry, you'll get to know everyone eventually."

"Who's that woman with the tattoos?" I say suggesting with my head which way he should look.

"You must be talking about Umeko Ando. Kind of intense right? She's really cool though. Come on, I'll introduce you."

Victor reaches out to grab my arm, but I pull away.

"What's wrong? Is it the files? We'll discuss it with everyone in a minute. Don't worry, we'll come up with a plan."

"I know your group will come up with a plan, and they'll figure things out for themselves, but I need to come up with my own plan."

"You're not alone in this anymore—we're a team."

"I understand that—and I do feel safer knowing I have a group at my back—but with the coming storm, I don't want to lose my family. It may be selfish, but I need to get them to safety. I need to find a way to convince Mother to let go of her fears, to break free from the prison she's built for herself."

"I don't think that's selfish at all. In fact, I think the whole group needs to be considering their families right now. I already know what direction Damian is going to try and take us, but if the both of us offer a less reactionary, level-headed response, we might be able to keep things from getting out of hand."

"So you think Damian is actually committed to fighting? Doesn't he realize that is what they want him to do? Violence against the Caretakers only strengthens their position."

"I agree—believe me, I do. I don't want to see Damian throw his life away, or anyone else's."

"Together then, we'll convince them to approach this rationally."

Victor smiles. The swelling is virtually gone, but his eye is still black and blue. The commotion in the kitchen dies down for a second—Charles is here. Charles Standish.

He walks straight into the crowd shaking hands and saying his pleasantries. He seems so much more alive than I've ever seen him before. It's amazing how different people are when they're surrounded by friends. Damian stops pacing and retakes his spot of authority.

"Nice of you to make it, Charles. Okay everyone, gather around the computer terminal. Victor is going to project what we've found. Try and keep your comments down until we've gone through the information. After that, I would like to propose a plan of action."

Stepping out of the corner, I inch toward the growing huddle.

"Victor and I also have a plan we would like to propose." A sea of quizzical faces blink at me. "I look forward to meeting you all." They are all smiles and nods—I want to puke.

Only Standish seems unsure of how to act. We make eye contact for an instant then he starts incessantly glancing at the door. Damian interjects before I can walk over to him and convince him that I'm not my mother.

"Play it, Victor."

Victor's fingers dance on the keyboard bringing the terminal to life. The videos, images, and spreadsheets we uncovered project onto the small screen. Everyone shuffles a little closer to see.

"The first thing I'm going to show you is a video conversation between Margaret Waters and Undersecretary Ursula Fowler, the subversives' program operator. This video was shot without Fowler's knowledge."

The video glows to life. The familiar, bright living room comes on the screen. Everything is neat and clean. The time stamp on the video shows it was taken almost two years ago. Fowler enters the room and takes a seat in an armchair. Margaret brings tea, sets it on the coffee table, then sits on the couch as far away from Fowler as she can.

"The tea is a touching gesture, but this is not a social call. I'm here to discuss the terms of your parole."

"Which terms do you mean?"

"The contract you signed upon release obliged you to work for the Great Society if ever the Caretakers required. Well now is such a time." Fowler leans back—her eyes narrow as she chooses her words. "I oversee a program that is desperately short of personnel. You will act as my recruiter."

"What kind of program?"

"That is none of your concern. You need only do what you are told."

"And what If I don't?"

"Then I'll throw you back in a cell, or I'll send you to the coal pits. It all depends on how generous I'm feeling that day."

Margaret picks up her mug. Her quivering hands splash most of the tea out on the way to her lips.

"Recruiter? I don't know very many people, and how do I know what kind of people to recruit if I don't know what the program does? Maybe I'm not the woman for the job."

"Believe me, you are. You won't have to find the people yourself. We'll find them and push them in your direction. All you have to do is answer the door, pour them some tea, and convince them that they are on the right path."

"And which path is that?"

"Mine. I'll give you a script of what to say and things to give them. You are a stepping stone for them, nothing more, but a vital stepping stone. You will weed out the smart and the driven and send me the docile and dependent."

"You seem capable. Why not just do it yourself?"

"Because I don't have to. You will do it, or I'll find someone else. It's a simple choice, really. Where would you like to wake up tomorrow?"

Margaret gulps down the rest of her tea. Her hands quivering, she sets the mug down with a clank.

"Tell me what to do then."

"Wise choice."

The video cuts out. The murmuring in the group grows into a buzz.

"Settle down everyone. I know that you have a lot of questions, but Margaret has put together spreadsheets and documents outlining what Fowler's plan is. She's already pieced it together for us. Here, this should fill in the blanks."

Victor's fingers twirl on the input projection making the documents and spreadsheets appear.

The crowd grumbles.

"What does that say?"

"It's too small I can't read it!"

"Simmer down everyone," says Victor. "I encourage you to read them over at your own leisure later, but Evelyn and I have already read through them, so I will do my best to summarize. We already knew Fowler oversaw the subversives' program and that she was close to activating it, but what we didn't know is that she has her own agenda. The last time the program was activated, she determined that with enough pressure and prolonged violence she could set the stage for a successful coup against the Caretakers and seize power for herself. Over the last two years, she has been building her army in secret. Using the Oracle Device, she indoctrinates her initiates far beyond the level Peace Officers and Guardians receive. She's totally rewired them to her way of thinking."

"How is that even possible?" asks a voice from the crowd. "Yeah, your brain turns to mush right?" asks another. The group mumbles and nods.

"We're not sure exactly," Mr. Herrington says. "But we believe it has something to do with the Oracle Device itself. It seems to be more capable of this kind of brute-force brain rewiring than even the modern imprint devices. If you study the power consumption records, you can see that it's drawing nearly as much power as Einsam itself."

The group is abuzz. Victor waves his arms to regain their attention. "According to Margaret's estimation, Fowler has ten thousand fully indoctrinated subversives ready to launch her coup."

There is a collective gasp. Rising voices threaten to carry the conversation in a hundred different directions. Mr. Herrington raises his hands and they quiet down.

"That's not the worst of it—there's more. Margaret was able to learn the zero hour for Fowler's operation—daybreak tomorrow."

The groups' murmuring erupts into a cacophonous roar. Damian seizes the moment. His booming voice cuts through the din. He stands by the bolted lockers—everyone turns to face him.

"There's no more time for talking—we need to act. The people need to know what's going on. They need to know who the subversives really are—that Fowler is about to set the world on fire. We need to strike now."

"Hear, hear!" the group cries out.

"I propose we arm ourselves and gain entry into the television broadcast center. From there we can communicate with everyone—the whole nation—all at once. Once the message is out, we'll go to the Under City, empty the factories and march with legions of workers at our back. We'll march all the way to the Halls of Power!"

Mr. Herrington grasps Damian by the shoulder. "This is madness! And with what weapons..." his voice trails off with his hand. He staggers over to the bolted lockers. Damian puffs up.

"It's no secret that our methods have always been..." he

lingers a dramatic beat, "…Passive. That may be well and good, but it's too late for that. The hour is upon us. I accepted Nightingale's assistance on our behalf," he gestures to the row of lockers, "and now we have the means to swiftly, and decisively, act. Who's with me?"

A pause. Tension boils the air. Murmuring. Everyone is spinning, trying to figure out where their neighbors stand.

"About bloody time."

"Death to the Caretakers!"

A near-unanimous cheer rises from the group. Ice pours down my back. One middle-aged man in a finely tailored suit with gray nipping at his temples turns and runs out the door.

"Let the coward run," Damian says swatting the air with the back of his hand.

I flinch as the door slams shut. Mr. Herrington is wobbling and vacant. Victor is backing away from the group.

I scamper up onto a chair so that everyone can see me. "What Damian wants to do is wrong, and you all know it. We want to unseat the Caretakers from power *because* they resort to violence, fear, and intimidation. If you march armed into the streets, you are committing the very acts you rebel against! You cannot win freedom from oppression with bullets and fists. It's too late for us to stop Fowler, but we need to stay resolved as a group. We need to champion peace, not stoke the flames of revenge. Instead of fighting, we should all be making sure our friends and families are safe. We need to be patient. We need to lay a proper foundation."

"Enough talk!" says Damian. "This girl speaks as if she has truly felt the weight of the Caretaker's boot on her neck. As if she has trembled in her sleep fearing the Peace Officer's baton. I will take up arms and fight alone if need be. Those who wish to slink away until the danger has passed, run off with Peter—be my guest—but know that when we've won our victory, I'll not suffer a coward beside me."

Victor, sensing that we're losing the crowd to Damian's fiery rhetoric, clambers up onto his own chair.

"Evelyn may not be from the streets, but she knows how the Caretakers think, how they'll spin our actions against us. Please, I beg you. Don't do this. If you go out now, the people you claim to be fighting for will mistake you for subversives. Killing Peace Officers will only galvanize everyone against us. Fuck Nightingale. Did you stop to think maybe they're wrapped up in Fowler's plot? You're playing right into their hands. Don't do this, Damian. We all need to stop and think about this."

"I've had my whole life to think, Victor. I'd rather die this instant than live another day licking boot."

"I..." Tears stream down Victor's face. Mr. Herrington stands motionless beside him—his eyes glassy and distant. Damian locks eyes with Victor—disgust curls his lips.

"To arms!"

His call to action whips the group into a riotous fervor. Chest up, shoulders back, he strides with pride to the bolted lockers, produces the key, opens the padlocks, and flings the doors open with a dramatic flourish. *Can he not see himself? Does he really think he's the hero?* The lockers are bursting at the seams with assault rifles, ammunition, and grenades. Damian picks up a rifle, slams in a magazine, and racks the charging handle. *Shick clack.*

The group hesitates—events have gone from figurative to literal—and even the most zealous among them can't stop the anxious gnawing in their guts. Each of them weighs their next course of action against what they think their neighbors will choose. A lanky thirty-something man with deep-set eyes breaks out of the huddle and picks up a rifle. Damian embraces him.

"Come on," the man says. He follows Damian across the room to the exit.

Umeko steps up and takes a rifle. The tide shifts. The group surges to the lockers, arming themselves to the teeth. Mr. Herrington, Victor and I are frozen, helpless to stop them. Person after person, gun after gun, they file by the locker and out the door—all except one: Mr. Standish.

The last person exiting the safe house slams the door behind them—it reverberates like a cannon blast. We linger in the echo trying to regain our composure. Mr. Standish breaks the silence.

"That didn't go well."

"No," I say. "Not at all."

"When I saw you here," Charles says walking over to join us. "I thought we had been infiltrated—given who your mother is. But hearing you speak just now, I have no doubt you're one of us."

"Thanks, Mr. Standish. Sorry I couldn't stop them."

"Please, call me Charles. This wasn't on you to stop. I can hardly believe what just happened. Damian's been planting those seeds for so long—I never thought they'd bear fruit. We should have never gotten tangled up with Nightingale, but it's hard to see how we're going to do this peacefully."

I turn to the now empty lockers and shake my head. "I wish I had an answer for you. All I know is that we need to get our families, and ourselves to safety. We can't lose hope."

Mr. Herrington's composure finally breaks. He falls to one knee. Tears stream down his face. We rush over to him and help him up into a chair.

"I failed him."

"You didn't fail him, Bernard. You gave him every opportunity—showed him the right way." Mr. Herrington clasps his hands on Charles's cheeks.

"Perhaps you're right. But it hurts Charles—I can hardly breathe."

Charles pulls Mr. Herrington into his hulking arms.

"It's going to turn out all right Bernard. You'll see."

"Thank you, Charles." Mr. Herrington closes his eyes, fills his lungs, holds it, then lets it all go. His eyes blink open. Everything bottled back up, he turns his attention to me.

"Your plan is a good one Miss Brennan, but alas, you three are the only family I have left."

"The same goes for me." Victor rubs at his good eye. "Olivia—my sister—she moved to Lufthaffen years ago, and besides her, this group is it. Was it…"

"What about you Charles?" A tinge of guilt grips me for not knowing if he even has a family.

Charles nods his head. "This might work. We can pick up Cornelia and Georgette from Centrum Arcadia when we go to pick up your father—kill two birds with one stone, so to speak."

Embarrassment flashes across my face. "You and your family—you live there too?"

"Really? You must have seen us."

Shame clobbers me in the gut. I can't manage any words, so I shake no.

"Can't say I blame you, we don't get a lot of visitors in the basement."

Mr. Herrington cuts in before I burst into flames. "Doesn't Miss Brennan have a mother you're forgetting about?"

"No, he's right, Mr. Herrington," I say. "We should go there to get my father. My mother won't leave."

"That's a shame. I do hope you can convince her to come with us. Regardless, Victor and I will do everything we can to help."

"Hopefully Damian left us the van," Victor says turning to look at the door to the garage.

"I hope so—I'm no spring chicken. And I don't think Charles wants to have to carry me all the way there."

Charles laughs. "Come on you old bird." He waves for us to follow him.

By some miracle, the van is still there. The last one out, I switch the lights off behind me then pass through the door into the garage.

CHAPTER TWENTY-FOUR

THE KEYS ARE STILL IN THE IGNITION. I get in first and let Charles close the door. Victor helps Mr. Herrington into the front passenger seat then buckles in behind the wheel. The van rumbles to life. Flipping the lights on, Victor opens the garage door and pulls out into the lamp-lit street.

"If you head straight six blocks, then take a left and go two more it'll be on the corner. Can't miss it," Charles says.

"Sounds like a short trip then," says Mr. Herrington. "Keep your eyes open for Peace Officers, subversives, anyone that looks out of place. Fowler knows where Evelyn lives so they might be laying a trap for her. If the front is being watched do you know a back way into the building?"

"Of course. One block up there is an alley. It's real narrow, but it leads to the garbage pickup and service entrance. You need a code to get in, so I doubt they'll be watching it."

"If that's the case," Victor looks back over his shoulder, "let's just head straight there. No reason to risk being spotted in the front if we can go around back."

"Agreed."

Even with a plan, I'm drowning in anxiety. With Charles's knowledge of the building, I don't think we'll have any problems getting to our families unseen, but convincing Mother to leave gives me pause. She is so attached to her reality that I don't know if there is a way to get through to her. No matter how minuscule the chance is though, I have to take it.

The streets are choked. Traffic surges and stops in sporadic jerks. The harsh neon of the billboards above colors the chaos red. Vehicles backed up at traffic lights belch black exhaust to mingle with the relentless shower of soot and ash from above. Like the belly of a malevolent beast, the tides of filth turn without end.

The world outside the van mirrors the maelstrom of nerves writhing in my stomach. With each passing minute, we grow closer to the apartment, and I grow closer to nausea. How will I convince Mother to leave? Will I be able to get her out the door? Will she let me leave again or will her fingers dig into me and never let me go? Even if I get her to leave with us, Father may not be home. He has been getting home so late it could be another hour or two before he stumbles through the door. Could I wait that long? Could I stall Mother, keep her from changing her mind?

The questions, doubts, and fears of the coming confrontation have been brewing for months, but up until now, they were fictions, another day's hardships. Now that they press upon me, I fear I'm not ready to answer them.

As Victor turns into the alley, the roaring volcano inside me threatens to burst. I have to close my eyes and breathe in through my nose to keep myself together. I take another deep breath and hold it. Calming my racing mind, I take these final moments to regain composure.

Cutting the headlights, Victor pulls the van behind the massive garbage bin. The service entrance shares little resemblance to the polished façade of the entrance hall. Ash mounds high beside a small mountain of trash waiting to be collected.

"After you two go inside, I'll turn the van around and keep it ready to go. I don't know how long it will take you, so we'll wait patiently. But be as quick as you can. The city feels off tonight—on edge." Victor's words are steady, but his darting eyes betray his anxiety. The ride over must have been plaguing his mind too.

"Don't worry Miss Brennan, I won't let him leave without you." Mr. Herrington says, smiling. Even now he radiates with a collected calm I couldn't fake if I wanted to.

"I appreciate that, Mr. Herrington." In a flash, images of him parenting me dance gleefully in my mind. A different childhood, a different life, but a better one I think.

I lean forward and give Mr. Herrington a kiss on the cheek.

"For luck," I say.

Charles opens the door and clambers out. I jump out after him.

"Stay close. I'll take us through some maintenance passages to the service elevator. From there I'll let you go up to the top, and I'll head to the bottom. When you have your parents, it should be as easy as retracing your steps," says Charles.

He sprints to the door lit up by the single yellow bulb hanging above it and punches in the code. The door clicks open, and we waste no time getting inside. The wind grabs it slamming it closed behind us with a crash. The point of no return.

Charles starts down the hallway. I stop him with a hand on his shoulder—he turns to look at me.

"Good luck, and thank you, Charles."

Charles grins then leads the way down the service hallways. The farther we venture into these utility tunnels, the more it strikes me how little I know of this building. The areas I normally use are shining and clean. At their narrowest, the hallways are wide enough to stand two abreast, and the lofty ceilings are filled with soft white light. The service paths, on the other hand, are hardly distinguishable from the alleys outside. The veneer of civilization is paper-thin.

We twist and turn through the building at Charles's urgent pace. Without him here to guide me I don't know if I'd ever make it to the elevator. In a repeating pattern of concrete walls snaked with wires, the elevator could easily be missed. Charles pulls open the control box and calls it.

"We'll head to the top first. That should give you some more time. It should be easy for me to grab my family, they've been ready for a day like this, but I think you're going to need a miracle to get your mother out of that apartment."

"Good thing I saved my last one."

I give Charles a sarcastic wink. He grins in amusement. The elevator opens breaking our moment of levity. I step in first. A heavy odor of garbage, oil, and coal hangs heavy in the stagnant air. Charles follows and presses the button for my floor. The elevator jerks to life. I reach out and grab the wall to keep from falling. Instead of the soft whirring I normally enjoy in the residence elevator there is a high-pitched squealing and grinding. *Great, we're going to die in this stupid thing.*

The elevator jerks again at the top and the doors grind open.

"Just retrace your steps, and I'll see you and your parents in the van."

"It will be nice to meet your family," I say.

Charles smiles. I crouch low and step out. The elevator doors close behind me with a sense of finality. Alone in the hallway, I scan my surroundings to get my bearings. Looking at the door numbers, I should be able to turn the corner in front of me, go down six doors, and be at my apartment. At least it's close.

Crouching up to the corner, I take a quick glance up and

down the hallway in both directions. Empty. Standing up, I run down the hall. One, two, three, four, five. Stopping on six I take a quick breath then grab the knob. The door is unlocked and swings in at my touch. This can't be good. Not ready to face what's inside, I press on anyway.

The room is brightly lit. Looking straight down the hallway I see Father sitting on the couch facing me. His face is pale—he's dancing a lit cigarette on his knee. Mother is out of sight, but already I know something is very, very wrong.

The television's light isn't blaring in the windows and Father is making no attempt to greet me. I'm walking into a trap, but what other options do I have? I step cautiously down the hall. Passing the empty kitchen, I step into the living room.

The trap is sprung.

Mother stands by her bedroom door—she's not wearing her mask. For the first time in months, I can see her face. It's a far cry from what I remember. Her eyes are sunken into black pits. Her skin has faded to the point of being nearly translucent—even across the room, I can see the web of slender blue veins crisscrossing underneath. She looks dead inside.

I could have stayed locked on her for hours, studying the decay, but a looming presence in the background pulls my eyes away. Standing behind her are two Peace Officers—their rifles low and at the ready.

"Arrest her!" His words hack through me to the bone searing

through my nerves like fork-tongued lightning.

I have been tortured, stabbed, bashed, and pushed to the edges of human endurance but this overshadows everything. I'm dumbfounded. I thought he loved me. I had assumed Mother could do something like this, but never Father. I didn't know him at all. The realization of how little I know cripples me. Whatever love he has for me is weaker than his duty to the state.

The Peace Officers obey his command. They swoop in, rifles leveled at my chest. Incapable of processing what's happening, my legs turn to concrete, and I can do little but tremble in the doorway. Everything is slipping away. They're nearly on me. Their eyes are void—their breaths metallic and unnatural. They're beside the couch now. Only a few more steps and it's all over.

There's no way out.

In a flash, Mother springs forward and grabs hold of the lead Peace Officer's rifle.

"Run!"

Her words reawaken me. Without hesitation, I spin around and run as fast as I ever have.

Bang! Bang! Bang!

Three gunshots ring out. My world explodes. I stumble to the ground—everything liquid static. My body picks itself back up and forces me to run—my mind ripping and pulling on my sanity trying to free itself from this nightmare. Tears stream down my face. Only Mother's desire for me to live keeps me from giving up. All that I love has been ripped away in a muzzle flash.

I reach the service elevator and hit the call button. Survival and adrenaline push my agony aside—the world blurs into a tunnel of intense focus.

The doors aren't opening.

I slam the heel of my fist on the call button in a frantic flurry. Charles lives in the basement—the elevator may not be able to climb fast enough to reach me before they find me. Trembling, I move to the corner. Maybe I can take the rifle from him before he uses it on me and by then the elevator will come? No sooner have I thought about the rifle than one of them bursts into view.

I react on instinct. Grabbing the barrel of the rifle, I shove it back into his face as hard as I can. The butt of the rifle connects with his rebreather with a sharp crack. It jars him enough that he loses his grip on the weapon.

I flip the rifle around without thinking—borrowed instincts at my command. My sweaty hands clutch desperately to the handle. The Peace Officer raises his baton, ready to strike. I squeeze.

Bang!

The Peace Officer crumbles to the floor. A heartbeat passes, and the second Peace Officer lines up in my sights.

Bang! Bang!

Both rounds rip through him. Holding his chest, he slumps down the wall painting a red streak on the silver foil wallpaper. A pool of bright red blood spreads around his motionless body.

Breathing hysterically, the rifle falls from my quivering hands.

Ding.

The elevator doors grind open. Backpedaling, I trip into the elevator. Picking myself up off the floor, I mash the button for the service entrance. A fleet of brushbots has already materialized from the walls to investigate. The gory scene shrinks away between the narrowing gap in the doors.

The elevator jerks. The world slides over itself.

Mother died to give me a chance and Father just sat there. Now two men are dead because of me. This can't be happening. In less than five minutes I've lost everything. I've lost my family. My principles. My future. How can I hope to show others the truth when I didn't even know the truth about my parents? How can I preach peace with blood on my hands?

I buckle under the weight of it all and weep.

Ding. The elevator opens into the service corridors. I pull myself together and scramble out before the doors close. The tears in my eyes have turned the world into a swirling blur. I reach out and use the hot metal pipes that run exposed along the walls to guide me. Half delirious, I press through the door to the alley.

The amber light above the door sears a jumping red sphere into my vision. I stagger through the deluge of falling ash back to the idling van. I pull the door open and hop inside. Mr. Herrington turns around. The panic in his eyes showers my wounds with salt.

I gulp for air between sobs.

"What on earth happened?"

"No time—look!" Victor says pointing through the front window with a trembling hand.

Four Peace Officers—rifles raised—are coming down the alleyway.

Run!

Mother's fire rekindles my will. "Punch it, Victor—if we stay, we're all dead."

"Hold on," interjects Mr. Herrington putting his hands up in protest. "What about Charles and the girls?"

I lock eyes with him. "Peace Officers were waiting for us… They're not coming."

Mr. Herrington slumps as though someone cut the last string that had been holding him up.

Victor slams the accelerator and the van surges forward.

We hurtle toward the squad of Peace Officers forcing them to jump aside to avoid being hit. They recover fast. Crouched, they take aim and open fire.

Whiz-snap. The rear window shatters and falls away in a shower of broken glass. Bullets ping and thud in the body of the van. The front window quickly follows. Tiny shards of glass cascade off Victor and Mr. Herrington. Dozens of bullets zip through the van before Victor can turn out of the short alleyway.

There is only a narrow opening in traffic for Victor to turn into. Cars slam on their brakes and honk. Victor swerves us into oncoming traffic and narrowly avoids catastrophe by flinging the wheel back hard to the right. My seatbelt yanks me back into the seat.

The car in front of us puts on their brakes to slow for the red light at the intersection. Victor pushes the van to its limits and rams us through the narrow gap between the cars blocking our escape. Metal squeals. Sparks fly. Dodging cross traffic, we zoom through the red light. Victor doesn't let up.

"Everyone all right?" Victor says.

My heart pounds in my chest like a galley drum. Totally numb, I run quivering hands over myself looking for injuries.

"I don't think I'm hit," I say.

"Mr. Herrington, what about you? Are you all right?"

Victor reaches back and grabs Mr. Herrington's shoulder.

His head falls forward, limp. Tears well in Victor's eyes.

"Damn it. Damn it. Damn it. Evelyn, see if he has a pulse."

Struggling against my seatbelt, I turn to inspect him. I push two fingers against the vein in his neck. His skin is clammy—nothing. I reach under his blazer to see if I can feel his heart beating in his chest. I pull back red dripping hands.

"No. No…" The words tumble out of my mouth like hot ash. Everything implodes. Victor wails.

Victor commands the van with reckless abandon. We lurch back and forth as he weaves us through the narrow gaps in traffic—the engine revving ever louder. Passing lights swell and recede into darkness revealing and concealing the blood-stained hands trembling before me.

CHAPTER TWENTY-FIVE

TIME PASSES IN AGONIZING DRIPS. The safe house is as silent as death. Pain and grief reverberate uninterrupted in my mind. My sobbing has long since stopped and has been replaced by a gripping ache in my chest. Victor and I are frozen, kneeling on the icy concrete floor. We clutch at Mr. Herrington's lifeless body in the naïve hope that he might sit up and wake us from this nightmare.

In the course of only a few days, my entire world has crumbled. Every death I've caused and foolish decision I've made since I allowed my hunger for the truth to consume me, replays with excruciating clarity. I'm finally at a point where I don't know how to go on.

Even if I could stand up right now and leave, where would I go? Everyone I know is either dead, missing, or in the same emotionally destroyed state that I am. A dark thought crosses my mind. If I went to the authorities and professed my sincerest regrets for my recent actions maybe they would let me go back to my old life and put all of this behind me.

As the thought bounces around in my head, a feeling brews deep inside my stomach then rises into my throat. Disgust. How can I even think that while lying before me is the body of a man who gave his life for the truth? A man who put his trust and faith in a young girl he had only just met? How can I think that while Victor, who has every reason to push himself away from me, has remained steadfast despite his pain?

The feeling grows stronger. It grows strong enough to break the bonds agony and grief have placed around my lungs. I pull myself off the floor. Electric sprites dance in my legs as blood returns to them. My head swirls. How can I even entertain such thoughts when Mother gave up her life so that I could have mine? Even by thinking such a repulsive and cowardly thing I disrespect the memory of all the people who have sacrificed their lives so that I could be here and possess the knowledge that I do.

I expunge the thought of giving up from my mind. Getting back on my feet has refocused me on the here and now—my aches and pains are first in line for my attention.

Taking one limping step after the other, I reach the kitchen. Opening the cabinet doors, I search through them for painkillers. In the fourth upper cabinet, I find a large white bottle with only the chemical name written out on the cover. I recognize it from the small print on the bottle of painkillers I had at home. Our bottles were always brightly colored sporting names like *Super Maximum Double Strength Ache Busters* or *Head-ache-be-gone.* I dump four of the large capsules into my left hand. I pop them in my mouth then get a handful of water from the tap. As soon as I swallow them, relief washes over me in a wave. Surely a placebo effect, but real or not, I welcome the relief.

The refrigerator holds dozens of plainly packaged meals. Caring little for their flavor at this point, I pull one of the silver packages from the top shelf at random and close the door. Inside are an assortment of other smaller silver packages. I take out one labeled "crackers" and rip it open. I munch on the bland, dry triangles as I walk back over to Victor and Mr. Herrington. I stop behind Victor. His left hand is interlaced with Mr. Herrington's while his right hand strokes his thinning gray hair.

"Are you hungry, Victor?"

Victor's hand stops mid-stroke. He turns and looks up at me—his face ashen. A mountain of sorrow lies behind his bloodshot eyes.

"Thank you, but no."

Ashamed with myself, I nod my head sympathetically and back away. I linger behind him unable to crunch into another cracker. Hunger can wait.

Wishing I had a time machine, I turn back toward the kitchen with the intent of setting the crackers on the counter. I pause mid step—a red diode on the computer terminal is blinking rapidly. Odd, I don't remember seeing that a moment ago.

"Victor, what does that light mean?"

Victor strokes Mr. Herrington's hair one last time, stands, then shambles over to the terminal.

"Blinking light…"

His voice cuts off as his bloodshot eyes register what he sees. In a burst of life, he rushes to sit at the terminal. His fingers dance in the projected keypad, and the screen comes to life.

"It's an alert. I have it set up to flash whenever the networks are transmitting an emergency broadcast. This is bad, this is real bad."

His fingers continue to dance, and as they do, the live stream from the central network fills the screen. What I see sets the hairs on my neck on end.

Standing center screen is Damian. He stands where Rourke normally sits to regurgitate his Caretaker-approved Nightly News. Bullet holes and the unmistakable splatter of blood glisten on the normally drab backdrop.

"People of the Great Society, my compatriots and I have seized the GSBN broadcast tower here in Einsam to put an end to the lies and deception that has spewed over this desk. We are here to give you the truth the Caretakers would rather stay hidden. There are many lies in the Great Society, but the biggest and most profound surrounds each and every one of you right now. The masks you wear. The airlocks you pass through a dozen times a day. The fear and paranoia we all feel. With every breath you take, you reinforce the lies designed to keep you in line. We have become so preoccupied with making sure each breath isn't our last that we've failed to see the atrocities the Caretakers commit against us. We toil in soot and filth, we live like rats in a cage, we have no freedoms, we are nothing beneath their boots! We are beaten and arrested for the most senseless of crimes. Every day thousands upon thousands find themselves in unemployment lines and living with the constant rumble of empty stomachs. Open your eyes! We are citizens, not sheep, and it's time we rise up! The Caretakers must act now or fall. Let them tremble at our collective cry for freedom!"

Damian punches into the air over his head. His eyes are wide and ravenous—a vein throbs in his forehead. Then everything changes.

A loud crack causes the speakers to sizzle with overload. Damian's head bursts open. His body falls out of frame. His blood and gray matter mix with Rourke's on the backdrop.

I double over and retch. My vision blurs. Static gunfire fills the room. I force myself to watch the screen unable to make sense of its projected jumble of chaos.

"What's happening? They killed him? Damian's dead?" I say, barely able to form the words.

"No, no, no. This can't be happening. That fucking idiot. Damn it. Damn it. Damn it all!"

Victor slams his fists on the desk. Fresh tears cover our cheeks. The frame of the camera stays fixed on the gore behind the desk. Only the sounds of rifle fire and shouting give clues to the gun battle raging beyond the frame.

Powerless, I watch Victor shake his head back and forth as he mumbles "Why?"

The sound of shooting stops abruptly. The screen cuts to black.

Victor bursts from his seat sending it clattering to the floor. Holding his hands over his eyes, he storms in my direction. I practically have to jump to get out of his way. Pacing between the kitchen and the terminal, Victor shakes his head and tugs at the hair on his temples.

The addition of Damian's death in his already vulnerable state must have broken the final thread of sanity Victor had. I'm not sure there is anything I can say or do to console him.

Staring at the blank screen, I focus on my breathing and try to digest this mess without shutting down again. A tall order.

Just breathe, Evelyn. Just breathe. A tiny voice guides me out of the depths and back to myself. Victor's pacing slows. He's still clawing his way out of the avalanche of emotions that buries him, but I don't think I've lost him.

The speakers beep sharply, and the screen changes to a gray-and-white image: *Please Stand By.* Victor lets go of his hair and makes his way back over to the terminal. Pulling the chair off the floor, he retakes his seat at the controls. The screen changes again, *5, 4, 3, 2*—the video stream resumes.

The gore-covered studio backdrop is gone, replaced by the yellow-lit cobblestones of Victory Square. In the frame are four of the people who left with Damian. Their arms are bound behind backs, their knees tremble against the harsh stones. Two of them I don't know. The third is the man who first spoke up for Damian. And the fourth is Umeko. Their faces are hidden by gas masks, but they are undeniably petrified.

Four Peace Officers loom over them pressing rifles into the backs of their heads. The sound of approaching footsteps reinforces the building dread—each step a timpani hit in an overture of terror. Entering the frame in front of them is a sinewy Peace Officer Commandant. Six silver diamonds gleam on his golden pauldron.

He snaps his heels together then, staring steadfastly into the camera, begins his address.

"Do not believe a single word these subversives have spewed at you. They are rotten lies meant to erode your faith in our Great Society. These rats offer you nothing but ruin. The Caretakers, on the other hand, are your humble servants. Everything they do, they do to protect you. They want only the best for you." He steps closer—the camera lights turn his eye ports into furnaces. "Loyal patriots I take no pleasure in what I am about to do, but I must clear away any place for doubt to grow in your mind. Watch as these subversive rats die by their own lies."

I brace for what I know is coming.

"Don't look away." He turns to face the prisoners. Umeko

lifts her head and stares straight into the camera.

The pause is sickening.

"Remove their masks!"

All four fight against the prying hands of the Peace Officers but bound and prostrated they struggle in vain. All but Umeko start gagging immediately. Their pain-racked faces screaming in soundless terror. Agonizing seconds of convulsions pass. Life spills out of them like water, and they fall hard and still.

Umeko holds her breath even as her eyes and nose rupture and bleed. The Peace Officer standing behind her thrusts the barrel of his rifle into her back.

Her ribs splinter—that sound will never leave me. Unable to keep her lips sealed, she cries out. Her final, defiant roar rips through me like a scythe.

Umeko falls to the cobblestones next to her three motionless companions. Her own twitches and convulsions quickly subside.

"This, citizens, is the truth of our Great Society. There is no secret here, only a painful and deadly truth."

The commandant pauses again. Death, pain, and sacrifice tear at my resolve.

"Stand by for a mess—"

A thundering boom and a burst of light interrupt the commandant. The camera whips around. A massive, flaming hole dominates the west side of the broadcast tower. Flames are lapping out of the cavity igniting the ash which falls as cinders to the plaza slick with fuel. Soon the sky is raining red embers, and the ground is awash with fire. The commandant shouts something incomprehensible just as another explosion in the base of the broadcast tower turns the camera feed into a garbled gray blizzard. The signal cuts out, and the screen falls to black.

"Victor, what's happening? Did Damian plant those bombs?"

"No, I don't think so—this is something else. This has to be Fowler. She must be exploiting Damian's speech to launch her coup. Damn, damn him." Victor's hands dig into his hairline. "He's always so short-sighted. We knew Fowler was going to launch her operation, so instead of waiting it out and presenting a voice of reason he just lumped us in with the real subversives! And they all died, every one of them. Why did they listen to him?"

His words threaten to send me spiraling. I shake them away and bring us back to more immediate concerns. "What can we do? Is there anyone else in our network?"

Victor's face burns red with anger.

"All gone, all dead, all ruined. A single day! One damn day and what took us years to build—what Herrington spent his life creating—gone… just gone."

Anxiety vibrates in the silence.

"Then," I pause, the words catching in my throat. "It's just us. What's our plan, where do we go?" I move to his side and pull his hands away from his scalp—a few yanked brown hairs fall away.

"We need to be someplace safe," I say trying to soothe him. "I don't think we'll have that here much longer."

"I don't know, I don't know," he says shaking his head.

"We have to think, Victor—it's just the two of us now. We have to keep trying to open people's eyes to the truth."

"How? Everyone's dead, and they died when their masks were taken off! How do we convince anyone—let alone the entire nation—that what they saw didn't happen? We can't! It happened, and now we're ruined."

Words of anger scramble into my mouth but I rein them back in before they can escape. Victor's right. What people saw was real, it was true. But it may not be the whole truth.

"Victor, were you recording that broadcast?"

"Always. Why?"

"I may know a way we can still show people the truth."

"I don't follow."

I push past him pointing at the projected light display.

"Go to the shot where the camera operator flipped the camera around to look at the tower. With any luck, he caught a glimpse of one of those silver trucks, like the one near the field the day they killed Cinnamon. Go frame by frame."

Victor pulls up the video and digs into it opening a timeline. The first frame showing the flash of the explosion fills the screen. It disappears, replaced by the next frame and so on.

Watching it slowly, frame by frame, after seeing it live is surreal. I nearly get vertigo telling myself that these images weren't ripped from a movie.

I watched them die. I watched the bombs go off. But through the screen, sliced up into frozen snapshots of time, it feels mundane, like the mindless flashes on the Nightly News.

A few dozen frames in, the camera levels out and the image is clear. The whole square is visible as is the street at its far side. Victor's hands pull back out of the projected light.

"I don't believe it—there it is."

In a total of six frames is the unmistakable shape of the silver truck with its mysterious tanks.

A muddy cocktail of emotions courses through my mind. *I wish I weren't right.* I fight through it, turning away from the computer.

"This isn't enough to prove to everyone that the real danger comes from the Caretakers, but now we have someplace to start. Can you load this footage and the details of Fowler's coup Margaret gave us onto an info disk?"

Victor nods—a plan brewing on his face.

"I can do you one better. I'll burn it into a storage sphere. The information gets etched into the crystalline structure, that way nothing can tamper with the data, and it'll be practically bulletproof."

"I like the sound of that."

Victor dives into the drawers under the computer terminal. Rooting around he pulls out a perfectly clear orb the size of a grape. He loads it into the cradle then turns his attention to the input board and hammers out the commands.

"Shield your eyes," he says as he strikes execute.

I hold my hand over my eyes, but the brilliance of the violet laser is so intense my fingers turn semi-translucent. The cradle whines and fills the room with the stench of ozone.

"*Write complete*," says a synthesized voice from the computer.

Victor plucks the sphere out of the cradle. It has metamorphized from nothingness to a galaxy of indigo and sapphire.

"Here," he says handing it to me. "It's still warm."

I run it through my fingers. A dichotomy of emotions floods into my head, and the weight of its potential challenges my grasp. I unzip the front flap of my jumpsuit and press it inside. *Zhhwhip.* Tucked away, I breathe out some of the anxiety swelling inside me.

"We can do this Victor, we can find out what's in those trucks and who orders them around. When we know that, we can finish what Damian started and accomplish what Mr. Herrington dreamed of."

Victor rises from his chair and envelopes me in a hug.

"Thank you. Thank you for keeping me on track. We may have lost everything, but I'm glad I haven't lost everyone."

I have no words to reciprocate. I hug him back hoping he knows I feel the same way.

Wrapped in his embrace, for an instant, the nightmare takes a back seat to the moment. But the nightmare cannot be kept at bay for long.

Whoosh-crack! The explosion and its tremor hit in the same instant with enough power to send Victor and me both sprawling to the floor.

"That was close," I say.

"That was in the building."

"They must have planted bombs everywhere. We have to do something. Should we run? Or should we wait it out here?"

Brushing himself off, Victor turns to face the far wall.

"Let's go see."

Running to the wall behind the bunks, Victor pulls down a composite panel revealing a thick triple-pane window that swings open onto a cramped steel fire escape.

"We can get to the roof from here and see what's going on out there," Victor says picking up our masks.

I take mine from him and, with a sigh, slip it on. "Lead the way."

Progress up the ladder is slow. Each rung is slick with soot. The bright orange glow of the city in flames has turned night to day. Reaching the top, the full scope of the bombings becomes evident.

Every building in sight is on fire. Updrafts caused by the inferno send burning ash high into the air. With everything covered in fuel the fire is spreading fast and burning hot. Hundreds of fire trucks choke the streets. Fire Officers rush about below—the blaze reflects blindingly off their silver suits. Great torrents of water spray from thousands of hoses, and still, the fire spreads.

The city is in chaos.

The fire's crackle and roar meld with the whining of firetruck sirens to form the baseline of a sinister soundtrack. Automatic weapons fire and the *crack-boom* of bombs punctuate its score. I watch the world around me burn and can't help but think that it was I who lit the match.

CHAPTER TWENTY-SIX

THE DEAD ARE SO PEACEFUL. In the posters, they are writing and grotesque. But even with the world erupting in chaos outside, Mr. Herrington's body is still and calm. His face is placid—at peace with the life he lived. Yet the tranquility of his final fixed expression pierces my heart deeper than the posters ever could. The responsibility for his death tugs at my heart and I can feel darkness seeping into the cracks. I wanted to go back for my parents. It's my fault he died. It's my fault Mother died.

Tears stream from my eyes splashing onto the dried blood pooled around his body.

"We have to start moving, Victor."

The city is going to burn. We could leave him here, let the fire take him, but I can't stomach it. His death is on my hands. I didn't know him long, but I feel an overwhelming obligation to give him a proper funeral.

"It'll be easier to carry him if we wrap him up in a sheet first."

Victor nods, holding back sobs and gags in equal measure. "There are clean ones on the bunks." He manages to point me in the right direction before he needs his hand back to hold himself together.

It feels like I'm pulling myself through water—each step and action labored and slow. The wool blanket is tucked in tight. I tug at it, then all at once, the bedding comes away collapsing into a jumbled pile at my feet. I sift through it pulling out the white sheet still starched and clean.

I lay it out flat on a clean patch of floor as close to him as I can. Victor helps me straighten the edges then we step back steeling ourselves for what we're about to do.

"I don't think we'll ever be okay or ready for this. We just need to do it quick, like pulling off a bandage."

Victor nods. He's ashen, but he's managed to get his nausea under control. Victor moves to his legs, so I move to line myself up with Mr. Herrington's shoulders. In position, I look down. Locked open, his eyes stare up at me. I turn my head to the side to avoid his empty gaze, but the hairs on my neck won't let me shake them. I take rapid, shallow breaths hoping to calm myself down and avoid the smell, but it only makes it worse—now I'm light headed, and everything tastes of biting copper.

Victor squats low and grabs Mr. Herrington's ankles. His hands push up his pant legs just enough to reveal light brown socks patterned with white diamonds. I bend down to pick him up. A great sigh rushes out of me without intention.

Sliding my hands under his shoulders, I try and get a good grip. The abnormal sensation on my fingertips nearly pushes me to retch. His skin has turned solid and his body is rigid.

"Ready?" Victor nods. "Okay, here we go. On the count of three. One… Two… Three."

Exhaling on three, we heave his body up. The instant he lifts from the floor, the blood and secretions pooled underneath him splash out. A torrent of nauseous smells—sickly sweet and acrid—assaults my nostrils. Bile shoots into my mouth. I fight it down—my throat stinging like needles. His neck remains stiff as we shuffle him overtop the sheet keeping his eyes fixed on me. I shed my remaining tears.

He was such a graceful man. Full of dignity and class. Death, it seems, cares little for the character of the dead, and it treats them all with the same vile crudeness.

We set him down as gently as we can, but he's way heavier than I thought he would be. He lands on the sheet with a thud. I start to sob. This is awful, so fucking awful.

"You okay?"

I wave Victor off, doing my best to wipe my eyes with the crook of my arm. "We're halfway there. We have to keep going."

I fold in the corners and tie the bundle up. Fragmented memories of my days in the Blue Scarf Girl guide my clumsy, jittering hands. I can hardly see what I'm doing through the tears clinging to my eyelashes.

Stepping back, his clean, wrapped form feels almost comforting. Before I can process that, dread pours back over me. Dots of red are creeping up through the fabric—a bloom of poppies on a starched white field.

Kur-Whoom!

A shockwave rattles through the floor and into my teeth. We snap up sober.

"We're running out of time. Do you want to grab his head or his feet?"

"I think," Victor gulps hard, "I think I'll take his feet. You don't know your way through the sewers, and it will be easier for me to lead holding his legs. Let me go prop open the utility door." The oceans of sorrow behind his eyes have boiled away leaving behind dry red streaks down to his chin.

I nod my head, my mouth too parched for words. He is quick in his task, and I don't have to wait long for him to return. We shuffle into position. The *crack-boom* of bombs and the shrill cries of sirens reverberate in our ears—a ceaseless nightmare cacophony.

Mr. Herrington's passing demands stillness. It should be mourned with silence and contemplation. The universe itself should pause for a moment to grieve his exit. Instead, it wails and screams like a banshee—as if the gates of the underworld are opening up to receive him. The idea of it unnerves me. Storybook depictions of vile demonic forms pouring from the darkness to gather the dead ensnare me bringing with them further depths of pain. I won't let this be true. He was a good man, the best of us. Surely darkness cannot be what awaits us? But as hard as I try, I can't imagine that there is a paradise awaiting any of us.

"Here we go—masks on."

Victor locks eyes with me. His gaze pulls me from the darkness in my mind and back to our grim task.

Mr. Herrington is turning limp as we walk making him somehow heavier and trickier to handle. But soon we find a rhythm, shifting his weight from side to side as our arms begin to quiver with fatigue.

Passing through the utility room, we find our way to the long ramp down into the sewers. A few scattered lights flicker their sickly yellow glow over the refuse and stagnant water in the tunnel. Our masks do little to hold back the stench. Thick black water pours into the center channel through multiple connecting pipes. The smell of burning ash is pungent. The sounds of the inferno above have almost entirely disappeared, dissipated by the meters of concrete above us. The smell continues to remind us of what's happening above and refuses to let us forget our role in this tragedy.

With every step, my shoes fill with filth. Tiny particles of ash grate against my ankles and the pads of my feet. Grit pushes its way into a thousand tiny cuts. The stinging grows and becomes overwhelming setting my feet on fire—as if my legs have become a mass of stinging, biting ants.

Combined, the deadened roar of a dying city, the all-consuming darkness, and the unrelenting pain in my feet are pushing me to the brink.

I'm one misstep away from breaking.

I so desperately wish this were a nightmare. I could wake up and be free from this agony. But there is no waking up from this. I am more awake than I've ever been, and it fills me with no small amount of guilt to know that all I want to do is go back to sleep.

Victor's voice pulls me from the spiraling darkness of my mind.

"Get down! There are lights up ahead." His words began as a harsh whisper, yet in our cavernous surroundings, they quickly amplify to a shout. The loudness of the reverberation is jarring.

Unable to see past Victor, I try to remain composed—ready for the unknown. He too must have been trying to figure out what our next move should be. Unfortunately, he does nothing to communicate what he is thinking. He attempts to drop low, but his foot slips on some concealed slime on the bottom of the tunnel. His right leg shoots out from underneath him.

He throws his arms out to catch himself, and he unwittingly drops his grip. Mr. Herrington's feet splash into the water. The full weight of his torso slams into me. The sudden shock throws me off balance and the tunnel floor is unforgivingly slick. With the weight distributed between the both of us it was a nuisance, but now my feet might as well be banana peels.

Both legs shoot forward. I crash straight through the water to the concrete below. The crack of my tailbone reverberates up my spine and chatters in my jaw—pain blooms. Vile water seeps behind my mask and into my mouth. *I should have double checked my seal.*

My arms tremble from the effort of keeping Mr. Herrington's chest and head out of the water. I scramble to get out from under him, but I get no purchase in the slime.

I could let go of him and let him float around in the muck. This would get me out of danger, but I can't bear the thought of it. From being shot in the back, to lying cold and dead on a concrete floor, he has suffered enough indignity. I cannot let him drift around in the sewer like the corpse of a rat.

Unable to keep him up much longer, I lock my arms out in front of me. This pulls most of the weight from my muscles, but it forces my head under water. I've put myself in a terrible dilemma: If I hold him out of the water, his weight will drown me. If I let him go, I'll drown in regret.

Clenching my eyes shut, I see what must be the swaying of a flashlight as red streaks against my eyelids. I cannot hear what is happening above me, only the deep rumbling of a dying city.

The temporary relief of locking my arms has faded and now my joints ache from the strain. Muscles spasm. Coursing veins leach the air from my lungs. Empty, they pound at my throat. *Air. Air!*

A primordial panic emanates from the base of my spine. Pride and instinct rage inside me.

The world outside grows distant. Each beat of my heart sends throbs of pain through my veins. Temples grow hot. Instinct begins to take control. I thrash about, looking for the surface. *I can't let him fall into the muck. I can't let him fall into the muck.* My will struggles on, keeping me pinned to the tunnel floor. *What's taking so long? Why hasn't Victor pulled me up?* I dip into my last ounce of resolve and prepare to die with whatever dignity is left for me in this sewer.

The weight vanishes. Seeing its opportunity for survival, my brain suppresses thought or willful action. I burst from the ashen water and gulp deep the air.

Sight, smell, and sound rush back as though I crossed through the veil of death and back into the land of the living. Disoriented, and still euphoric from the rush of being alive, it takes a moment for my senses to come into focus.

Standing over me is a hulking man holding a flashlight in his outstretched right hand. Mr. Herrington hangs like a sack over his left shoulder. The man's face is concealed by mask and inky shadow. The light obscures my vision, but I can make out what looks like Victor slumped against the wall of the sewer clutching his head. Two shadowy figures loom behind, flanking him.

My will to fight burns hot. I get on my feet as quick as the filth-strewn sewer will allow. My hands clench into fists, but as I raise them in front of me, the man's face comes into focus.

CHAPTER TWENTY-SIX

"Charles?"

"Evelyn. Thank goodness you are all right. I heard the gun-shots, and well… I assumed you were all killed."

He sloshes forward a step. Charles extends his right hand toward me. Our eyes meet. Behind his mask his face is knotted thick with panic, sorrow, and rage.

"Here—take the light."

I grab it from him without hesitation. Stepping back, Charles drapes Mr. Herrington's body over his arms. I point the flashlight over to Victor. Under his hand, a tiny shimmer of red blood is peeking through. Standing over him is a woman and a young girl. They must be Cornelia and Georgette. I train my flashlight on them. Cornelia is wearing a long yellow dress with white lace trim. It would be beautiful if it weren't soaked and covered in ash. Georgette is wearing black from head to toe. It's impossible to tell if her clothes started out that color or were transformed from the soot.

"I still can't believe Bernard is gone. He was a great man," Cornelia says.

"I can't express how much it grieves me to hold him like this. Did anyone else make it?"

"No. Damian… everyone," Victor pauses, his bloodied hand trembling. "Peace Officers got them all. And then Fowler set off the bombs."

"Good God." Shaking his head, Charles turns to face Victor, "Sorry about your head."

I look down at the flashlight in my hand. There is a small splotch of red where the handle connected with Victor.

"I understand Charles—you were protecting your family," Victor says. The words are hardly out of his mouth before he tries to stand. His legs wobble, but Cornelia and Georgette rush in and prop him up.

"We have to keep moving," Victor says, his words trembling.

"Are you okay to walk?" Charles asks.

Victor shakes his head up and down with a moan. "We'll help him along, Charles," Cornelia says.

"All right then. There is a junction just down there to the left." Charles gestures down the tunnel with his head. "If we follow it straight we should emerge on the edge of the city. Evelyn, lead the way."

I nod and press on, illuminating the path before us.

CHAPTER TWENTY-SEVEN

WE PRESS FORWARD through the sludge. My light pierces the Stygian darkness revealing our putrid path. I don't know where I'm going, and each step feels like venturing into the belly of a monster. Despite the uncertainties, I feel strangely at ease. These past few months trudging through the darkness with only a sliver of light to guide me is all I've been doing. I've run full bore into the unknown, and I'm still here, still making it. But I can't help but think that everything is different now. I could have gone home. I could have dealt with the consequences and tried to return to the masquerade—the life I endured before. But it's all gone now. My family, that life, the ignorance. There is no way back. The only way forward is out of this tunnel—out of the darkness.

I shake my head trying to pull myself back into the present. The pungent odor helps. Refocused on the task, I glance back. Victor is still having trouble walking, but Cornelia and little Georgette are keeping him moving. Charles looks exhausted. His face is beet red—his mask's eye ports fog and clear with each quick and labored breath. I turn my attention back to the path ahead. The tunnel is beginning to climb, ever so slightly, and the walls are drawing together making the already narrow path claustrophobic.

"I think we're getting close now. Just a little further and then we can rest," I say, my voice surprisingly steady.

Charles' wet sloshing footsteps stop. "Good, I need it. How are you holding up darlings?"

"We're hanging in there, isn't that right Gette?"

"I'm all right dad, promise."

Victor grunts, "Still hanging in there."

There will be time for reflection—time to contemplate what I've done and who I've become, but now they need me to keep up my resolve. We're all feeling it—I know I am—but now is not the time. Best to push it down and box it up for later.

"All right then everyone, let's pick up the pace and get out of here."

I move as fast as the sludge and slime allow. Each step leaves behind a swirling wake in the thick black water. Our breaths grow heavy from the exertion of the hastened pace. With light in hand, I can feel the group's attention on my back. In this overwhelming darkness, I am the lighthouse that will guide them safely to shore.

A few minutes later, the end comes into view. Mire-slick steps lead up to a landing. A lonely tungsten bulb, partly obscured by the filth that coats everything down here, illuminates a gray metal service door. I climb the steps first. Now accustomed to the slippery ground in the tunnel, I make short work of them with judicious use of the handrails.

Nestling the flashlight between my cheek and right shoulder, I help the others up. One hand firmly on the railing and the other steadying them, we take our time and soon all six—I mean five—of us reach the landing.

Slowly setting Mr. Herrington down against the wall, Charles rests for a moment catching his breath, then turns to address us. "We're almost at the safe house. It's just through this door and then up another flight of stairs. There's food, water, hot showers, changes of clothes. This place was always meant for a worst-case scenario—Damian and I built it out of a utility closet—I never thought we'd actually need it."

"I never thought it would come to this either," Victor says, his voice trembling nearly as much as his hands. "What was he thinking? I'm so angry with him. I'm so unbelievably angry,"

"I know Victor—we're angry too," says Cornelia. "This was never meant to happen, but Bernard would want us to keep going. Keep fighting to make the Great Society a better place." She runs a gentle hand through Victor's hair. His trembling slows, and with a great sigh, his tears start again.

"I miss them both so much. They were everything to me. It's like I lost my brother and father all at once. I can't lose anymore… I can't lose any more of you."

Cornelia embraces Victor pulling his head into her chest. Deep, aching sobs pour out of him. Georgette joins in too, wrapping her little arms around them both.

"We're still your family, Victor. We won't let you lose anybody else."

Georgette's words bring a lump to my throat, and the lid on my box of emotions cracks open again. Hot tears pool in my eye ports. I join the embrace. Wrapping my arms around everyone, I squeeze them as tight as I can. Charles joins too, adding his sobs to the chorus. The enormity of our pain feels at first to be insurmountable but knowing that we're in this together begins to make it smaller, more manageable. We let the tears flow, and the sobs escape for a long, cathartic minute.

Crack-boom. A bomb detonates overhead—the light above the door flickers. Pushing my way out of the embrace, I inhale deeply and step back.

"We will make it through this. We're going to make it together. But now we need to get out of this sewer and get out of this city. Do you need help carrying Mr. Herrington?"

"No, that's all right I can manage. Keep lighting the way, it's not much farther now. Here," Charles produces a set of keys from his pocket and thrusts them into my free hand. "I can't remember which one. It's brass or silver I think."

I inspect the collection of brass and silver keys and shake my head.

"All right everyone, follow me we're almost there."

After going around the ring twice with no luck, a bulky brass key mercifully slips into the lock. It turns with a satisfying *clunk* and the door swings open into the ominous passage beyond.

I pause on the threshold to glance back at everyone lined up behind me. Responsibility laboring each step, I dispel the darkness with my flashlight and press forward.

I navigate the steep flight of stairs with great caution. Boots mired in filth, I ensure each step is secure before daring another. My aching calves delight upon reaching the top.

A narrow utility door stands alone on the concrete landing. I shine the light down the path revealing the tunnel's end and the metal ladder to the streets above. Charles's strained breaths rattle in the stairwell behind me. I turn my focus back to the safe house door. The keys clatter in my shaking hands, but I quickly find the small silver key—it slides in effortlessly. Just in time, Charles has ascended the stairs red-faced and heaving. I hold the door open for him, and he stumbles through. The others are just a few steps behind him. All accounted for, I pull the door closed behind us and throw the lock.

Small, and feeling cramped with all of us in it, the safe house is more accurately a safe *room*. In one corner stands a set of bunk beds surrounded by a series of dressers. On the opposite wall is a galley kitchen with cabinets stretching from the floor to the squat ceilings. A small table with four metal chairs fills the middle of the space. On the back wall is a door marked W/C.

Charles moves to the bunk beds and places Mr. Herrington down on a woolen blanket—the once white sheet is now indistinguishable from the splotchy brown-green of the blanket.

"I know this is packed," Charles says rubbing his right shoulder, "but we have everything we need to get moving again. Take turns showering and getting this gunk off us. You'll find clean clothes in the dressers," Charles points to the metal dressers on the wall behind the bunk beds. "We don't have much as far as variety, but the jumpsuits should fit us all nicely. While you are all doing that, I'll dig out the antibiotics we have stashed here. There is no telling what manner of filth we were exposed to down there."

"Gette and I will go first. You two get some rest—it's been a rough day." Cornelia looks at Victor and me with gentle, caring eyes.

I think deep down Mother felt the same way toward me, but her eyes could never show it like hers do. They rummage through the dressers for a minute until they find two jumpsuits that will fit—holding them arms outstretched to judge. They disappear into the bathroom.

Victor and I sit down at the table. The relief is exhilarating. The aching muscles of my legs, arms, and back whisper their gratitude. I can't wait for the shower. It's always been my place of refuge, but now more than ever, knowing that I can wash away the muck and mire feels like the only slice of paradise we are given in this world.

Charles scours the kitchen cabinets pulling out medicine and food. Most appealing are the cold bottles of sealed water he takes out from the fridge. Bright drops of pure water condense on the exterior of the green glass bottles. Water beads and falls in fat drips around the raised lettering *Purity Springs*.

As if he read my mind, Charles brings two of the jade, frosty bottles over and places them on the table. His hands are clean, so he twists off the caps for us.

"Thank you," the words are quiet, hardly making it past my parched lips. Charles returns to the cabinets, rattles around with various pill bottles, then comes back to the table with three small paper cups full of red, blue, and white pills. He sets one in front of each of us and keeps one for himself.

"Down the hatch." Charles throws back all his pills at once, gulps them down without water, then goes back to prepping our meal. I take my pills by the bottom of the cup, careful to keep my fingers away from the lip. With my other hand I reach out and grab my bottle almost in sync with Victor. I toss the pills in my mouth without hesitation and follow them with a mouthful of water. It's freezing cold and clean as a mountain spring. Hands down, it's the best thing I've ever had.

My stomach turns to ice as I drink it down in greedy gulps. Every sip is better than the last—I want to drink the whole bottle and then start on another. But my stomach is grumbling from the shock. I return the bottle to the table and watch its quarter remaining contents slosh around like ocean waves while

I catch my breath. Clasping my hands around it, I turn the clear droplets black.

Victor's staring at his water. His eyes trace the path of the droplets from the top of the bottle down to the table. He catches me watching him, and he looks up at me. His eyes seem hollow as if he'd been poured out like the contents of the bottle. *Do my eyes look like that?* I try to smile, to reassure us both that everything will be okay, but I can only manage a smirk. He blinks his eyes closed and holds them shut. For a dozen heartbeats, he sits as still as stone.

When his eyes finally open, they have a little glimmer of light in them. But he can't keep his eyes locked with mine, and they return to following the streaks on the bottle. I look away too. It's becoming unbearable to look at anyone, actually look at them, without stirring up the hornets' nest of pain that has burrowed into my chest.

The sound of the running shower stops, and a few minutes later Cornelia and Georgette emerge. Clean and bedecked in unsoiled smoke-colored jumpsuits, they look like a weight has lifted from their shoulders.

"You can go next Evelyn—I don't think I'm ready to stand up yet." Victor's eyes never leave the bottle.

Not wanting to argue, I push myself back and rise—the chair squeaks against the floor. I pull out four jumpsuits before I find one my size and then head to the bathroom. Georgette's already sitting at the table drinking from her own *Purity Springs.*

CHAPTER TWENTY-SEVEN

"I feel a hundred times better now! You will too," she says in between sips.

A genuine smile beams across my face. Even in the darkness, there is light. I close the door behind me and begin to pull off the filthy jumpsuit I'm wearing. I unzip the breast utility pocket then fish around until my fingers wrap around the glacial storage sphere. I hold it to the white light hanging over the small square mirror. A kaleidoscope of blue and purple fractals dance on the glass. It seems wrong that the sinister and gut-turning information within should gleam with such otherworldly beauty. I set it down on the ivory enamel sink then turn my mind from it.

A small basket in the corner holds the other discarded garments. Adding mine to the pile, I turn to the small stand-up shower. Hardly wider than my shoulders, this is a far cry from my shower in the penthouse. Long aimless hours drifting away under a steady stream of water is a luxury I've lost. Those days are gone for good.

Turning the knob, I'm assaulted by an arctic tsunami. My skin tightens, and I double over involuntarily from the shock. Thankfully, it warms quickly, and I'm able to stand up straight again. Leaning in to let the water hit my hair with full force, an endless stream of chunks and dark sludge pours off. I stare into the drain and watch the swirling water run black.

CHAPTER TWENTY-EIGHT

DROWNED OUT by the flow of water, the sounds of the conflict above fade into nothingness. But the instant I turn the knob off it rushes back. Bombs rumble. Bullets snap. Closing my eyes does nothing to deny the reality raging above me.

These new clothes are plain—a soft gray that will soon be black. Starched and stiff, I feel uncomfortable and out of place. I take up the storage sphere with a jerk—my arm overestimating its weight from the contents trapped inside. I zip it safely into the hidden pocket on the inside flap.

Opening the door, I realize I have a chest full of air I've been holding onto. Filling the doorway, Victor stands waiting—fresh light-gray jumpsuit in hand. I can't help but jump—the pent-up air rushes from my lips.

"Sorry—I didn't mean to startle you. I heard the shower turn off, so I thought I'd get in line."

I can't even express why I was startled. I think my nerves are just raw. They've been battered, beaten, and bruised so much over the past week that I feel wafer thin. The lightest breeze might shatter me.

"The shower feels nice," I say walking past Victor. I keep from making eye contact and go straight for a bunk.

I hear his mouth open to say something, but he thinks better of it then disappears behind the click of the bathroom door.

I lay down and I'm out.

Horrors swell in the darkness and I jerk myself awake—sweat drips from my forehead.

I pull myself up and join everyone at the table. Sliding into the chair, I retake my spot—someone went through the effort to wipe it clean. Before I can say thank you, Charles places a bowl of reddish-brown slop and a second paper cup filled with a rainbow of pills in front of me—I was out long enough for him to shower and change too. He offers me a spoon, and I reach to grasp it, but he doesn't let go of his grip. Our eyes meet, and I see deep concern stretched across his face.

"You'll be all right, Evelyn. We'll get through this." His words seem intended more for himself than me, but I force a smirk and nod.

"Yeah, I know we will."

An ear-to-ear smile crosses his face though the concern in his eyes remains entrenched. He releases his hold on the spoon. I turn my attention to the pills knocking them all back with a gulp of cold water. I want to be alone. Crawl up into a corner somewhere and process everything. But I can't. I can't escape what life has become.

Trying to find some solitude, I focus on the slop. I think it's chili, a staple of the safe house it seems, but it's lost much of its texture to age. Despite the mushy consistency, its warmth and savory flavors are welcome and almost enjoyable. Each bite feels a little like normalcy. Like dinner around the television—Mother's placid eyes, Father's distant stare.

Arrest her!

The vision of Father writhes inside me like a tangle of vipers. In an involuntary strike, my spoon slams through the chili to the bottom of the bowl. The world swirls. Chains tighten across my chest. The metal spoon digs into my fingers.

"That's not how you eat chili!"

Georgette barely contains her laughter. Her lightness pulls me back. She sits just higher than her bowl of chili—a Cheshire grin lights up her face.

"These spoons can be pretty tricky to get the hang of," I say.

"Oh, I know. It took me a while to get it down, but now I'm an expert. Look!"

Georgette shovels the chili into her mouth as fast as she can.

Cornelia smiles. "I'll race you, Evelyn," she says.

"You're on."

"Me too!" Georgette chimes in.

"Why not?" says Victor with a shrug.

"Charles?" Cornelia says, shifting her gaze to the kitchen.

His smile turns sour, and his face twists into disgust. "Really Cora? A food eating contest? Bernard is dead. Damian, everyone—they're dead. Bombs are falling overhead, and you want to act like we're at a carnival?"

Cornelia's face sharpens.

"You think we don't know that? That we aren't in the same room as you Charles? We had a chance to distract ourselves from this mess, even for a moment, and you've ruined it." Cornelia pushes the bowl away from her—chili splashes over the rim onto the table. Her spoon clanks loud in the growing air of tension. Their eyes lock onto each other. Their glare is so intense it's almost radiating heat.

Georgette has lost herself in her chili. Her neck and cheeks flush red. Staring into it, she sheepishly continues to take small nibbling bites. Victor's clammed up and smashed his eyes shut.

Feeling I must do something, I push off from the table edge scooting my chair back. The metal legs screech across the concrete floor.

"You know… I'm not hungry anymore."

I grab up my bowl and turn to Cornelia.

"Are you finished?" I say.

She nods ever so slightly. Her eyes, unblinking, stay fixed on Charles.

I grab up her bowl and head to the kitchen. Charles stands like a statue. His breaths deeper than normal—labored. I brush past him and drop the bowls into the sink. They clatter loudly.

"Thanks for the food. I'm going to go scout ahead. Come get me when you're done with," my hands twist in the air before me, "whatever this is."

My words sharp, tone irreverent. So what? He deserved it. Witting or not he made himself a lightning rod for the anger, fear, and anxiety roiling inside all of us looking for a way out. I grab one of the fresh masks hanging from hooks in the kitchen.

I take two large strides then slam the door behind me—its clang dissolves into the chorus of guns, sirens, and bombs.

The tunnel leading to the surface is murky and narrow. A dim light hangs every five meters or so along the ceiling giving off just enough light to see. Cramped as it is, it feels vast compared to that room.

Walking feels good, and it's helping take my mind off the swirling maelstrom of recent events.

Step, step, step.

Months ago—months that feel like a lifetime—I would have hated the regimented pace of my steps, felt suffocated by their uniformity. But now I can appreciate their order—their control. With everything slipping through my fingers no matter how hard I squeeze, even this insignificant ounce of control is euphoric. No wonder the Caretakers won't let it go and Fowler's willing to do anything to get it.

The tunnel's end draws near. A single lamp illuminates a ladder leading to a round metal sewer cover. My pace quickens. I reach the ladder, placing foot and hand on the rungs. Then I pause. The rubber straps of the mask nagging at my mind. They could be using the gas. The silver trucks could be out there on the streets. I take a deep breath.

Wear Your Mask.

The motions are automatic, familiar. So too is the dread. But this time, it's for what may be lingering in the air. Taking deep, carbonized breaths, I ascend the ladder. The distance is short, and I am soon up against the metal sewer cover. There is a stainless lever in the middle of the thick steel flanked by two steam cylinders. I try the handle, but it doesn't budge.

I lock my feet into the rungs as best I can and pull on the handle with all my might. It jolts loose. Steam hisses in the cylinders throwing the cover open.

The world ruptures in a shrieking whoosh.

Heat from the inferno above is sucking the wind from the

tunnel like an air-starved dragon. Air hisses past me in a torrent tangling and blowing my hair about wildly. And though it's night, the fires blaze brighter than daylight. My eyes squint tight, tearing from the sudden and unexpected brilliance. Falling embers land on my hands engulfing them in a momentary inferno before they exhaust themselves. The pain is intense, but I have to push through it and scout the path ahead. I reach through the portal and pull myself out. Getting to my feet, I am awestruck at the sight before me.

The haphazard skyscrapers are engulfed in flames. Their windows are bursting open belching torrents of fire so hot they appear almost white. Facades crumble from the heat; peeling away the stone and chrome reveals the bursting concrete and wilting rebar beneath.

The streets are empty. The only movement is blowing ash. Throngs of people milling about, and the choking, honking traffic, are eerily absent. In their place are the wisps of ashen ghosts and the unearthly flicker and roar of unquenchable fire.

I wade into the street. Ash—nearly to my knee—clings to my jumpsuit and crunches underfoot.

All around me is a vision of hell.

Life, however repressed, has been washed away into ash and soot—pain and flame. I struggle to catch my breath. Either from the sight or the rapidly depleting oxygen supplies, it's hard to tell.

There has to be a way out. We can't die here, not today, not in that tunnel. The city might be imploding, but I'll be damned if I'll let it take me with it. But looking around it seems like my resistance may count for little.

Wiz crack. Bullets fill the air around me. Their red tracers searing themselves into my eyes. I dive back toward the tunnel. Ash billows up around me forcing its way down the neck and cuffs of my jumpsuit. My heart hammers against my ribcage. *Thump. Thump. Thump.* Anxiety courses through me like stinging nettles—my skin electric and alive. My stomach tightens into a knot. I clutch at the asphalt desperate to pull myself closer to its relative safety. The sound of guns draws louder. The battle is still raging.

The growl of revving engines surges above the raging fire. Rising to a shrill crescendo then fading back into the background blur of fighting, bombs, and flames, the dueling automobiles pass. Their tires leave wakes in the ash like a boat's keel in the waves.

Alert, I pull myself into a crouch. There must be something I can do.

I see it before it rounds the corner. The flashing dazzling-blue lights of the ambulance stand out against the flames like the moon in the darkness. I keep low, so they don't see me and follow them with my eyes as they round the bend and pull up to a high-rise across the street from me. Lights whirling, its siren screeches in vain against the wailing chaos.

Paramedics in bleached, gown uniforms adorned with red crosses jump from the van. Leaving the doors flung wide open, they pull a stretcher from the back and rush into the building. Could we pretend to be wounded? Would they arrest us? Maybe they could get us out of the city. There's no time. I have to get everyone, and we have to get into that ambulance.

I rise, ready to sprint the short few steps back to the tunnel entrance when the world heaves. A concussion blasts me to the ground. The air is forced from my lungs. My head bangs against the tarmac. Blood and vomit push themselves through clenched teeth. A horrible ringing has replaced all sound. The world swims in swirls of bright and dark—can't make out solid shapes. But I can see well enough that the building the ambulance pulled up to is now more rubble than structure. As the dust settles, the twirling blue of the ambulance's siren emerges from the smoke.

I force myself to the ladder. I manage one rung before my trembling hands give way and my ash-covered feet slide out from under me. Falling to the concrete tunnel below, I catch myself on a rung with the crook of my arm. The metal digs to the bone forcing aside muscles and tendons. My screams go unheard in my ringing ears. I let myself fall the remaining distance to the sewer floor below.

Hurt and sorrow overtake me. Crumbled at the base of the ladder, every inch of me hurts, burns, or aches. They're dead. They ran in there to help people and as soon as they did that bomb went off. *They planned that.* They killed them—they murdered them innocent or not. How did they know they supported the Caretakers? This violence—this horror—it's too much to bear.

I rip the mask from my face releasing the trapped blood and vomit. I wipe at it with my ash-covered sleeve. It's almost no cleaner, but the act of trying helps me regain some semblance of control. Still sobbing, I limp to my feet and begin the journey back down the tunnel. My right ankle hurts so bad it might be broken. Each step is a symphony of sharp, shooting pain that dances up my legs and settles in my teeth. But I know I can't stop. They'll kill us too if we don't get out of here.

Grabbing the doorframe to keep from falling, I throw it open.

"Evelyn? What's going on out there? Are you all right? We need to—" I cut Charles off. I grab a new mask from the wall, take one long stride to the table, and grab Georgette's wrist. Her sweet eyes churn with panic and trust.

"There's no time!"

Even as the words exit my mouth, I've turned back to the tunnel. My body gains strength from its connection to Georgette. She follows me without question—her faith in me overpowering her fear of the streets above. Almost to the ladder, the echoes of sloshing feet multiply. Cornelia, Charles, and Victor have caught up. We stop at the ladder and wait. Cornelia, already wearing her own mask, slips one over Georgette's head and yanks the straps tight. Georgette whimpers but offers no further complaint.

"Across the street, there is an abandoned ambulance."

"How do you know?" Charles interjects.

"There's no time to explain. We need to get into it as fast as possible. Victor, can you drive it?"

Victor nods in affirmation. I pull my mask on and yank it tight.

"Follow me," I say my voice now both strained and distorted.

Up the ladder, final rung, over the lip, across the street.

My ankle rages like a kicked anthill. I can't get distracted—I have to focus, or we'll die. I keep my eyes fixed on the open double doors at the back of the ambulance. Every part of me is screaming in protest—not now!

The distance closes in a blink. I scramble into the back of the ambulance—Georgette's right behind me. We collapse onto the bench seat against the right wall. Her little arms are wrapped around me. Her grip is tight—her fingers are pushing into my back. The sensation instantly recalls Mother's fingers digging into me.

"You can't let them get you, Evelyn… you can't."

Mother's actions come into focus with stunning clarity—I fight to keep from falling to pieces. She did love me, and I never let her know that I loved her too.

Cornelia jumps into the back giving me something external to focus on. Charles is right behind her, Mr. Herrington's body slung over his shoulder. Through the cacophony of flame, bullets, and blasts it's impossible to hear, but his chest is heaving like a bellows. Cornelia grabs hold of Mr. Herrington and pulls his lifeless form onto the floor of the van. She slams the doors shut. Then nearly at the same time, Charles and Victor jump into the two front seats.

"Punch it, Victor," says Charles.

Victor's foot replies, pressing pedal to metal. We lurch forward—I throw my arm out to keep from sliding off the bench.

The world spins. Fire surges across my skin. Darkness pulls on my eyes.

"Don't stop. Don't stop…" the words tumble from my lips as consciousness falls from my mind.

CONTINUED IN THE GREAT SOCIETY TRILOGY BOOK TWO:

BURNED

ABOUT THE AUTHOR

G.K. Lamb writes speculative fiction, science fiction, and fantasy. His debut young-adult dystopian series is the *The Great Society Trilogy*: *Filtered, Burned, and Broken.*

Trained as a historian and documentary filmmaker, he explores themes of memory, history, and truth through a cinematic lens.

He holds a BA and MA in history from Northern Arizona University. He lives in the Sonoran Desert with his wife, two cats, and dog.

Thank you for reading! Please add a short review on Goodreads, Amazon, or wherever you like to discuss books.

We'd love to know what you thought!

If you would like to learn more about G.K. Lamb's other publications, please visit: www.geraldklamb.com

www.ingramcontent.com/pod-product-compliance
Lightning Source LLC
Chambersburg PA
CBHW051531100726
47898CB00005B/1651